A Sam & Friends Mystery

Book One

Dracula Madness

MARY LABATT · JO RIOUX

KIDS CAN PRESS

Kids Can Press acknowledges the financial support of the Government of Ontario, through the Ontario Media Development Corporation's Ontario Book Initiative; the Ontario Arts Council; the Canada Council for the Arts; and the Government of Canada, through the BPIDP, for our publishing activity.

Published in Canada by
Kids Can Press Ltd.
29 Birch Avenue
Toronto, ON M4V 1E2

Published in the U.S. by
Kids Can Press Ltd.
2250 Military Road
Tonawanda, NY 14150

www.kidscanpress.com

Based on the book *Spying on Dracula* by Mary Labatt.

Edited by Karen Li
Designed by Kathleen Gray
Printed and bound in China

The hardcover edition of this book is smyth sewn casebound.
The paperback edition of this book is limp sewn with a drawn-on cover.

CM 09 0 9 8 7 6 5 4 3 2 1
CM PA 09 0 9 8 7 6 5 4 3 2 1

Library and Archives Canada Cataloguing in Publication

Labatt, Mary, 1944–
Dracula madness / Mary Labatt ; illustrated by Jo Rioux.

(A Sam & friends mystery)
Interest age level: For ages 7–10.
ISBN 978-1-55453-418-0 (bound). ISBN 978-1-55337-303-2 (pbk.)

I. Rioux, Jo II. Title. III. Series: Labatt, Mary, 1944–.
Sam & friends mystery.

PS8573.A135D73 2009   jC813'.54   C2008-903253-5

Kids Can Press is a *corus*™ Entertainment company

To my family — M.L.

Thanks to Joseph Dafoe — J.R.

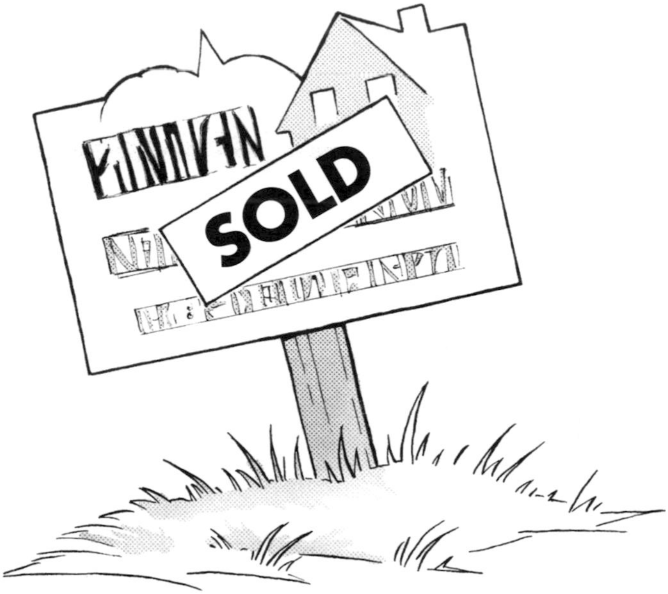
SOLD

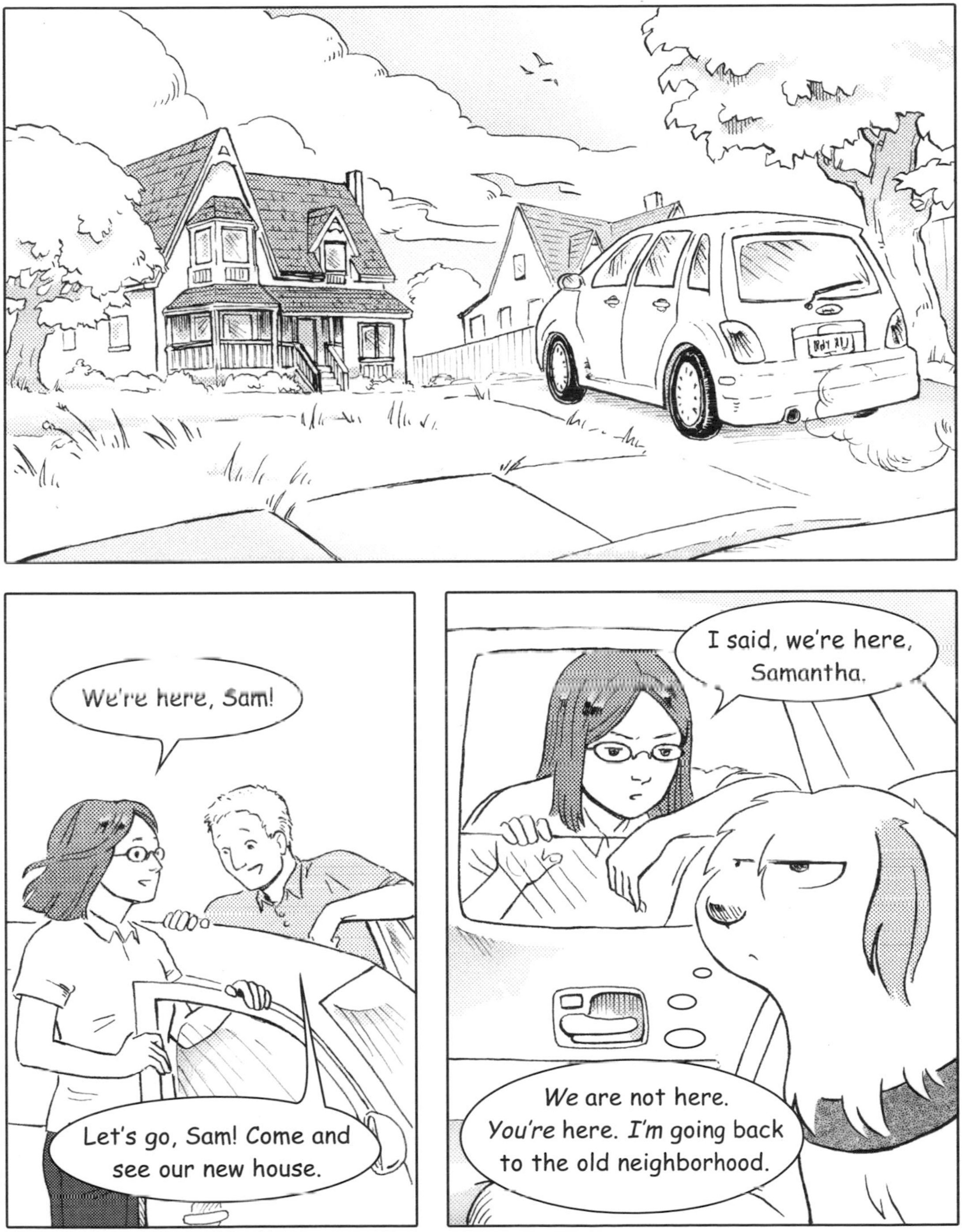
We're here, Sam!
Let's go, Sam! Come and see our new house.
I said, we're here, Samantha.
We are not here. You're here. I'm going back to the old neighborhood.

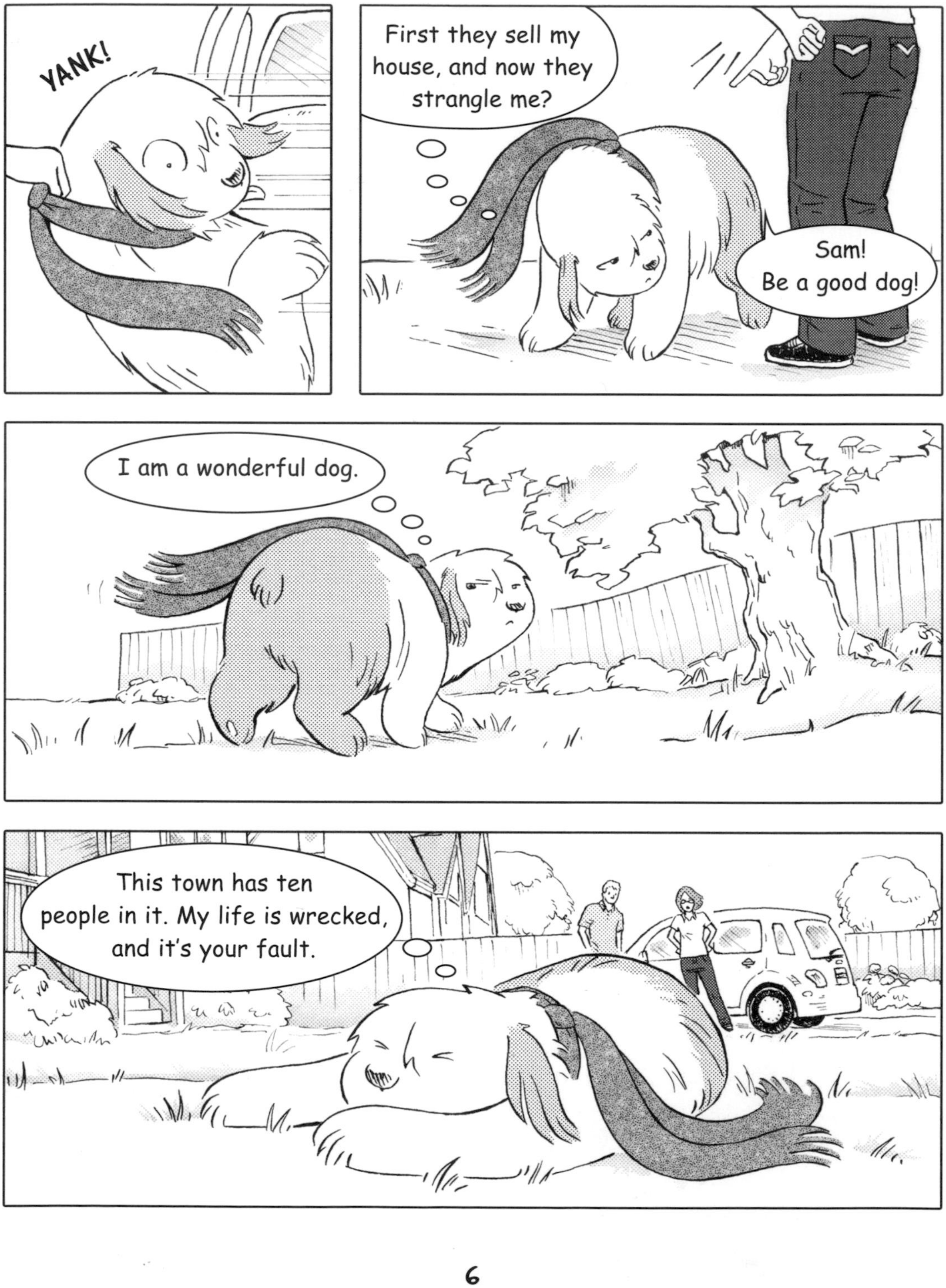
YANK!
First they sell my house, and now they strangle me?
Sam! Be a good dog!
I am a wonderful dog.
This town has ten people in it. My life is wrecked, and it's your fault.

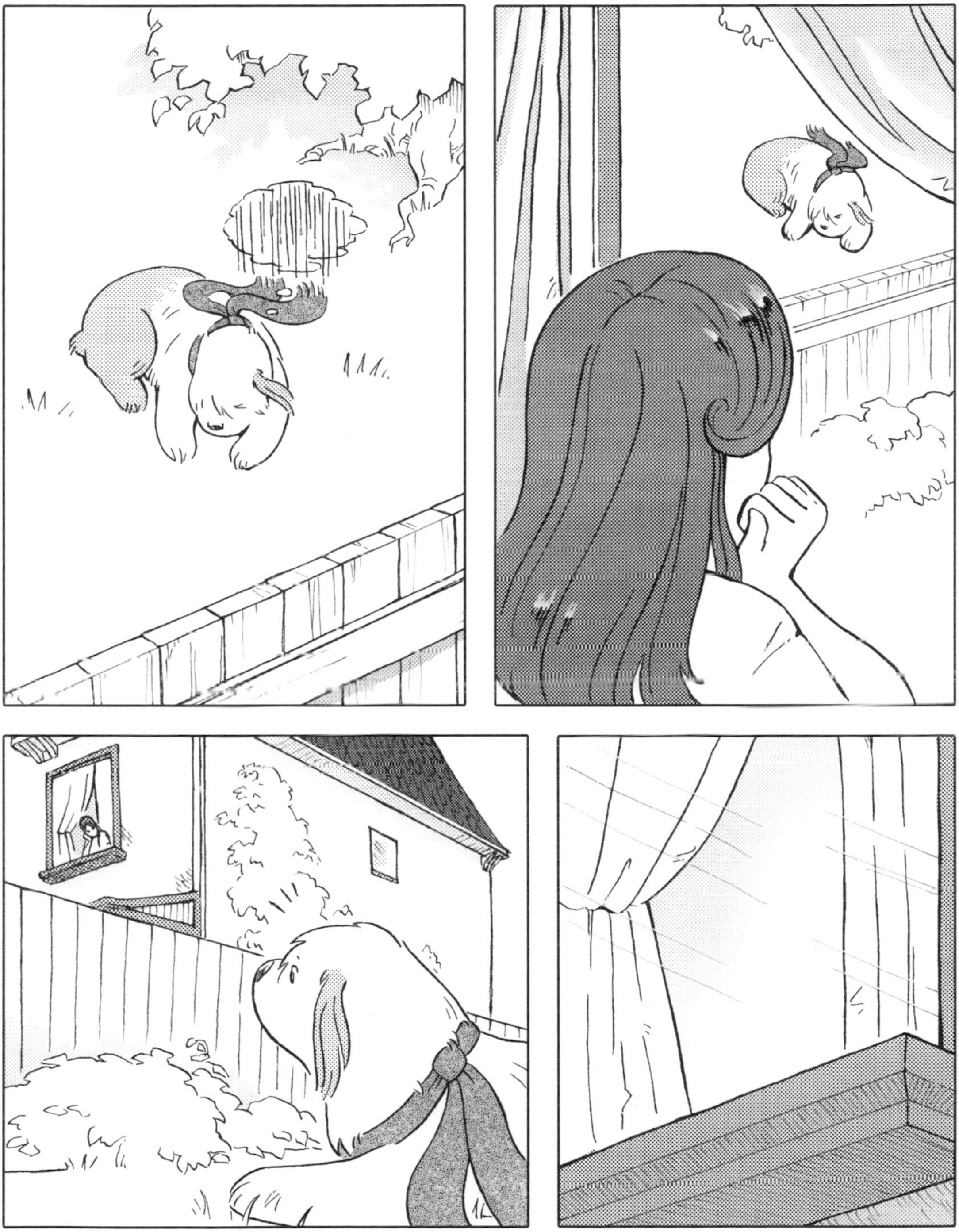

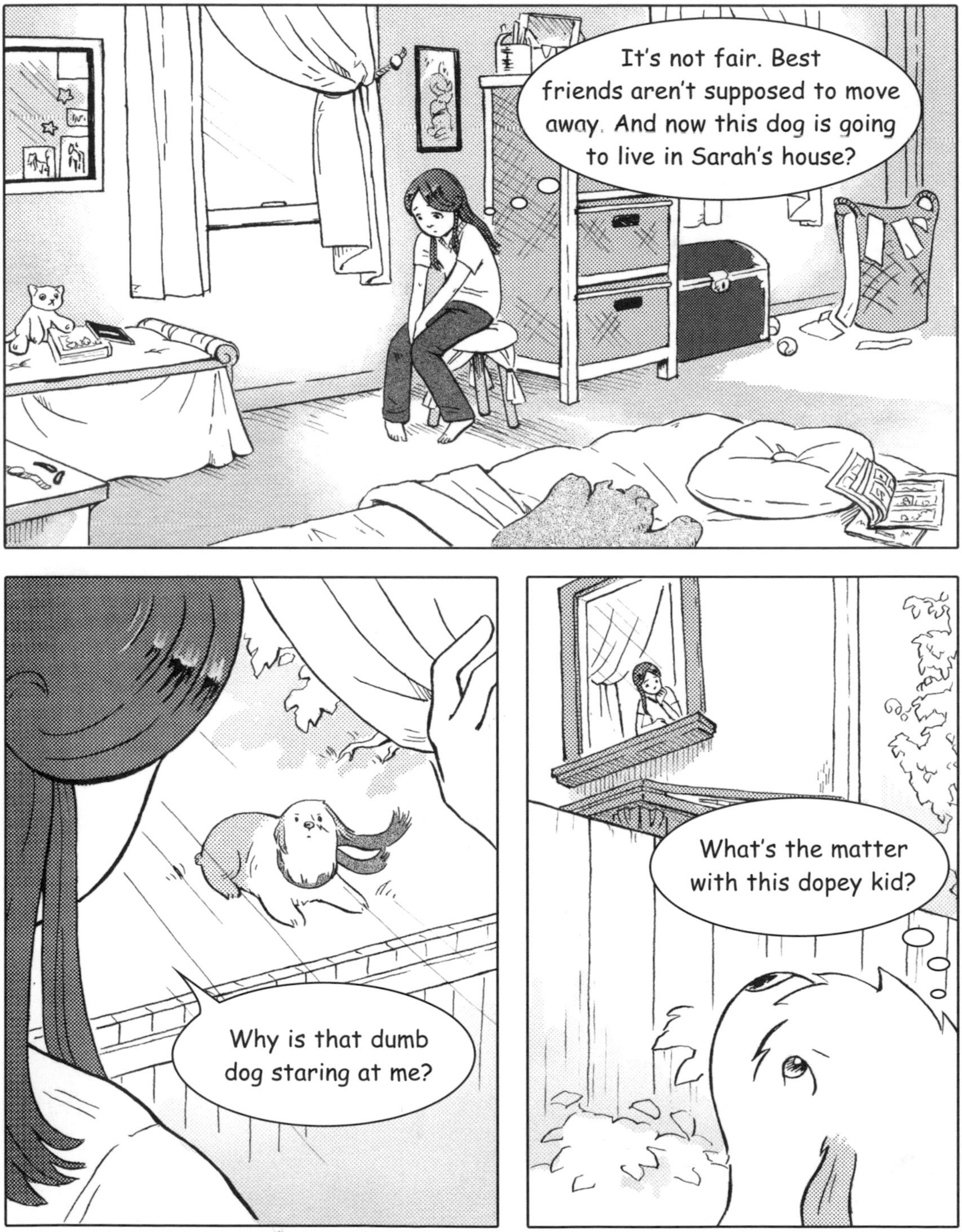
It's not fair. Best friends aren't supposed to move away. And now this dog is going to live in Sarah's house?
Why is that dumb dog staring at me?
What's the matter with this dopey kid?

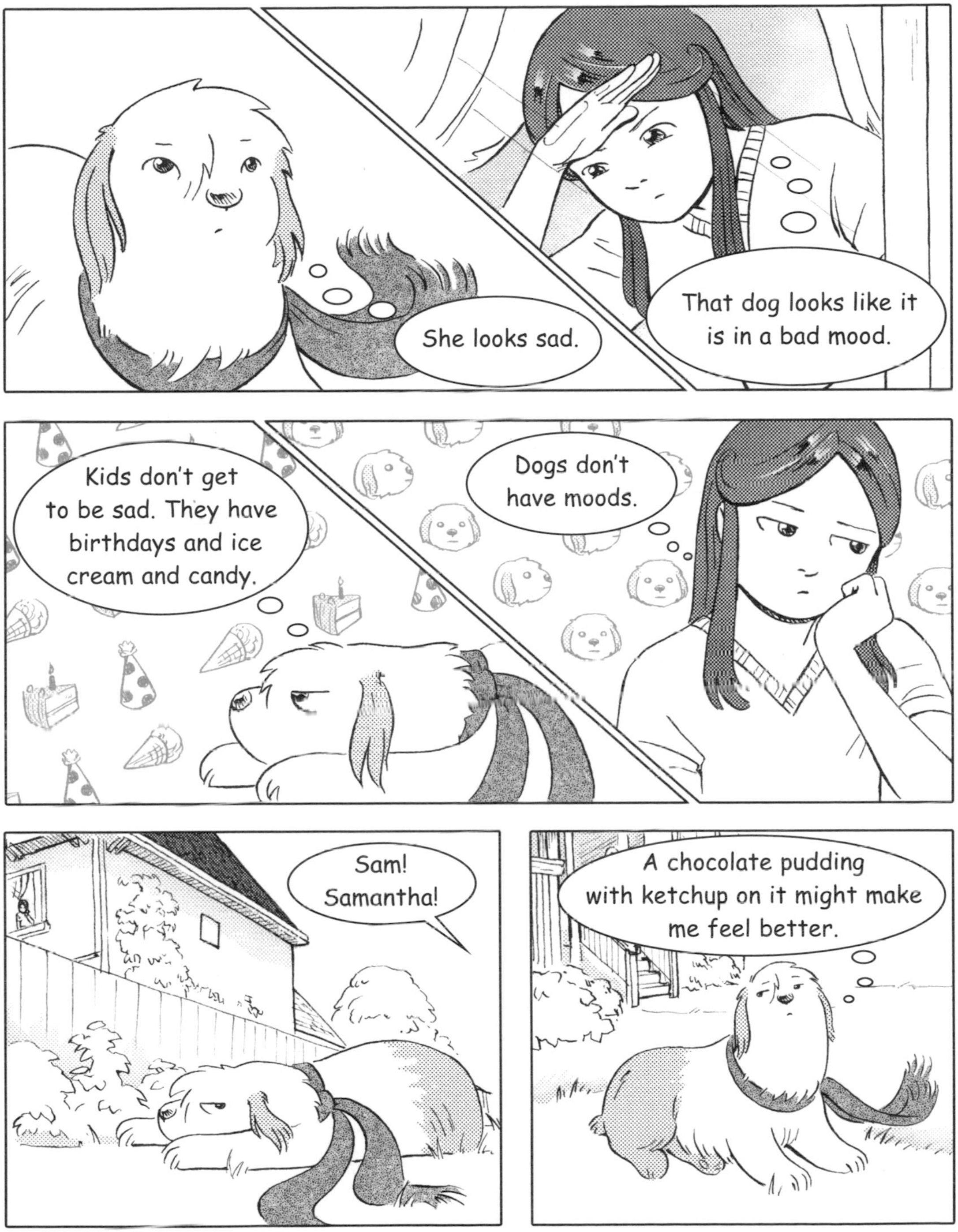
She looks sad.
That dog looks like it is in a bad mood.
Kids don't get to be sad. They have birthdays and ice cream and candy.
Dogs don't have moods.
Sam! Samantha!
A chocolate pudding with ketchup on it might make me feel better.

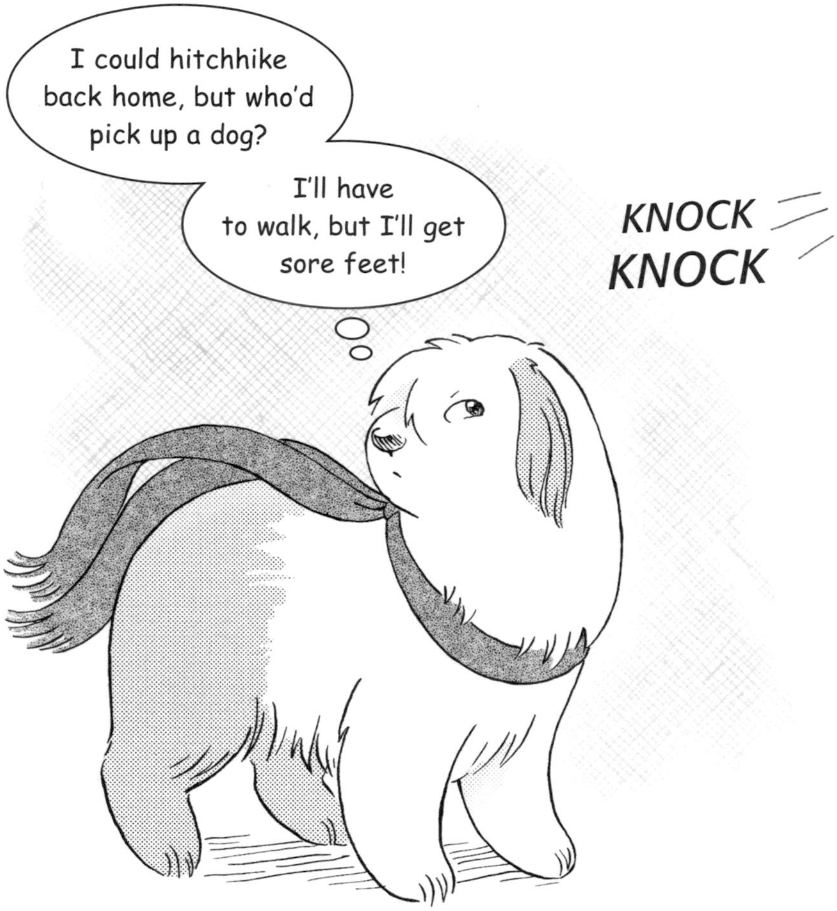
I could hitchhike back home, but who'd pick up a dog?
I'll have to walk, but I'll get sore feet!
KNOCK KNOCK

The next day ...

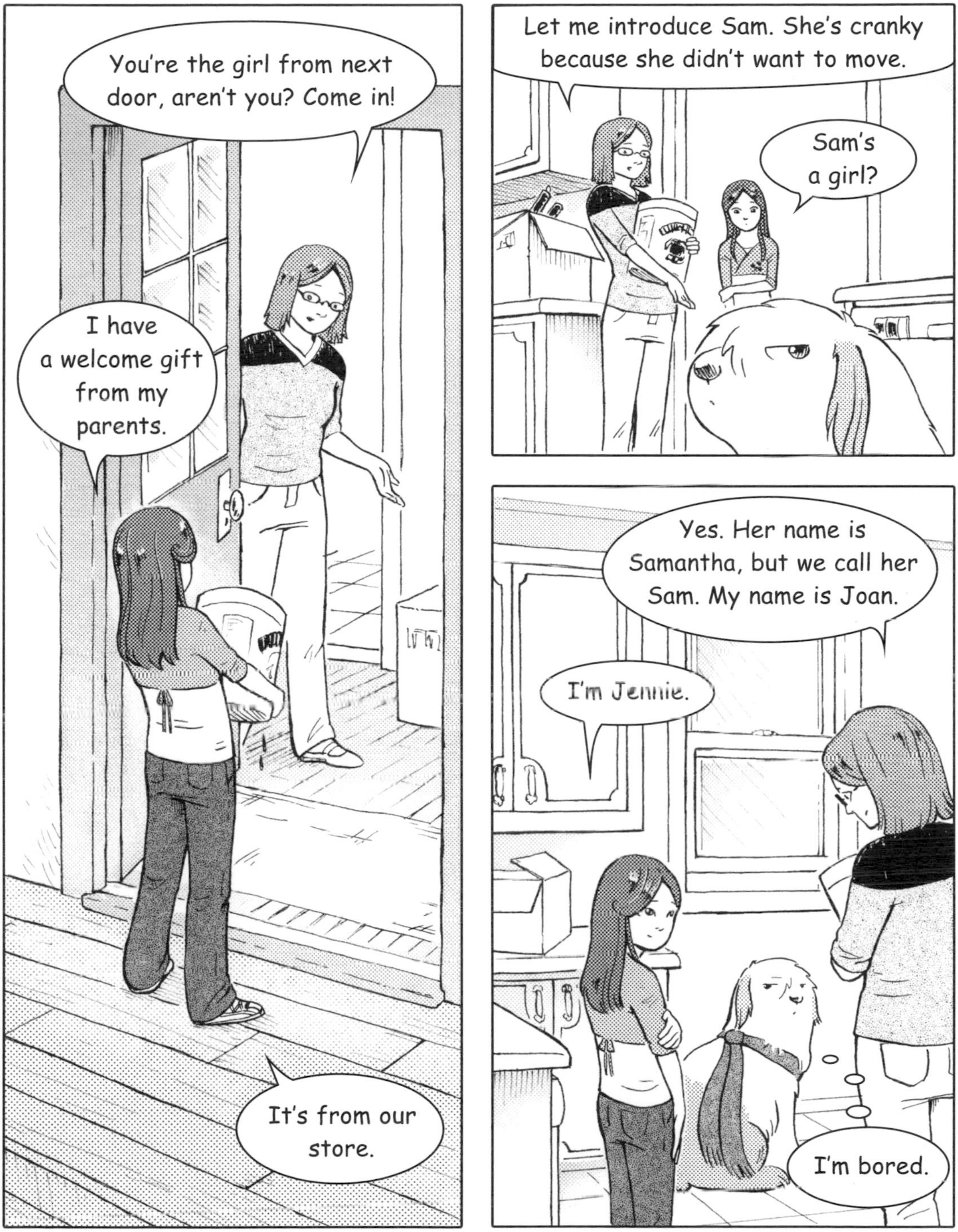

You're the girl from next door, aren't you? Come in!
I have a welcome gift from my parents.
It's from our store.
Let me introduce Sam. She's cranky because she didn't want to move.
Sam's a girl?
Yes. Her name is Samantha, but we call her Sam. My name is Joan.
I'm Jennie.
I'm bored.

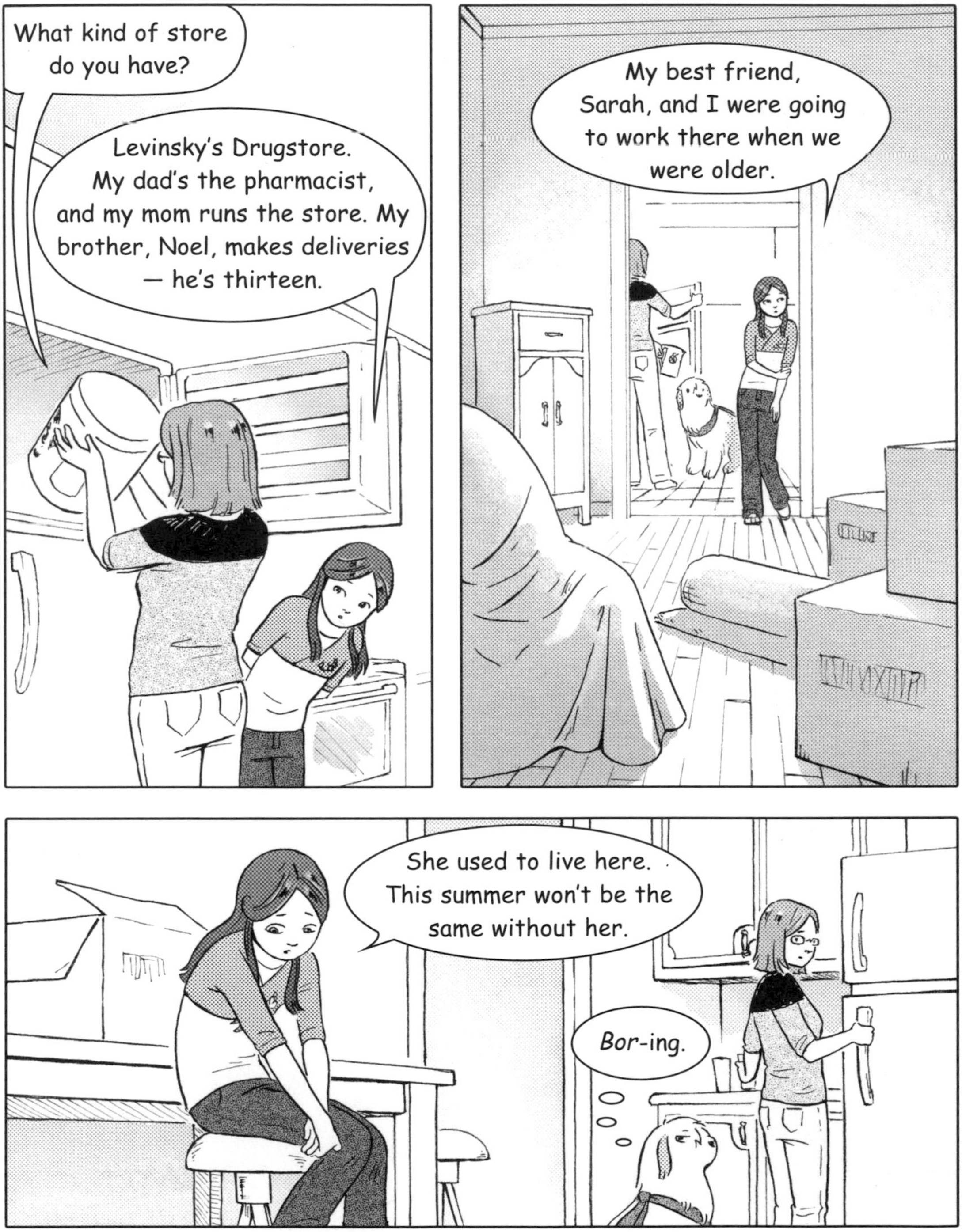
What kind of store do you have?
Levinsky's Drugstore. My dad's the pharmacist, and my mom runs the store. My brother, Noel, makes deliveries — he's thirteen.
My best friend, Sarah, and I were going to work there when we were older.
She used to live here. This summer won't be the same without her.
Bor-ing.

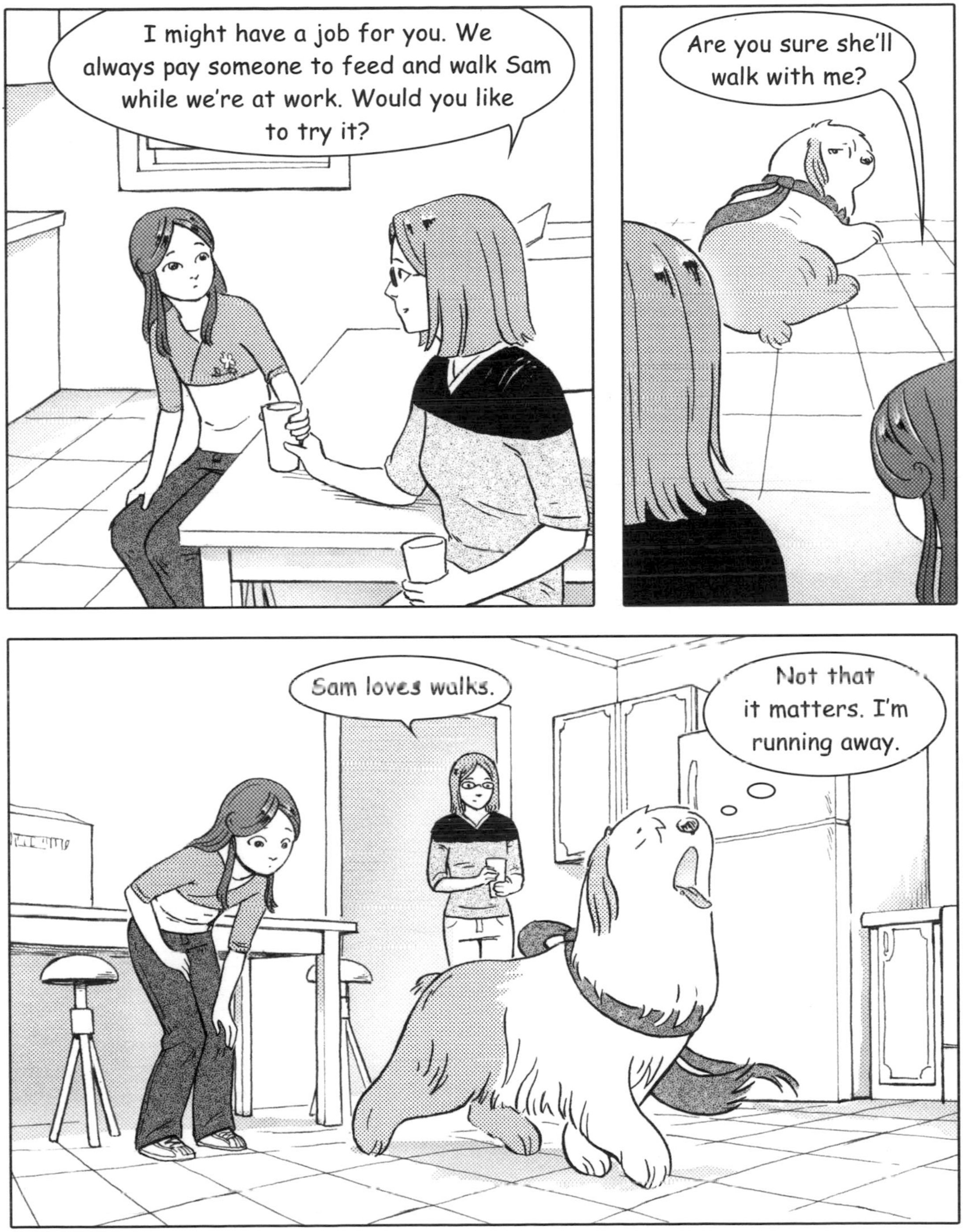
I might have a job for you. We always pay someone to feed and walk Sam while we're at work. Would you like to try it?
Are you sure she'll walk with me?
Sam loves walks.
Not that it matters. I'm running away.

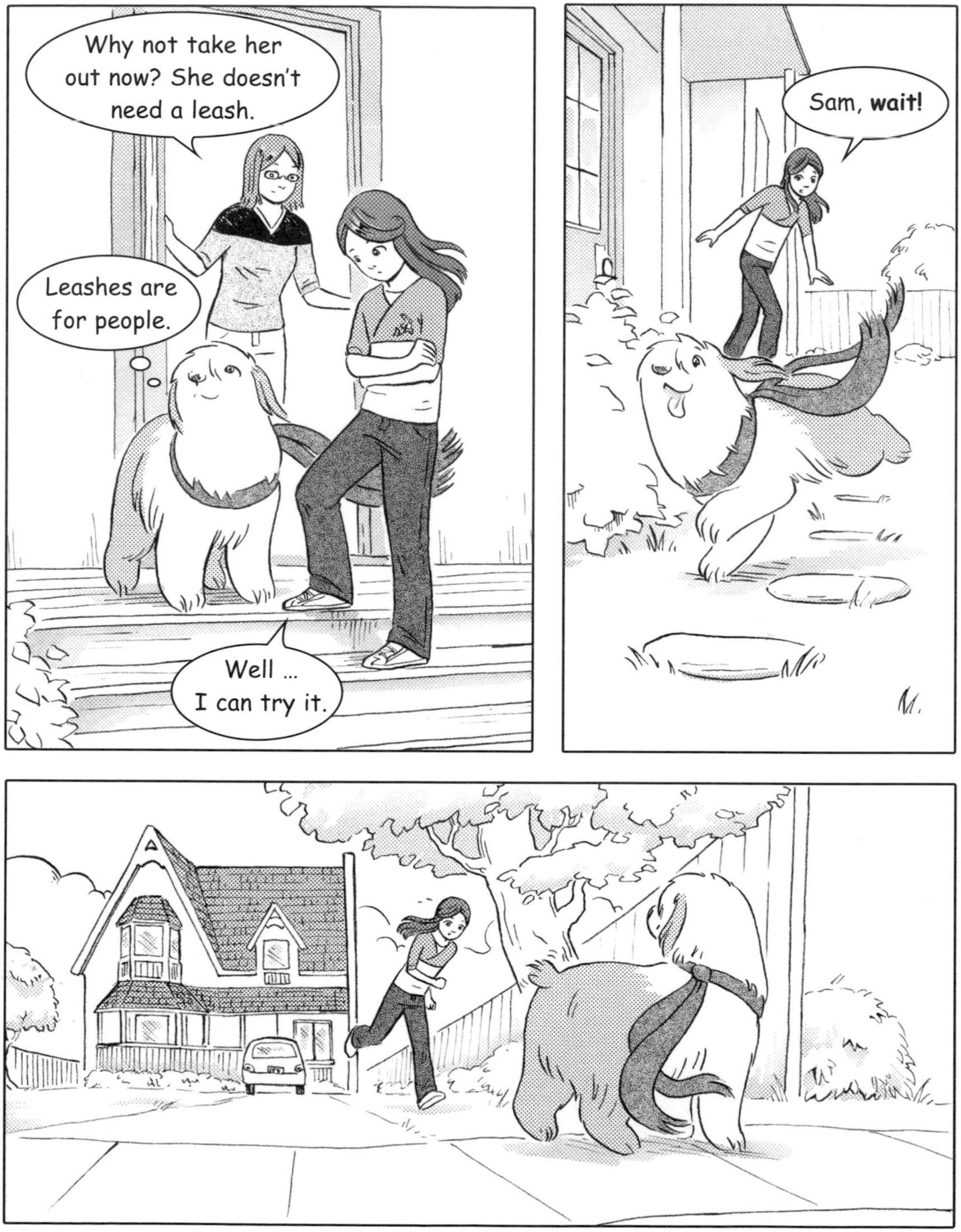
Why not take her out now? She doesn't need a leash.
Leashes are for people.
Well ... I can try it.
Sam, **wait!**

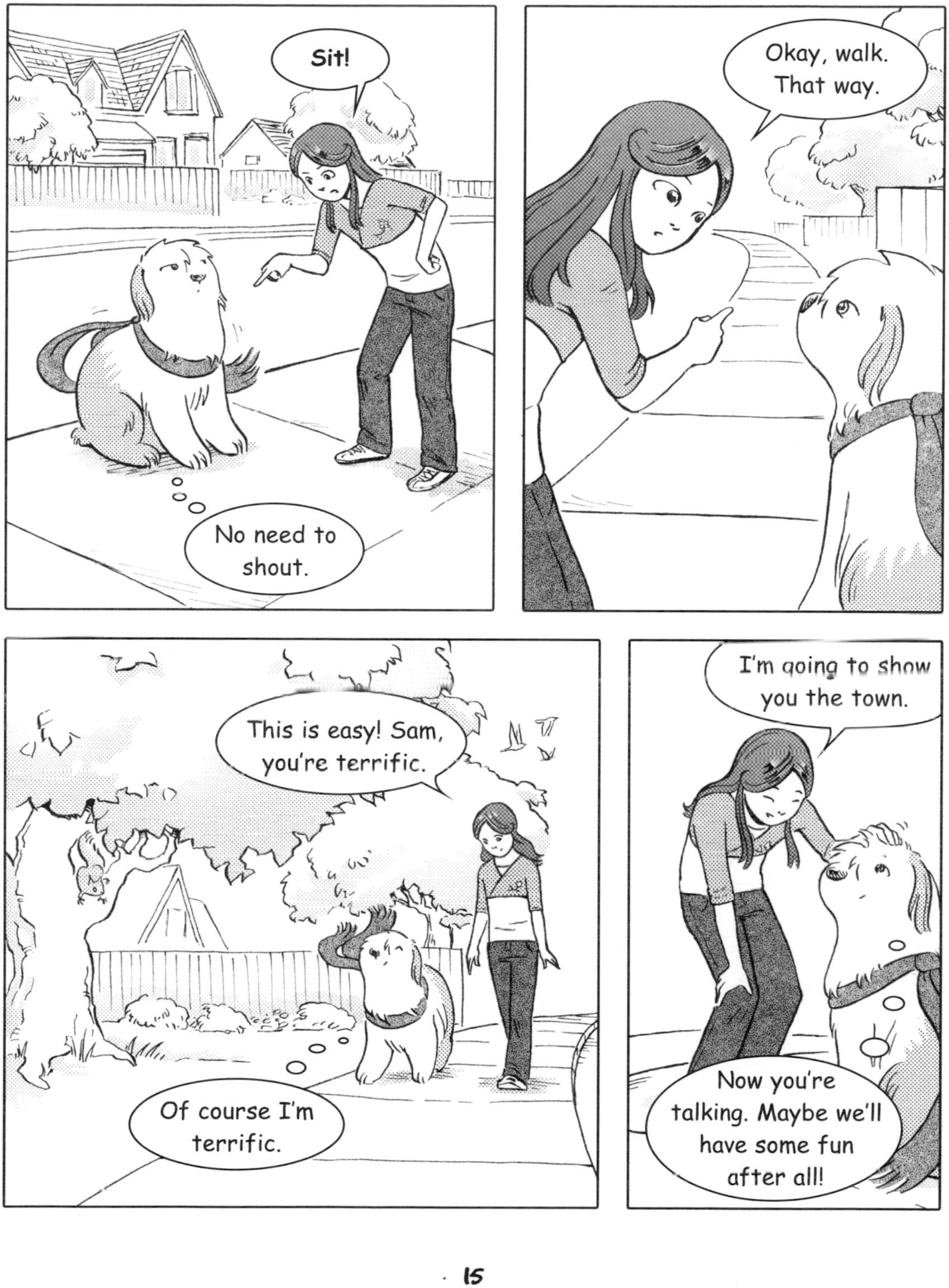
Sit!
No need to shout.
Okay, walk. That way.
This is easy! Sam, you're terrific.
Of course I'm terrific.
I'm going to show you the town.
Now you're talking. Maybe we'll have some fun after all!

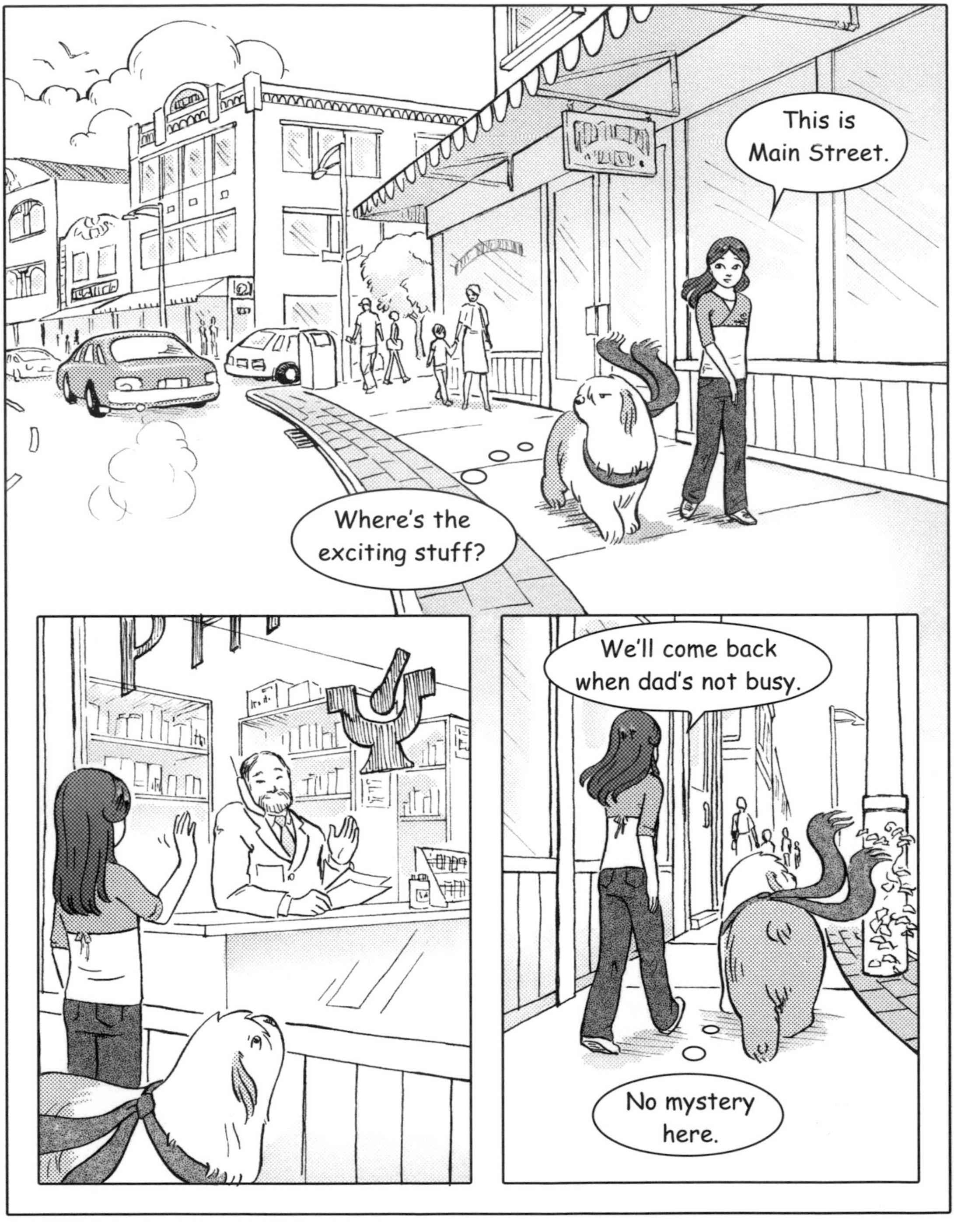
This is Main Street.
Where's the exciting stuff?
We'll come back when dad's not busy.
No mystery here.

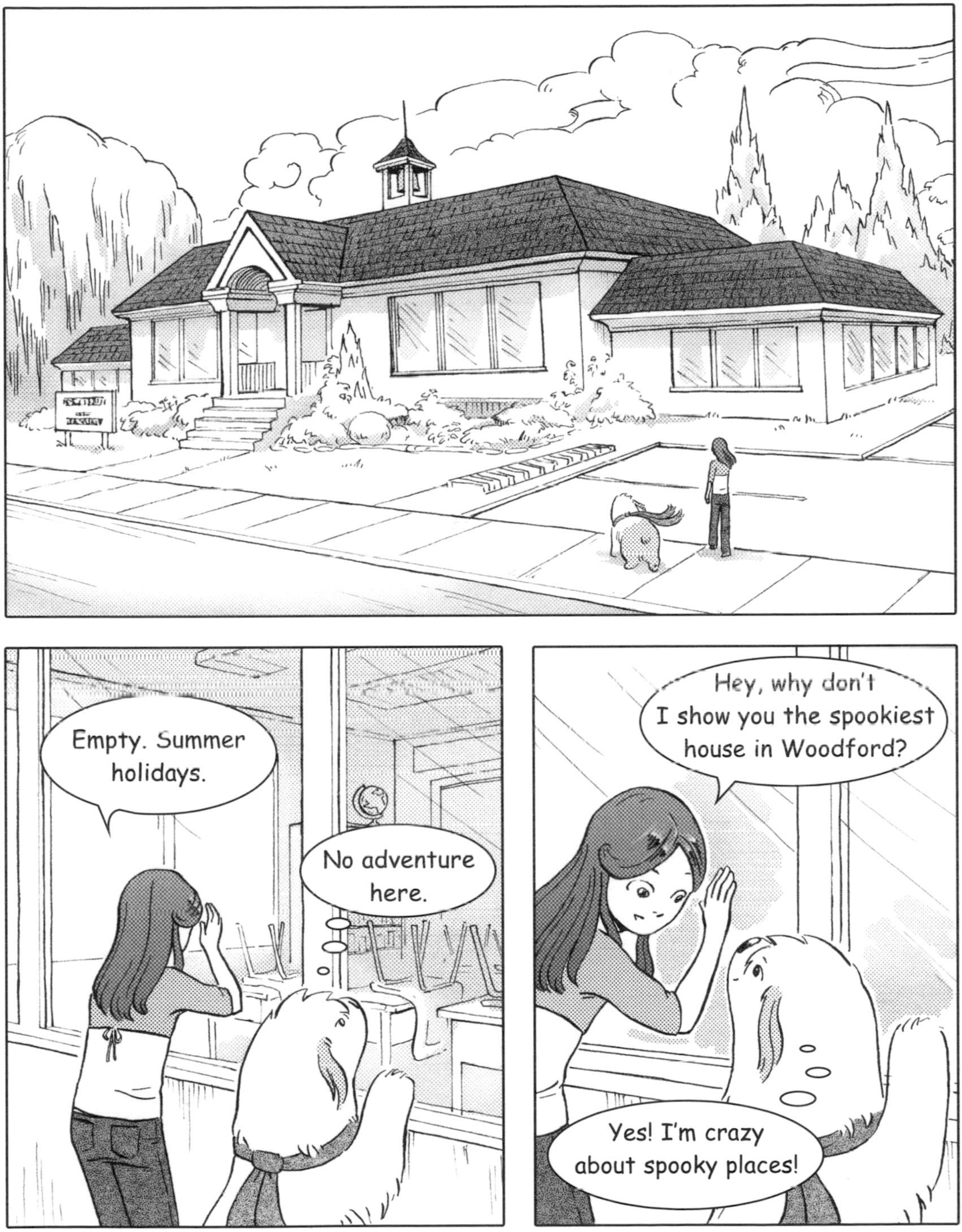
Empty. Summer holidays.
No adventure here.
Hey, why don't I show you the spookiest house in Woodford?
Yes! I'm crazy about spooky places!

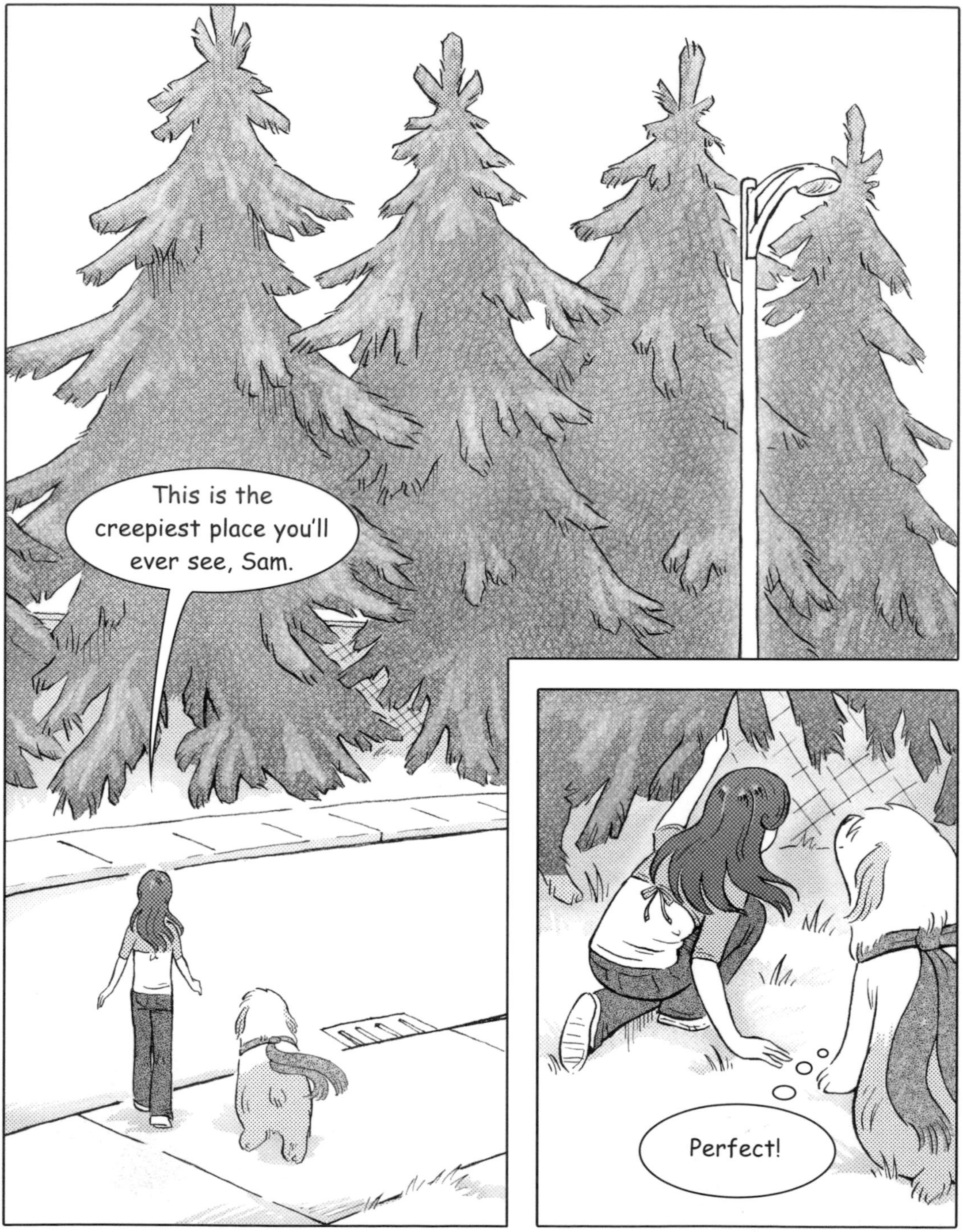
This is the creepiest place you'll ever see, Sam.
Perfect!

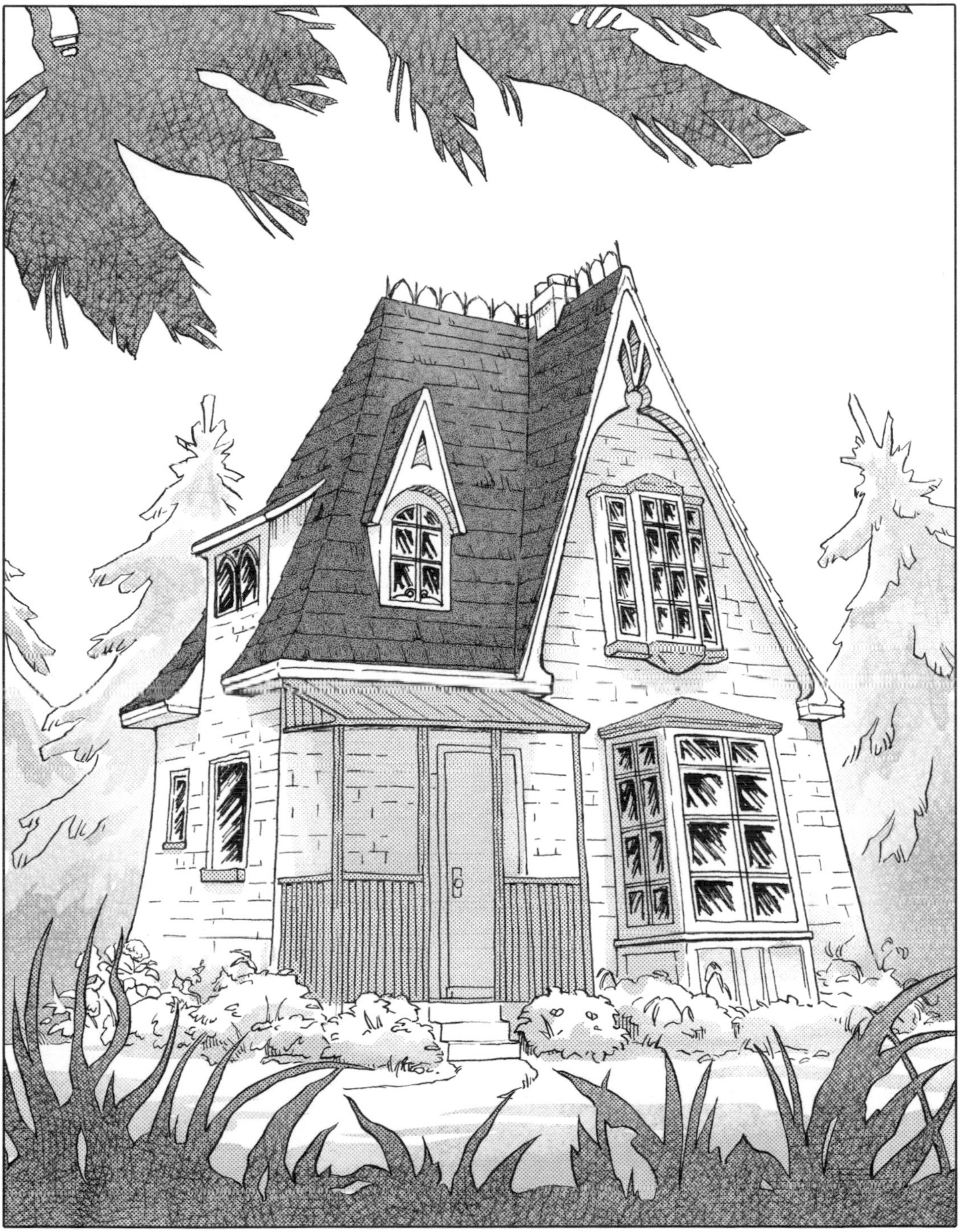

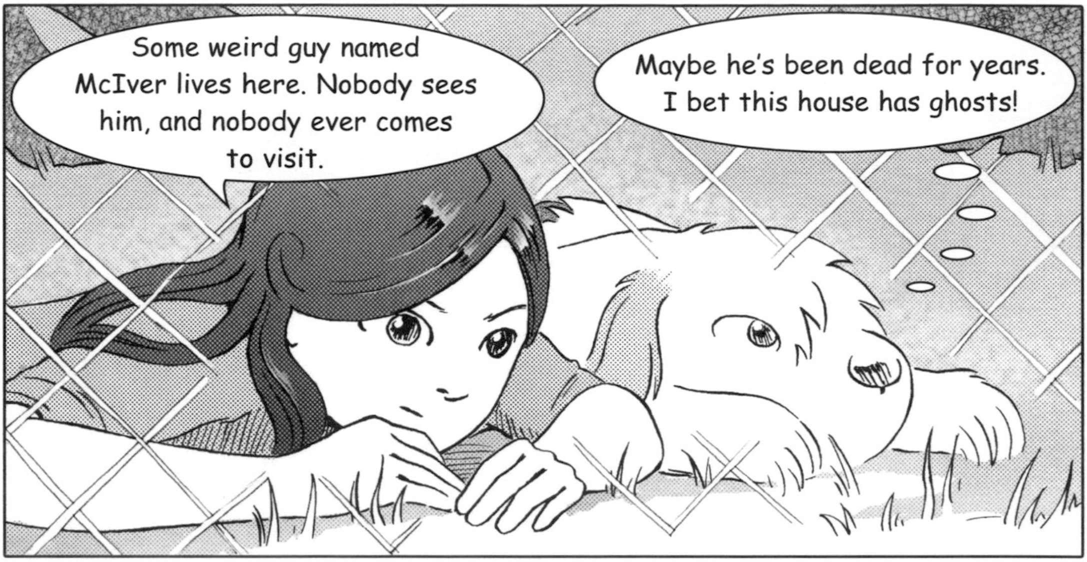
Some weird guy named McIver lives here. Nobody sees him, and nobody ever comes to visit.
Maybe he's been dead for years. I bet this house has ghosts!

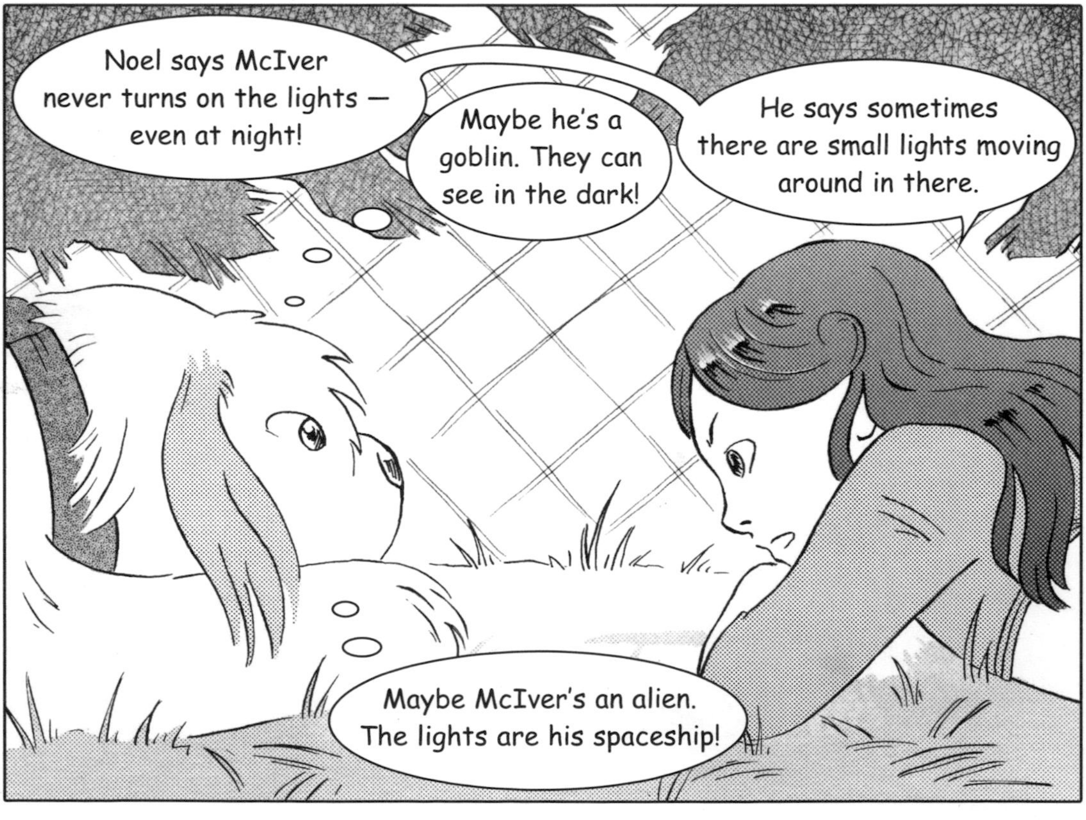
Noel says McIver never turns on the lights — even at night!
Maybe he's a goblin. They can see in the dark!
He says sometimes there are small lights moving around in there.
Maybe McIver's an alien. The lights are his spaceship!

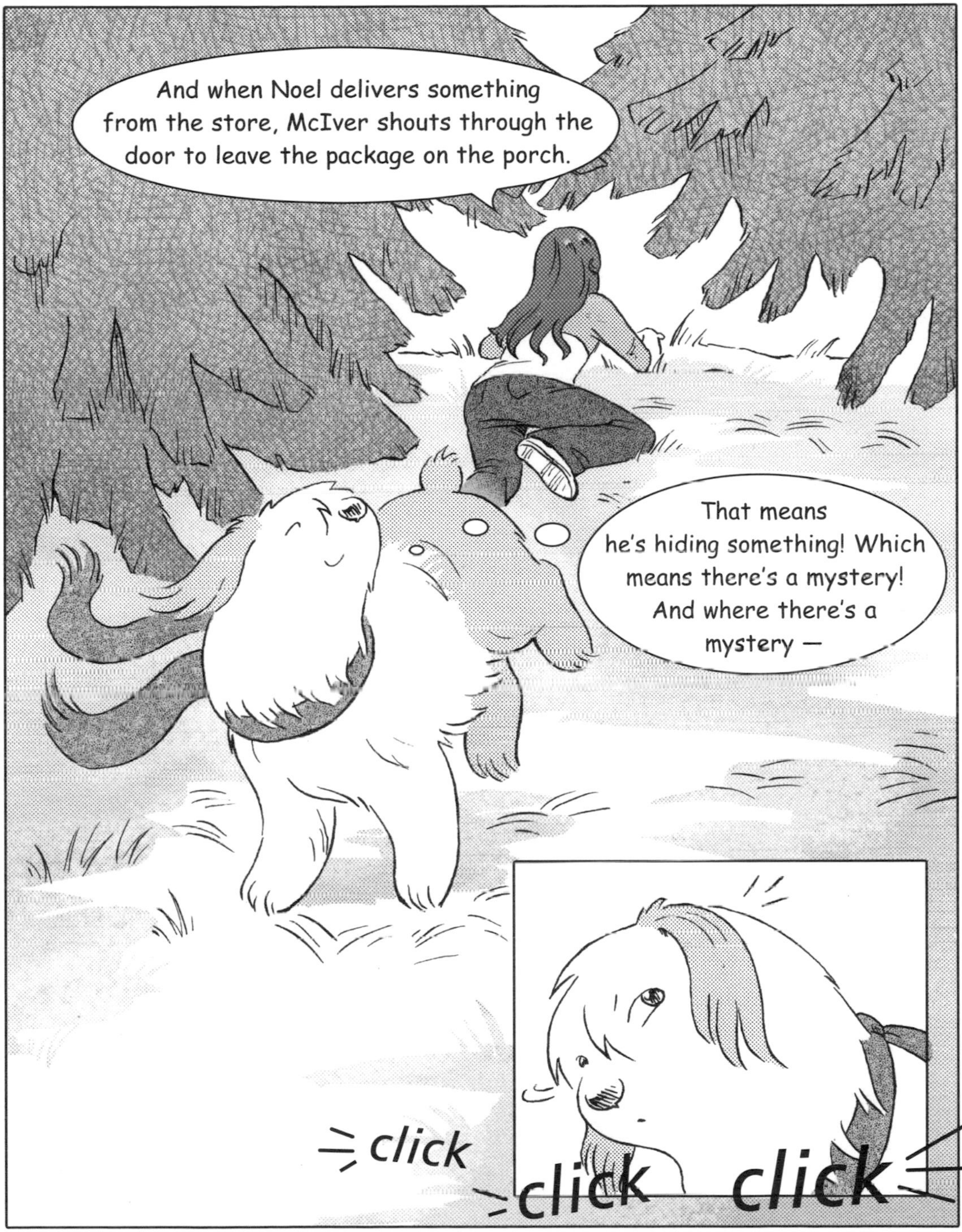
And when Noel delivers something from the store, McIver shouts through the door to leave the package on the porch.
That means he's hiding something! Which means there's a mystery! And where there's a mystery —
click
click
click

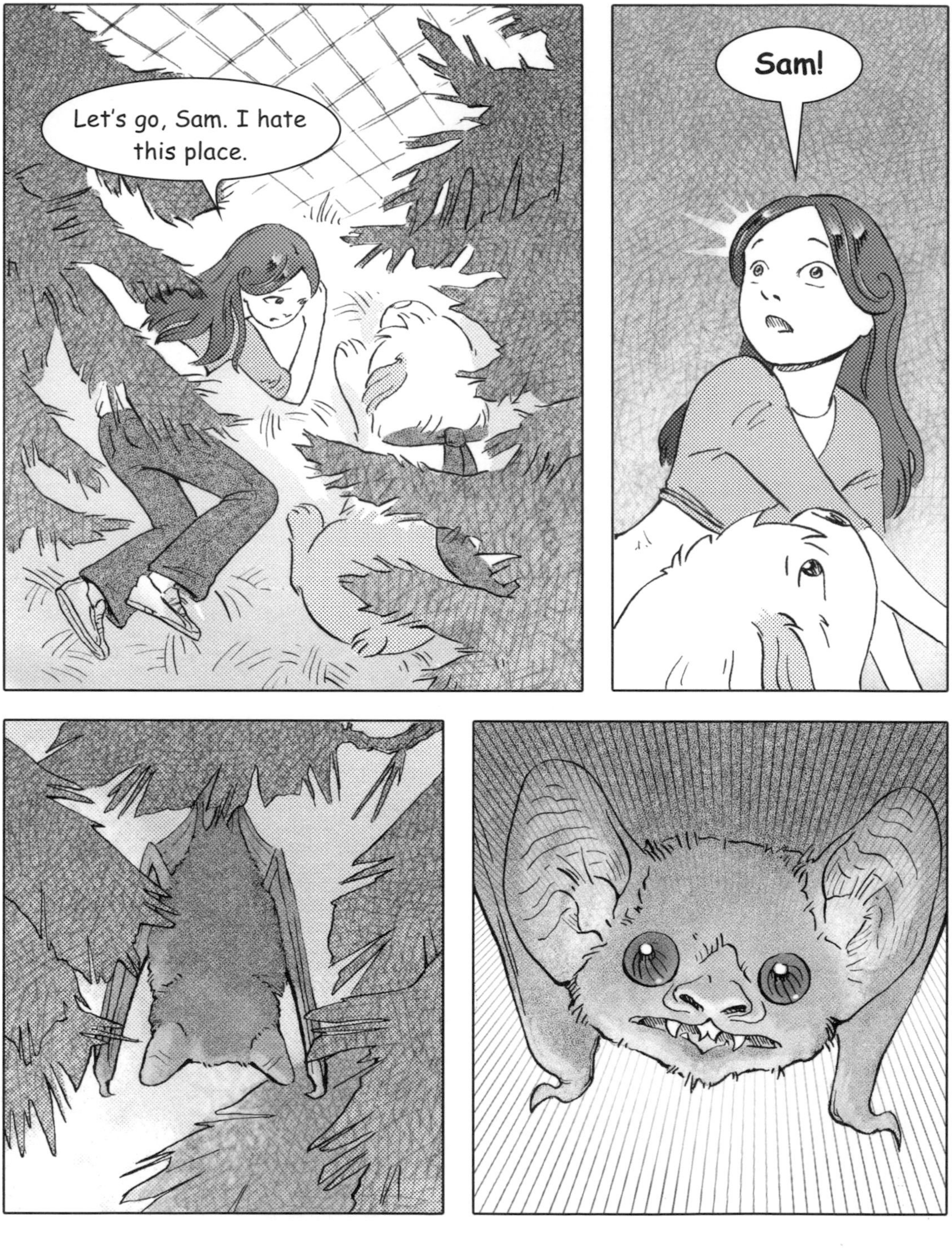
Let's go, Sam. I hate this place.
Sam!

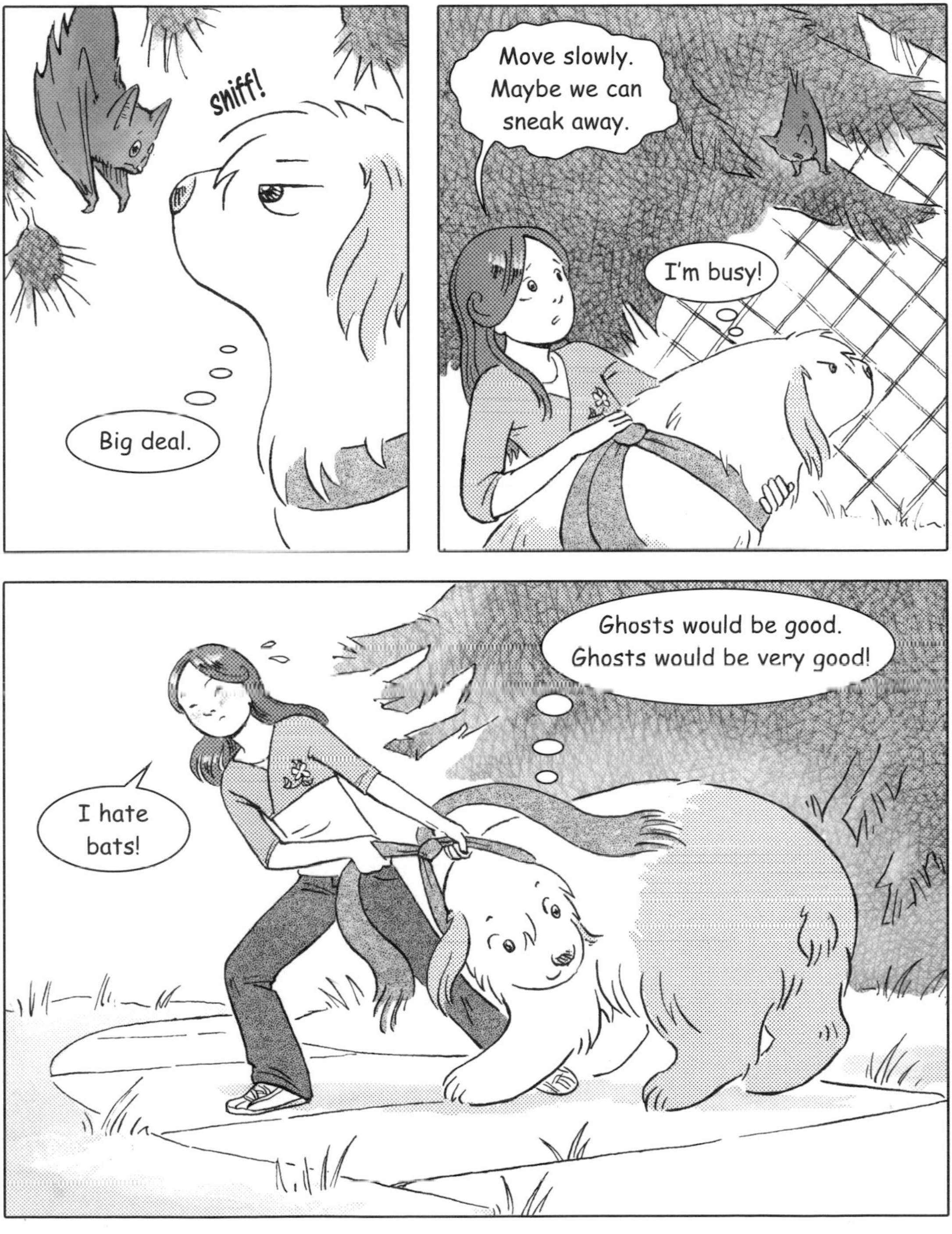
sniff!
Big deal.
Move slowly. Maybe we can sneak away.
I'm busy!
Ghosts would be good. Ghosts would be very good!
I hate bats!

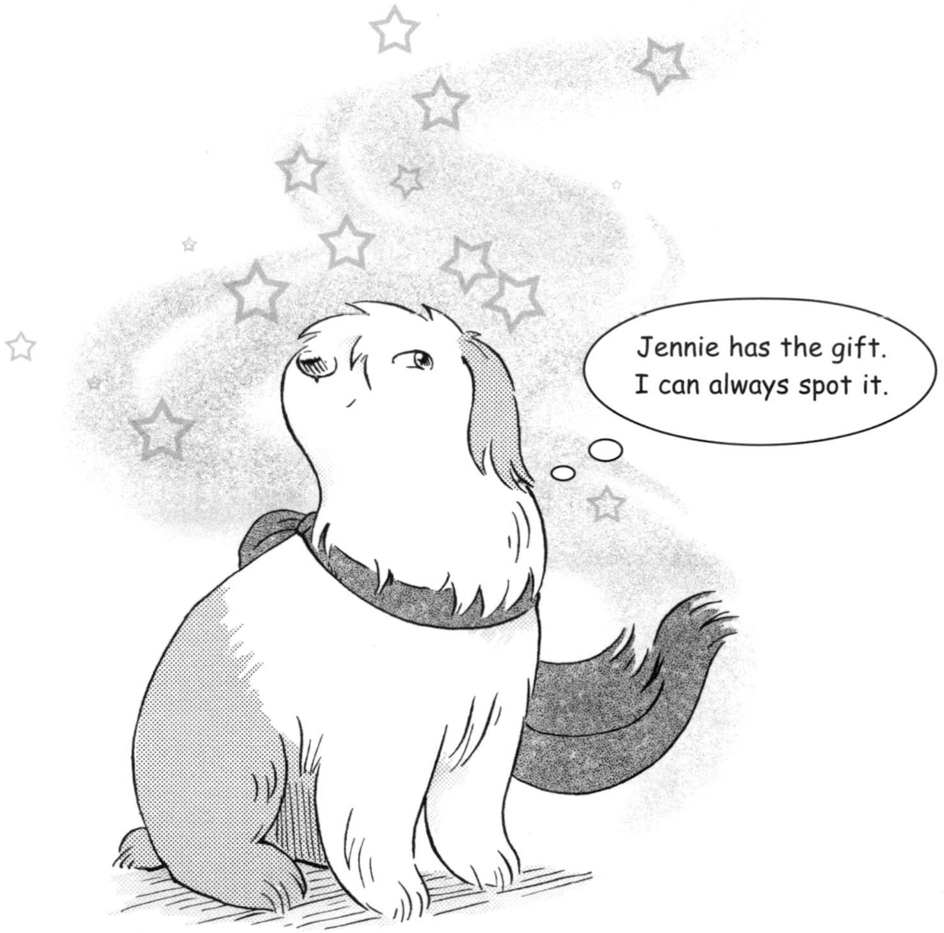
Jennie has the gift.
I can always spot it.

The next day ...

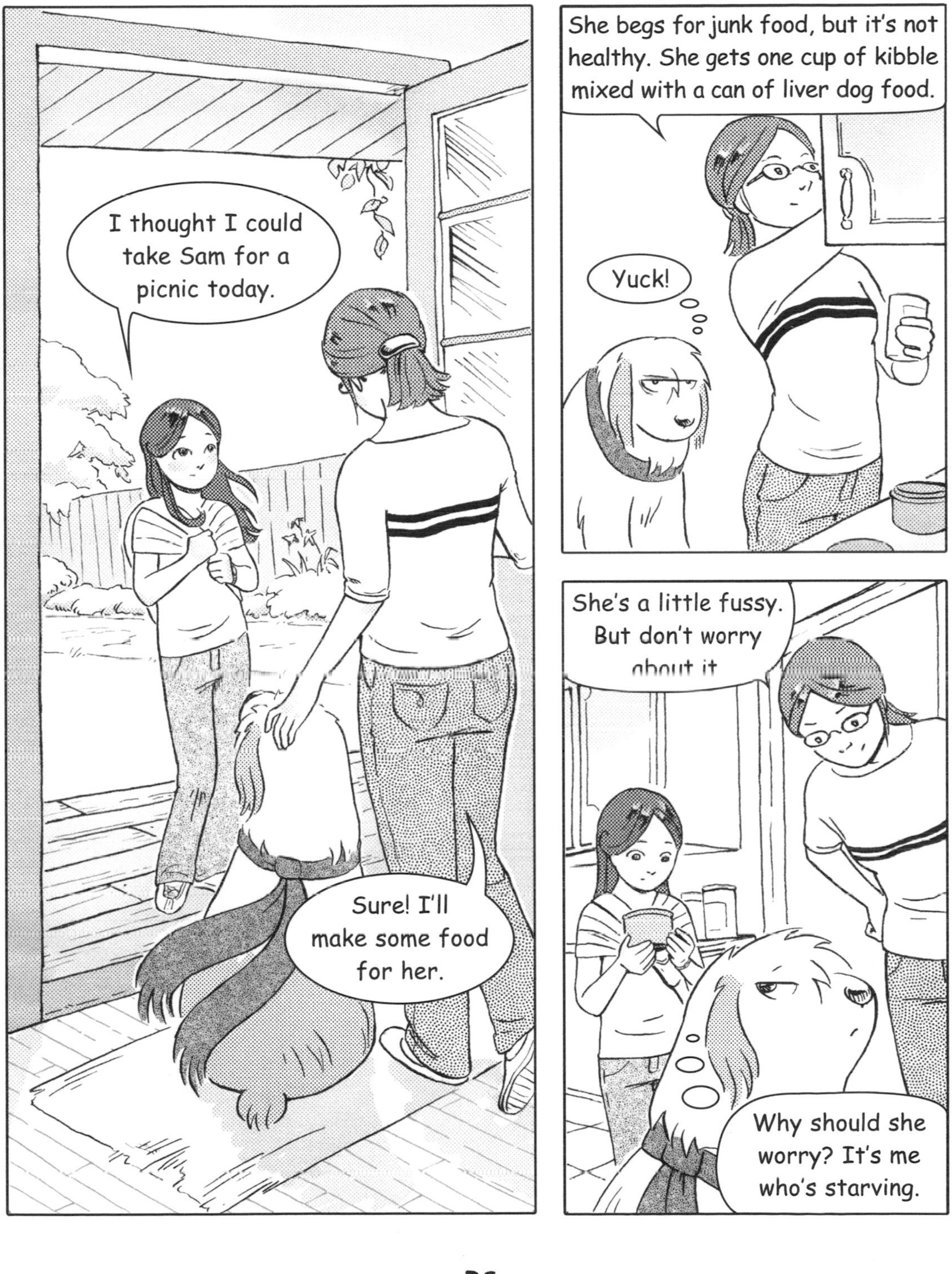

I thought I could take Sam for a picnic today.
Sure! I'll make some food for her.
She begs for junk food, but it's not healthy. She gets one cup of kibble mixed with a can of liver dog food.
Yuck!
She's a little fussy. But don't worry about it
Why should she worry? It's me who's starving.

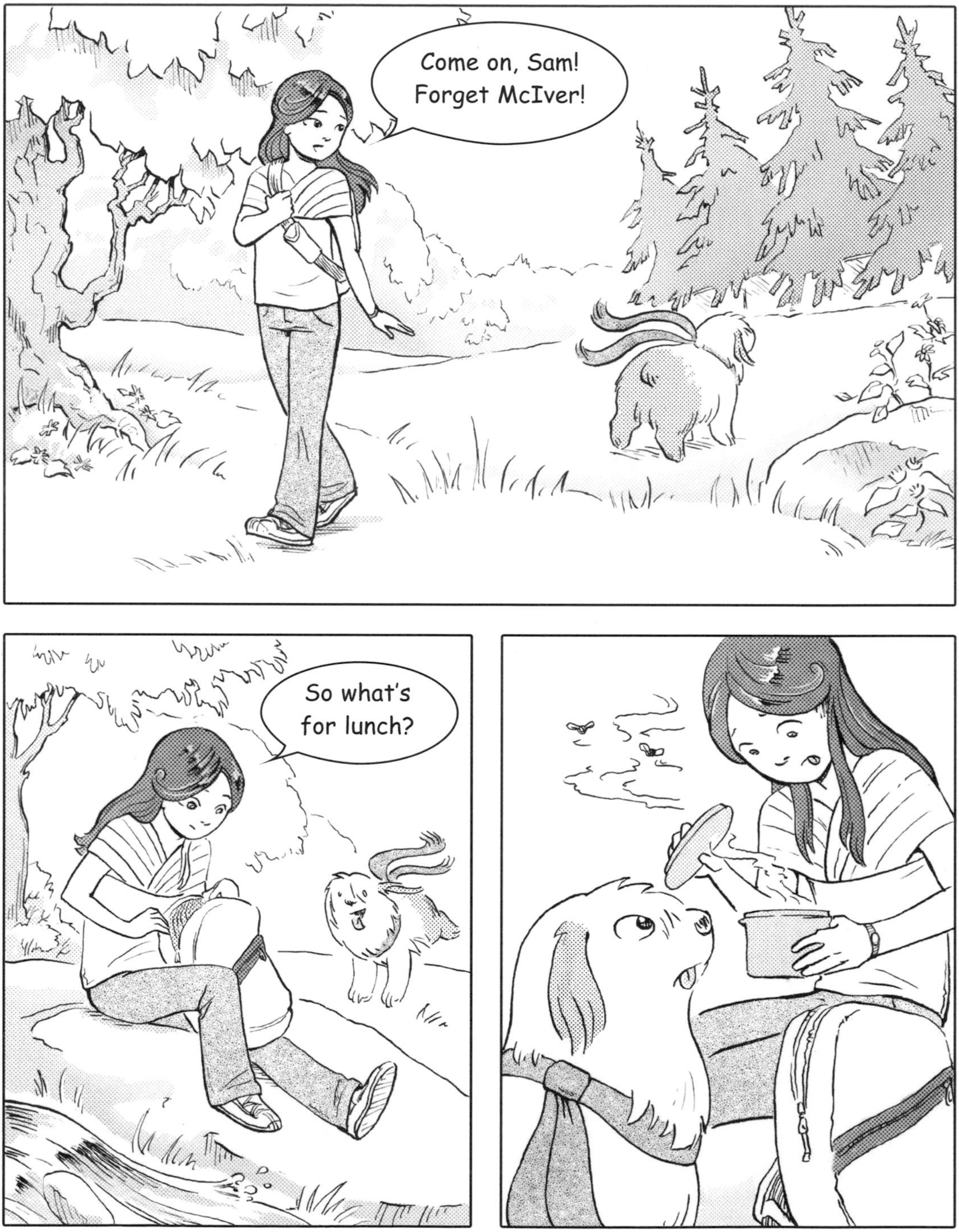
Come on, Sam! Forget McIver!
So what's for lunch?

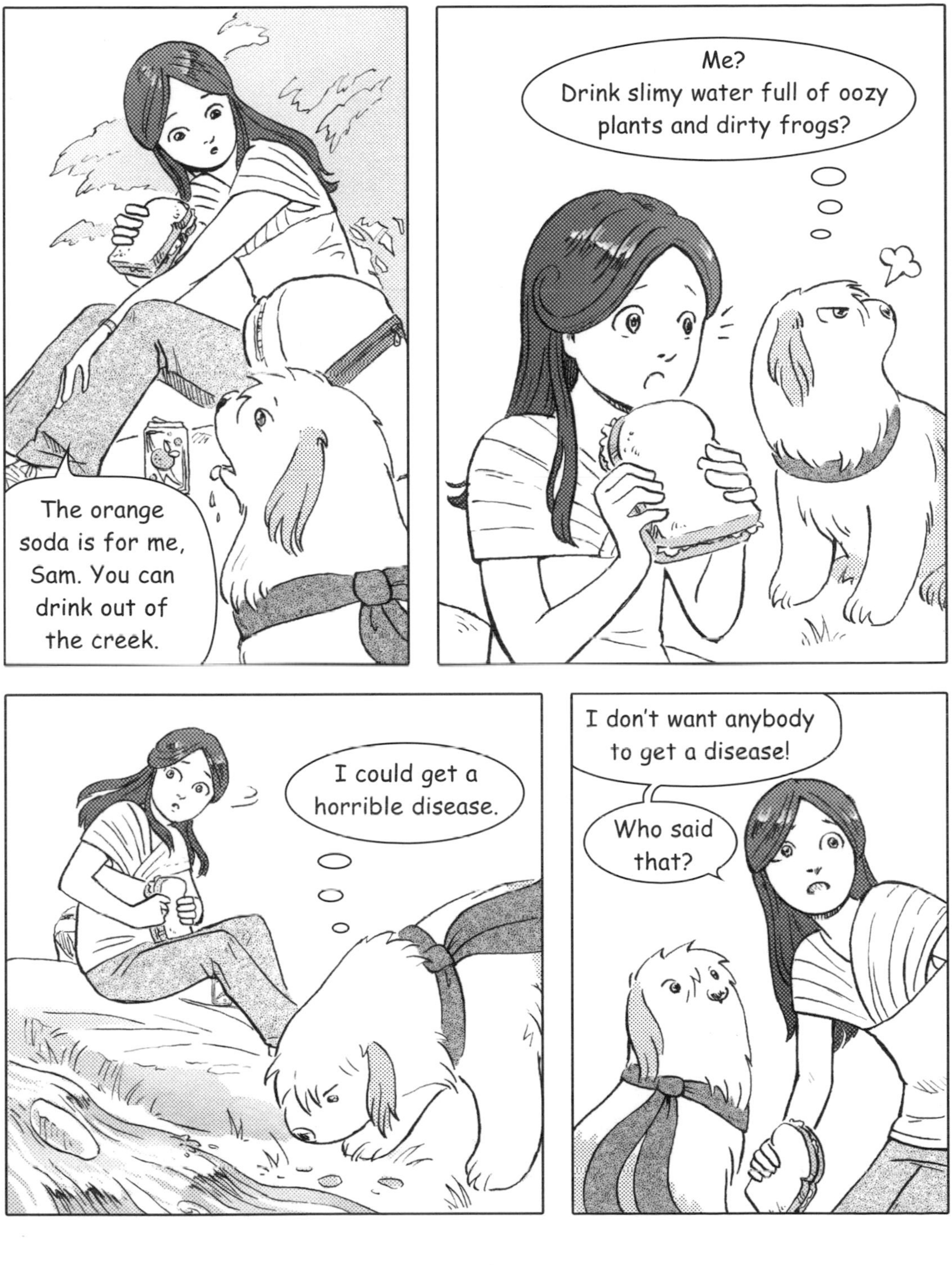
The orange soda is for me, Sam. You can drink out of the creek.
Me? Drink slimy water full of oozy plants and dirty frogs?
I could get a horrible disease.
I don't want anybody to get a disease!
Who said that?

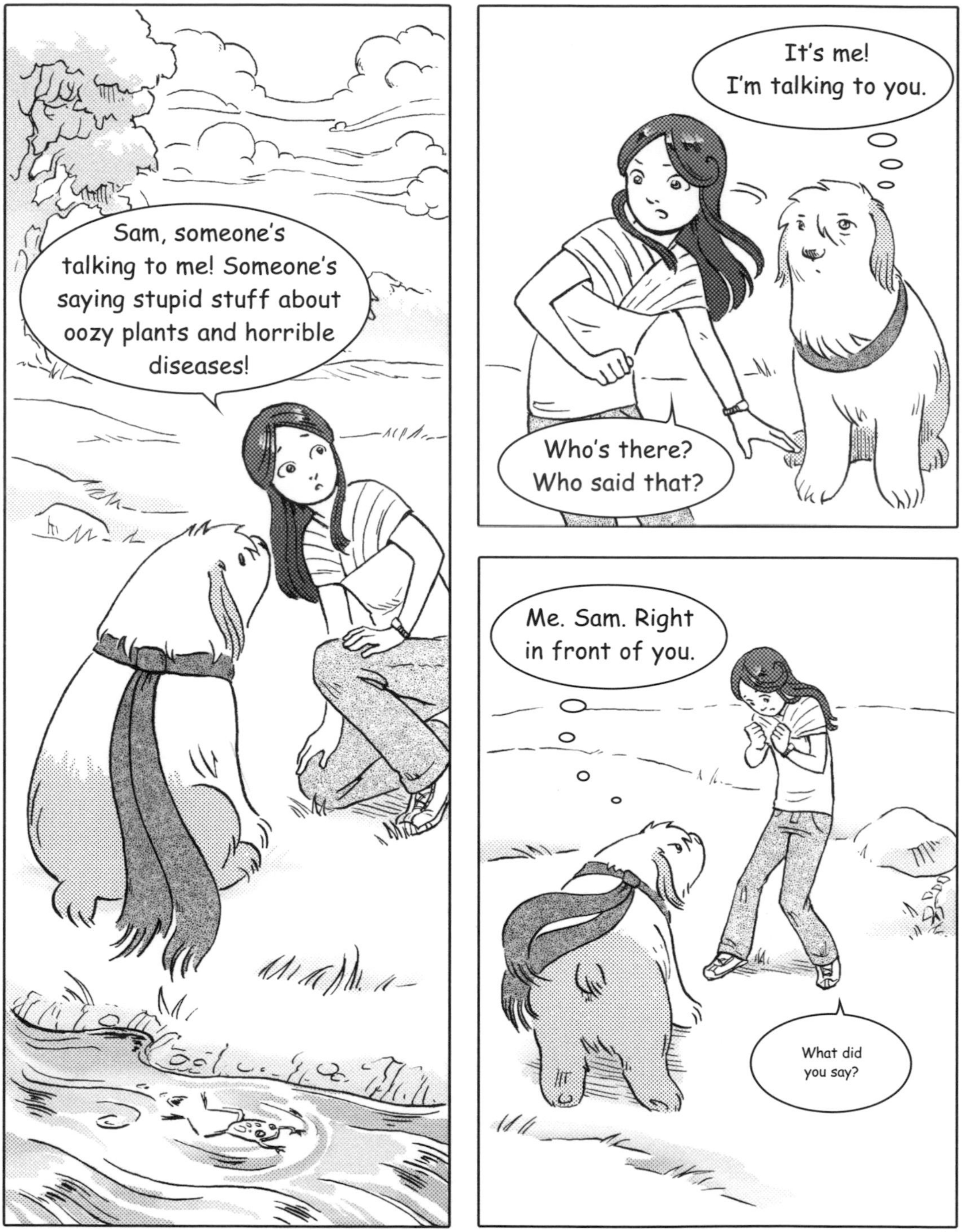
Sam, someone's talking to me! Someone's saying stupid stuff about oozy plants and horrible diseases!
It's me! I'm talking to you.
Who's there? Who said that?
Me. Sam. Right in front of you.
What did you say?

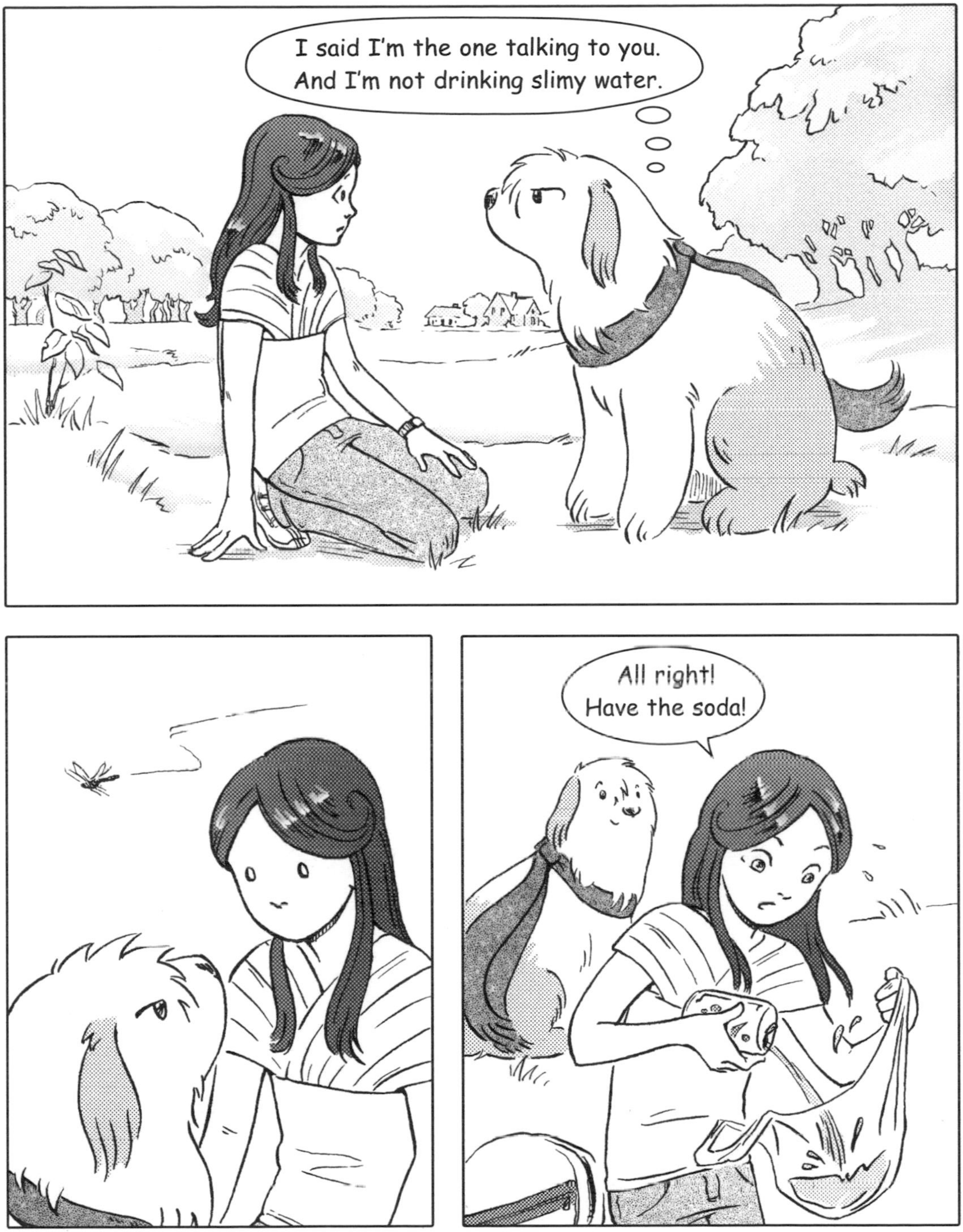
I said I'm the one talking to you. And I'm not drinking slimy water.
All right! Have the soda!

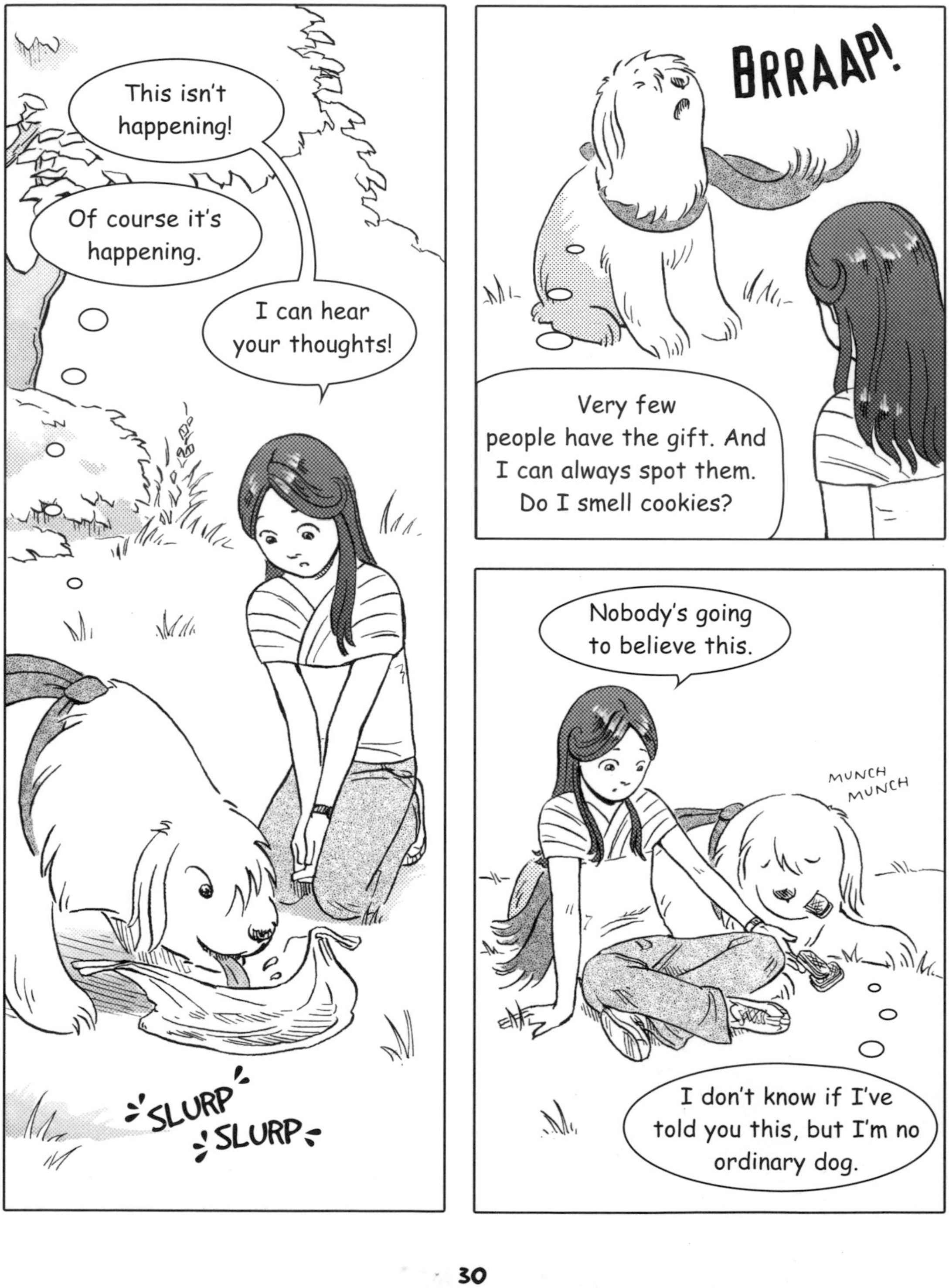
This isn't happening!
Of course it's happening.
I can hear your thoughts!
SLURP SLURP
BRRAAP!
Very few people have the gift. And I can always spot them. Do I smell cookies?
Nobody's going to believe this.
MUNCH MUNCH
I don't know if I've told you this, but I'm no ordinary dog.

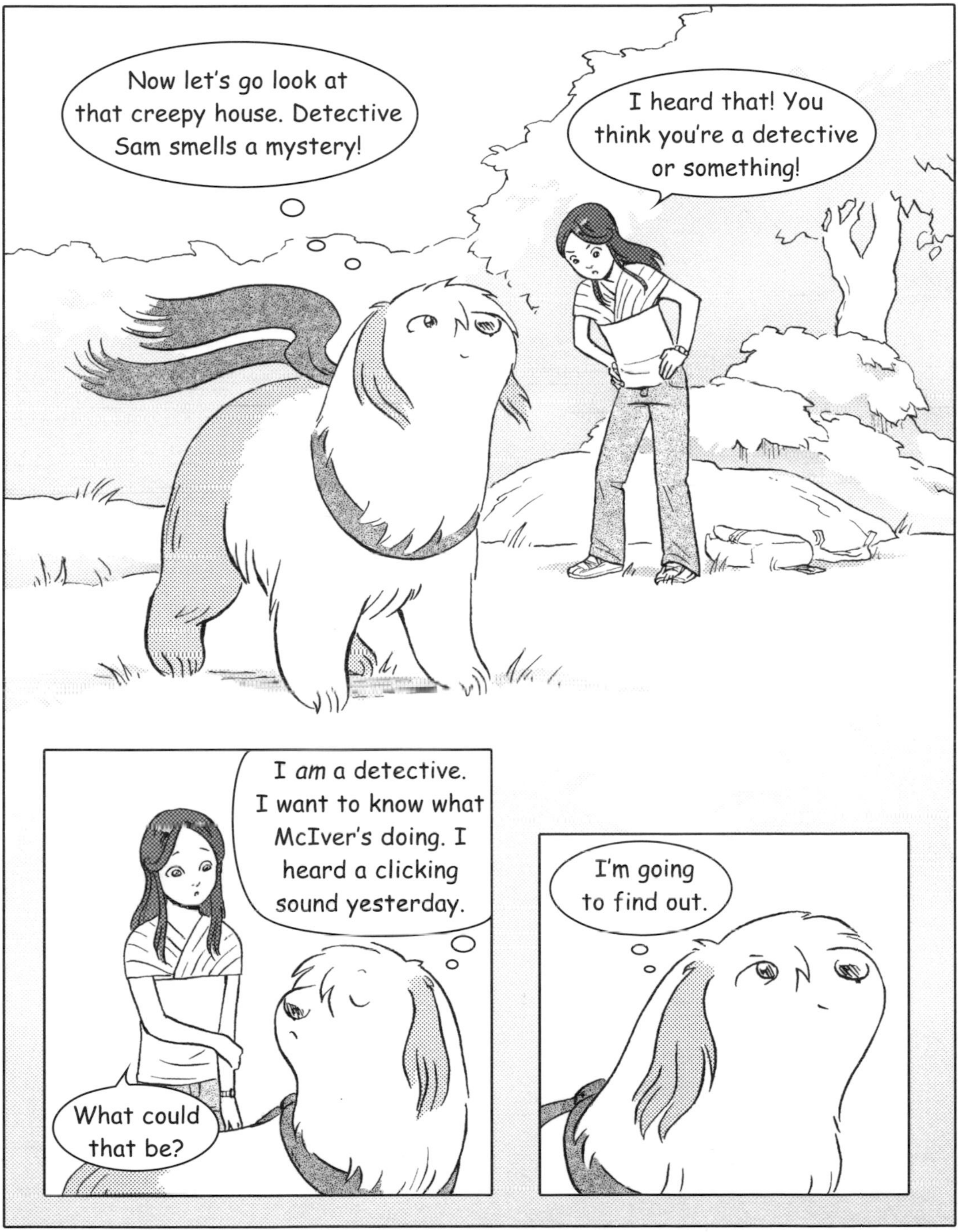
Now let's go look at that creepy house. Detective Sam smells a mystery!
I heard that! You think you're a detective or something!
I *am* a detective. I want to know what McIver's doing. I heard a clicking sound yesterday.
What could that be?
I'm going to find out.

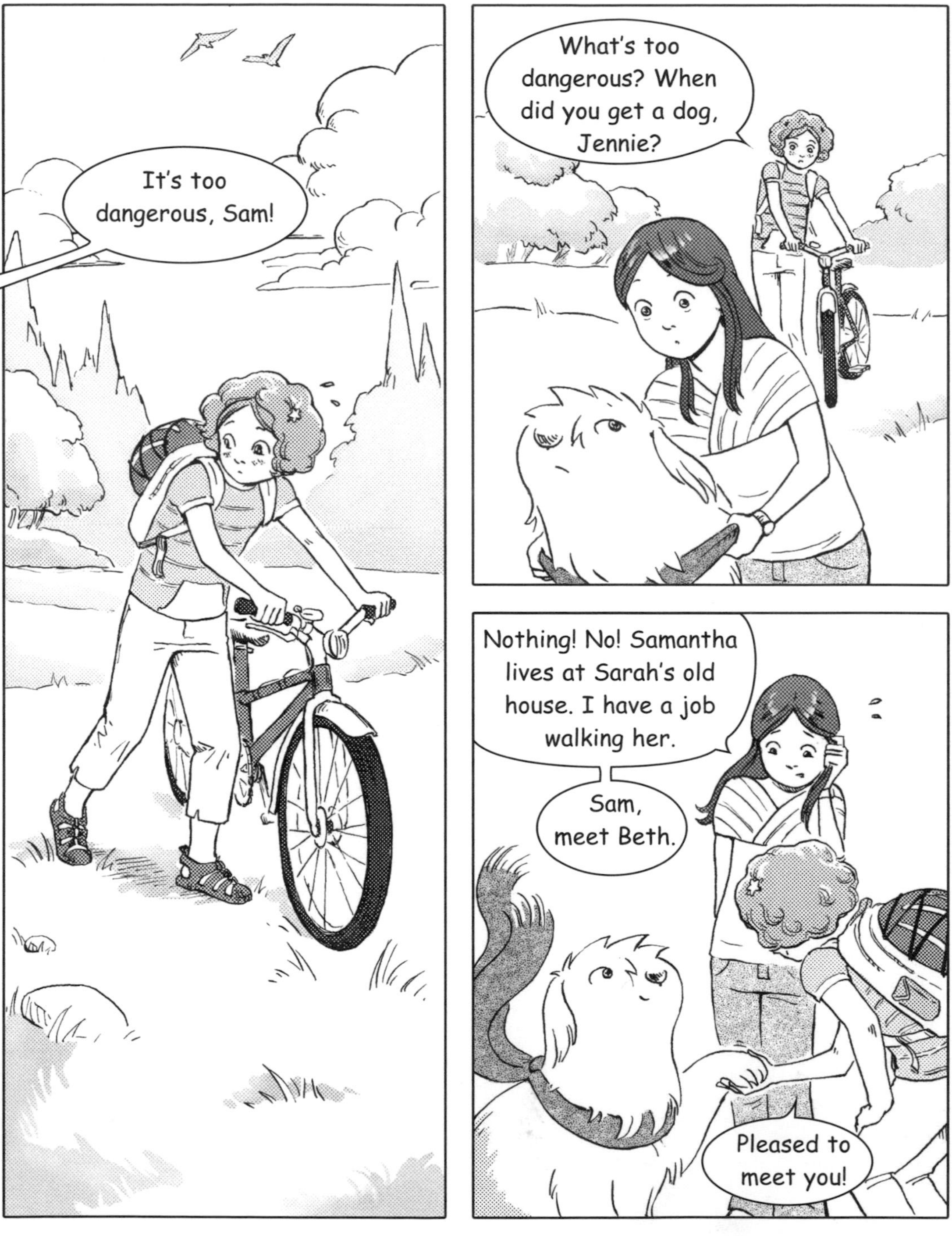
It's too dangerous, Sam!
What's too dangerous? When did you get a dog, Jennie?
Nothing! No! Samantha lives at Sarah's old house. I have a job walking her.
Sam, meet Beth.
Pleased to meet you!

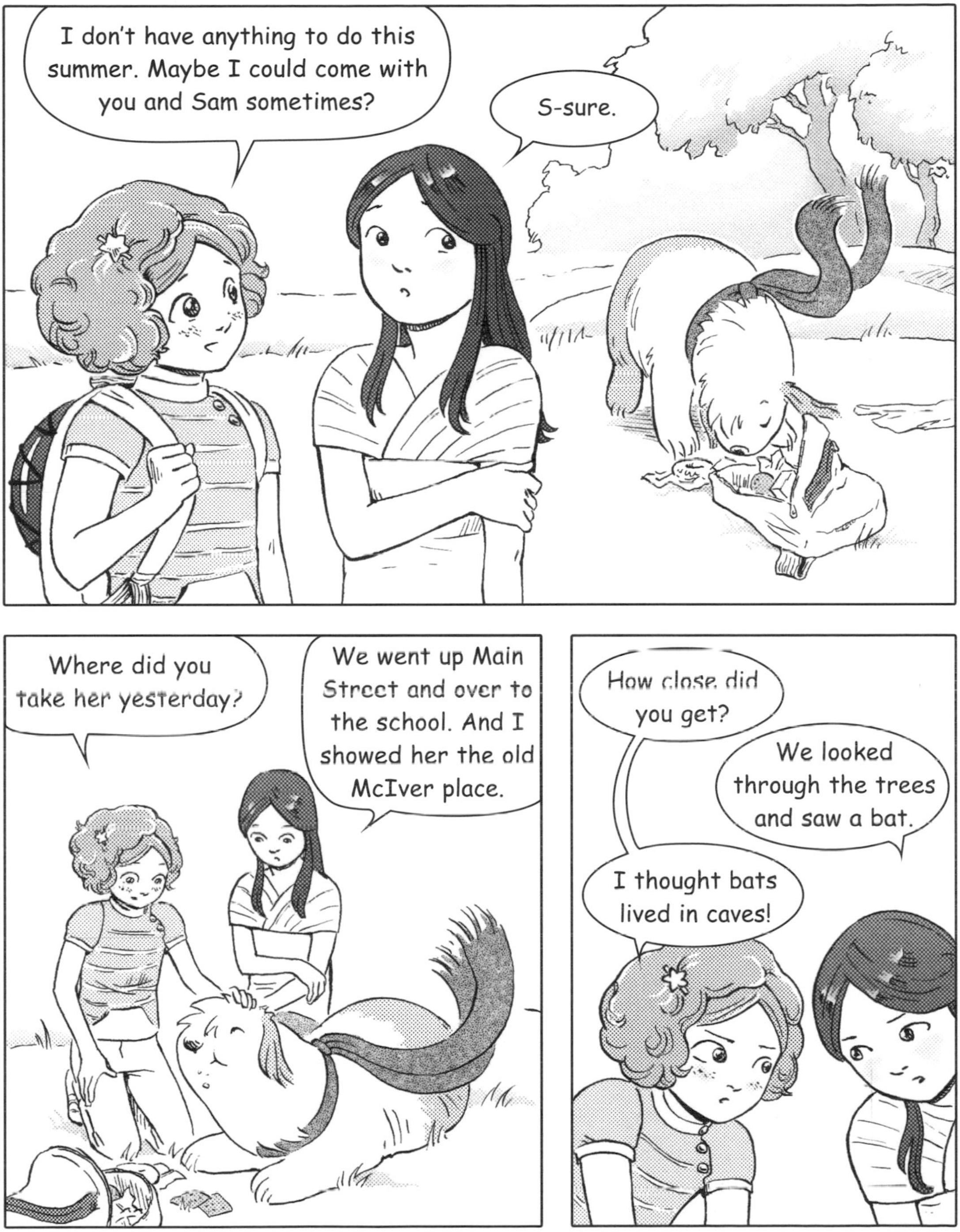
I don't have anything to do this summer. Maybe I could come with you and Sam sometimes?
S-sure.
Where did you take her yesterday?
We went up Main Street and over to the school. And I showed her the old McIver place.
How close did you get?
We looked through the trees and saw a bat.
I thought bats lived in caves!

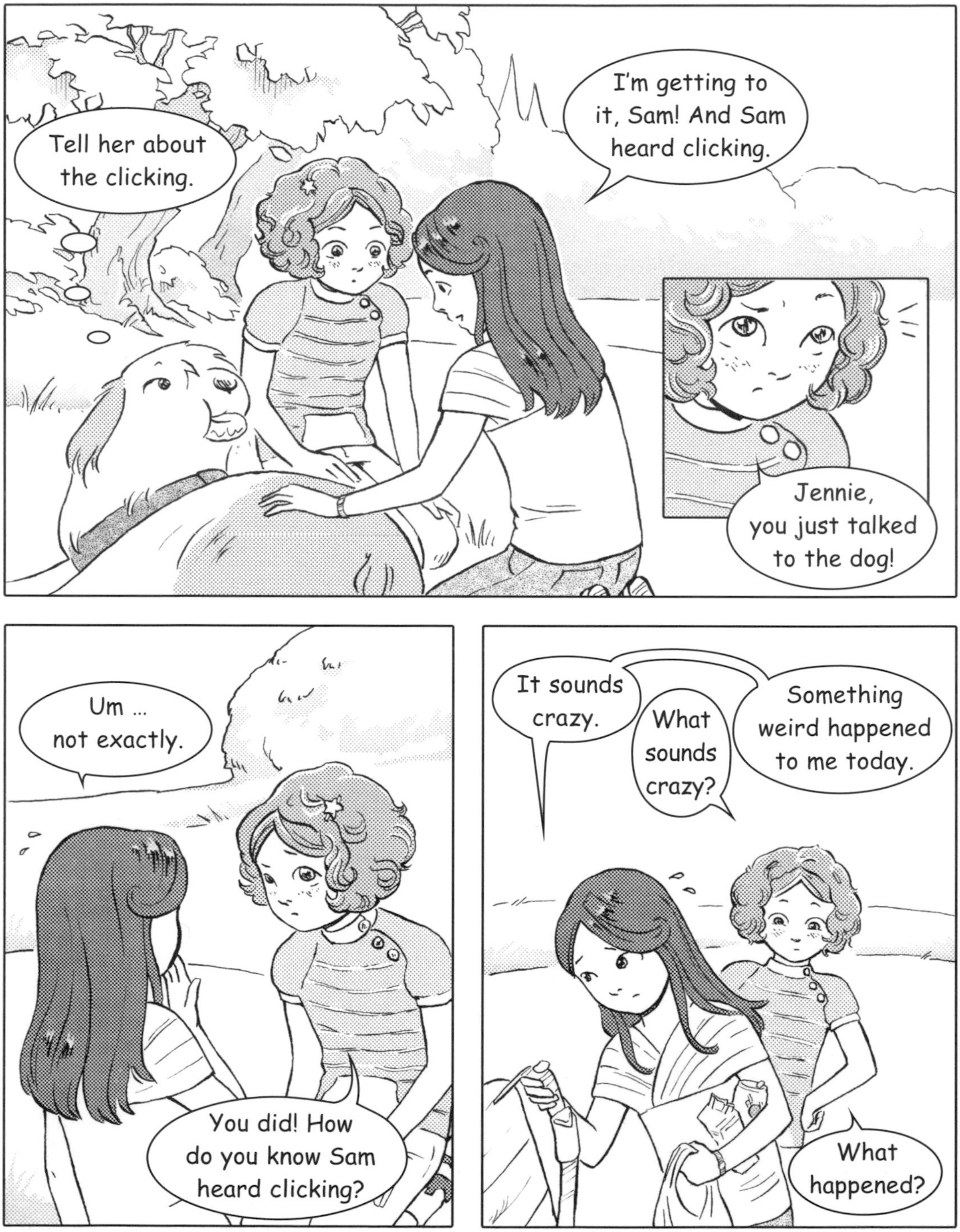
Tell her about the clicking.
I'm getting to it, Sam! And Sam heard clicking.
Jennie, you just talked to the dog!
Um ... not exactly.
You did! How do you know Sam heard clicking?
Something weird happened to me today.
It sounds crazy.
What sounds crazy?
What happened?

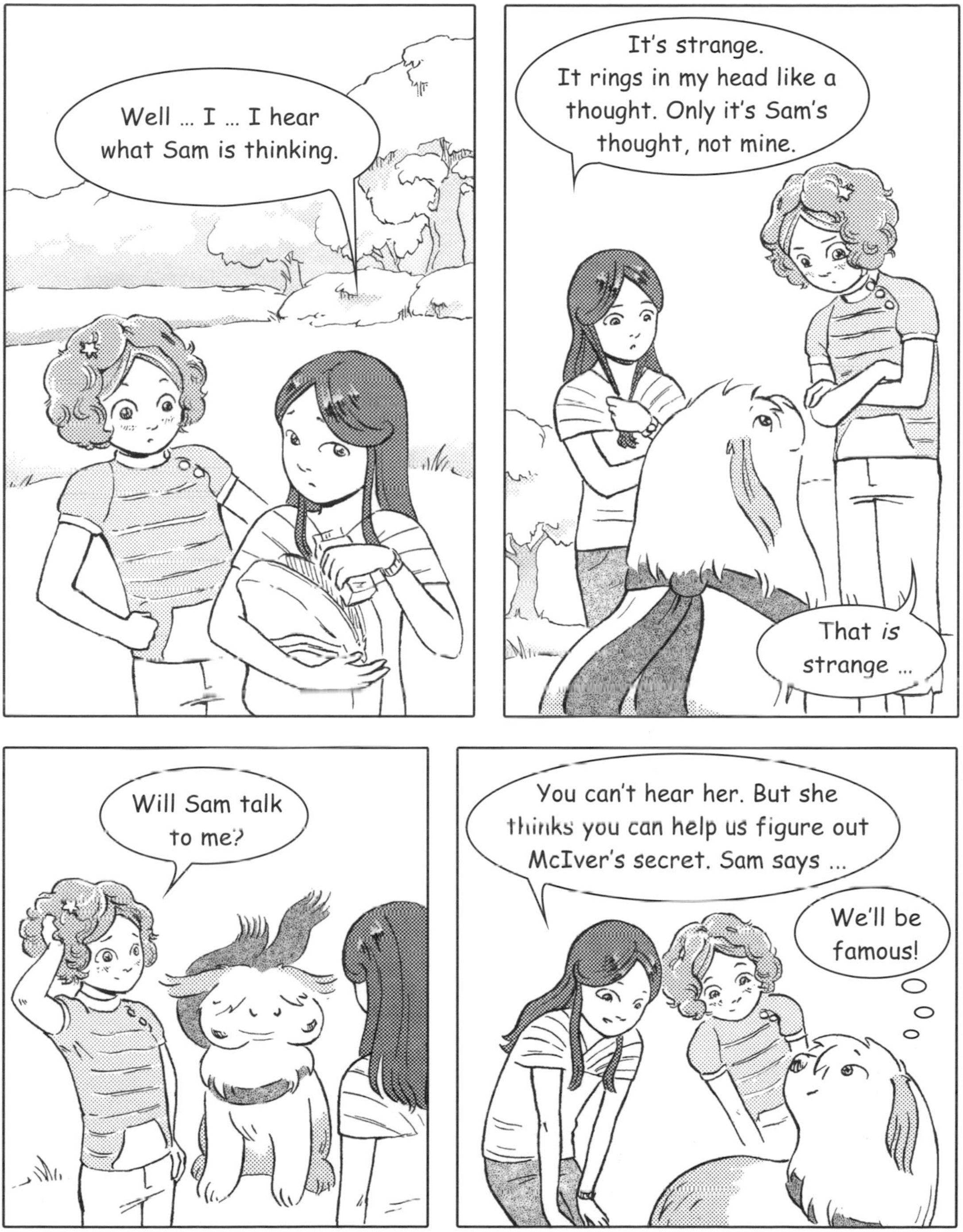
Well ... I ... I hear what Sam is thinking.
It's strange. It rings in my head like a thought. Only it's Sam's thought, not mine.
That *is* strange ...
Will Sam talk to me?
You can't hear her. But she thinks you can help us figure out McIver's secret. Sam says ...
We'll be famous!

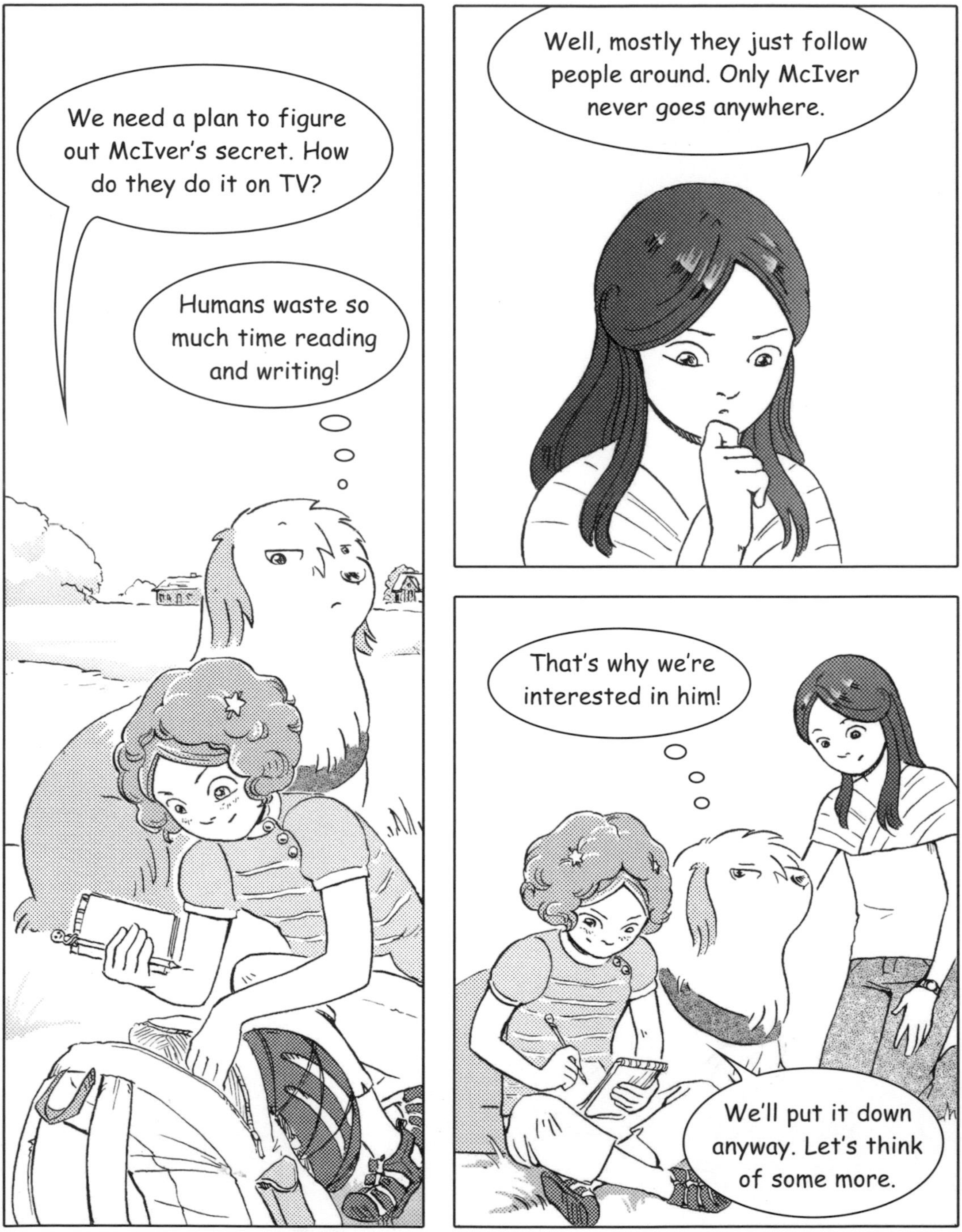
We need a plan to figure out McIver's secret. How do they do it on TV?
Humans waste so much time reading and writing!
Well, mostly they just follow people around. Only McIver never goes anywhere.
That's why we're interested in him!
We'll put it down anyway. Let's think of some more.

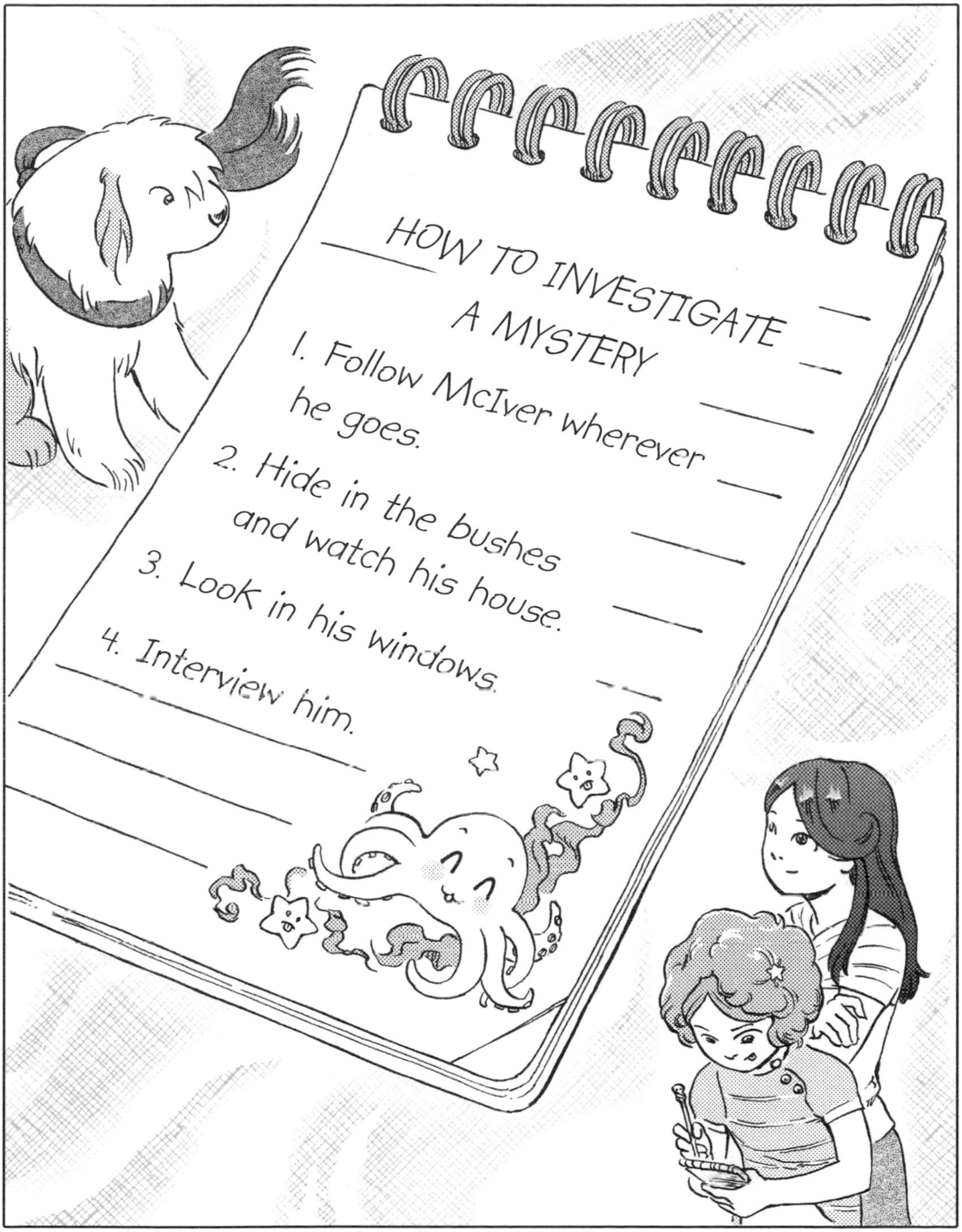
HOW TO INVESTIGATE A MYSTERY
1. Follow McIver wherever he goes.
2. Hide in the bushes and watch his house.
3. Look in his windows.
4. Interview him.

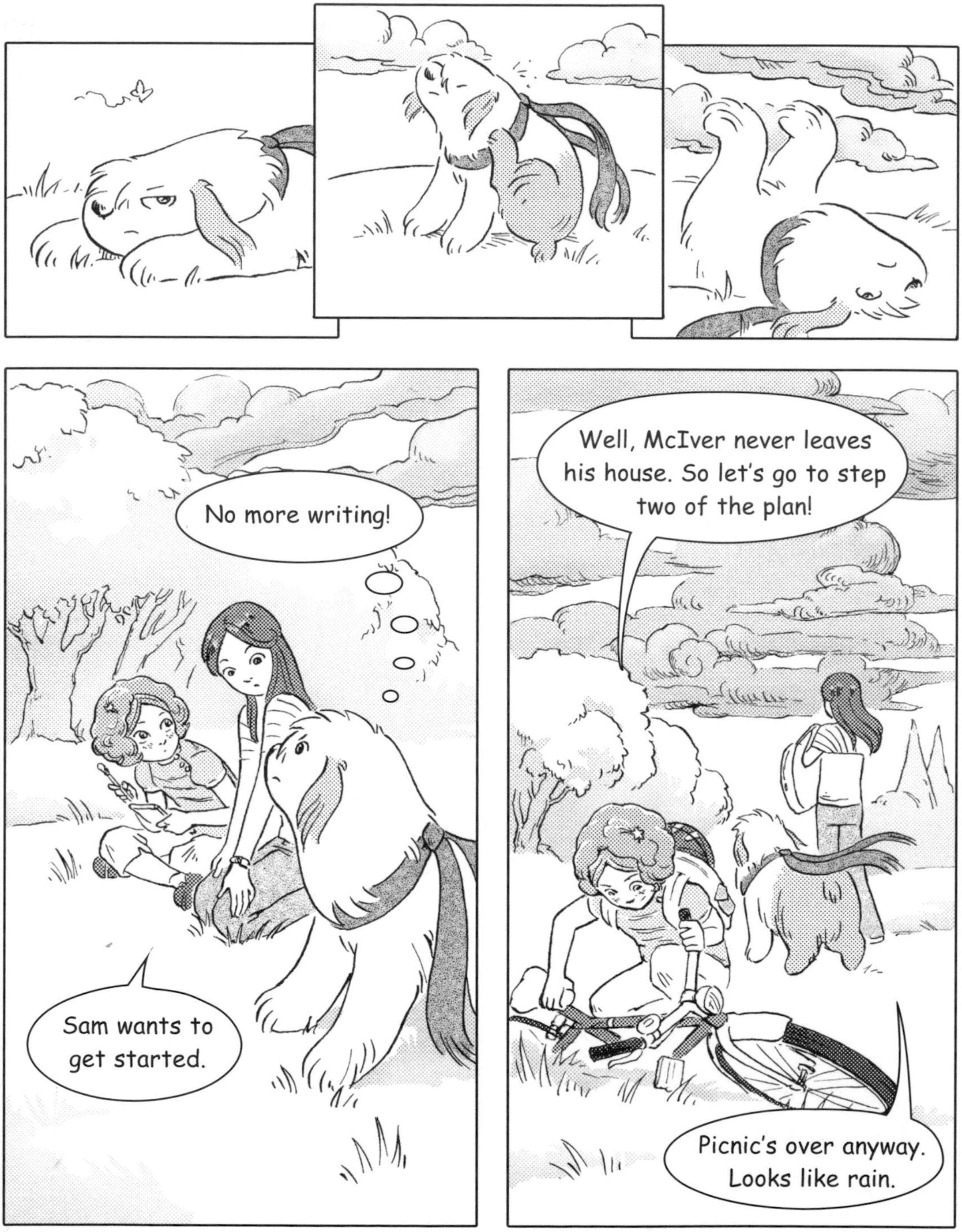
No more writing!
Sam wants to get started.
Well, McIver never leaves his house. So let's go to step two of the plan!
Picnic's over anyway. Looks like rain.

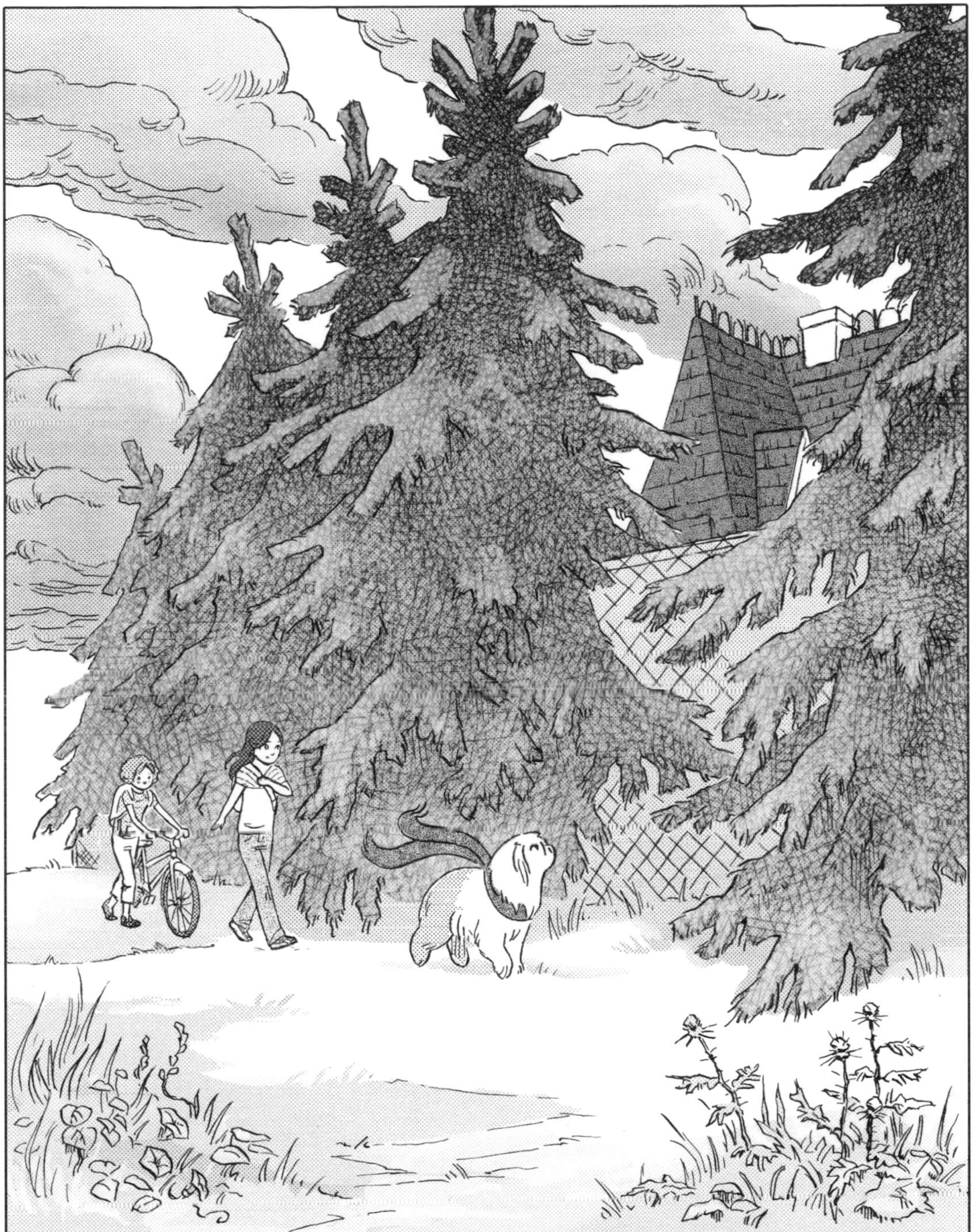

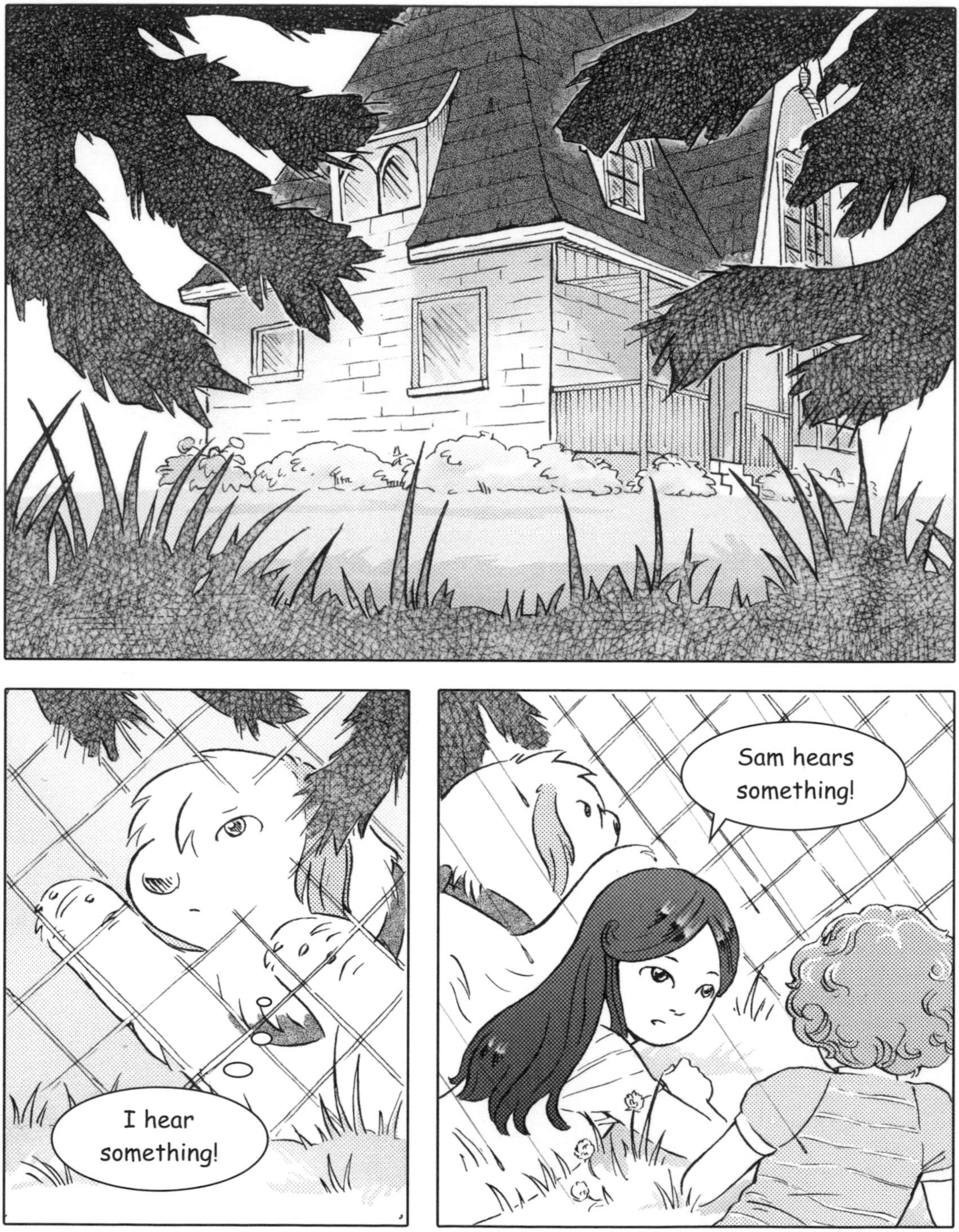
I hear something!
Sam hears something!

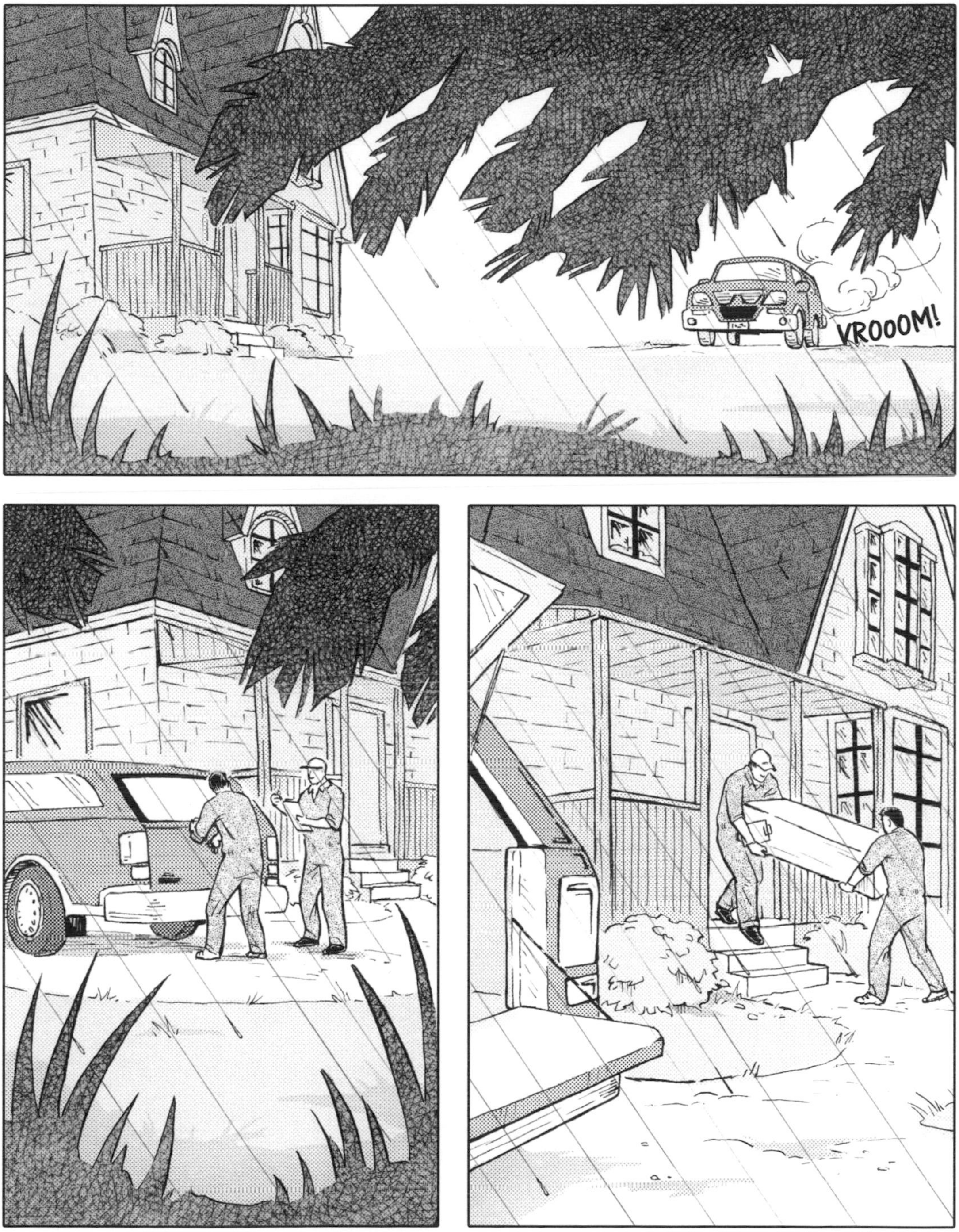
VROOOM!

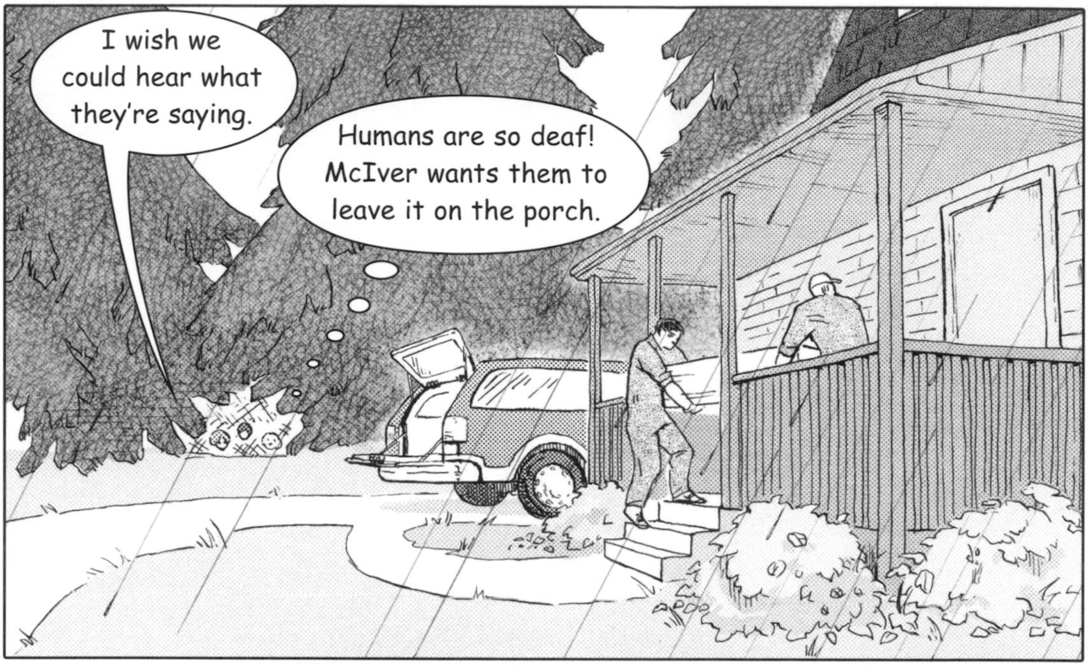
I wish we could hear what they're saying.
Humans are so deaf! McIver wants them to leave it on the porch.

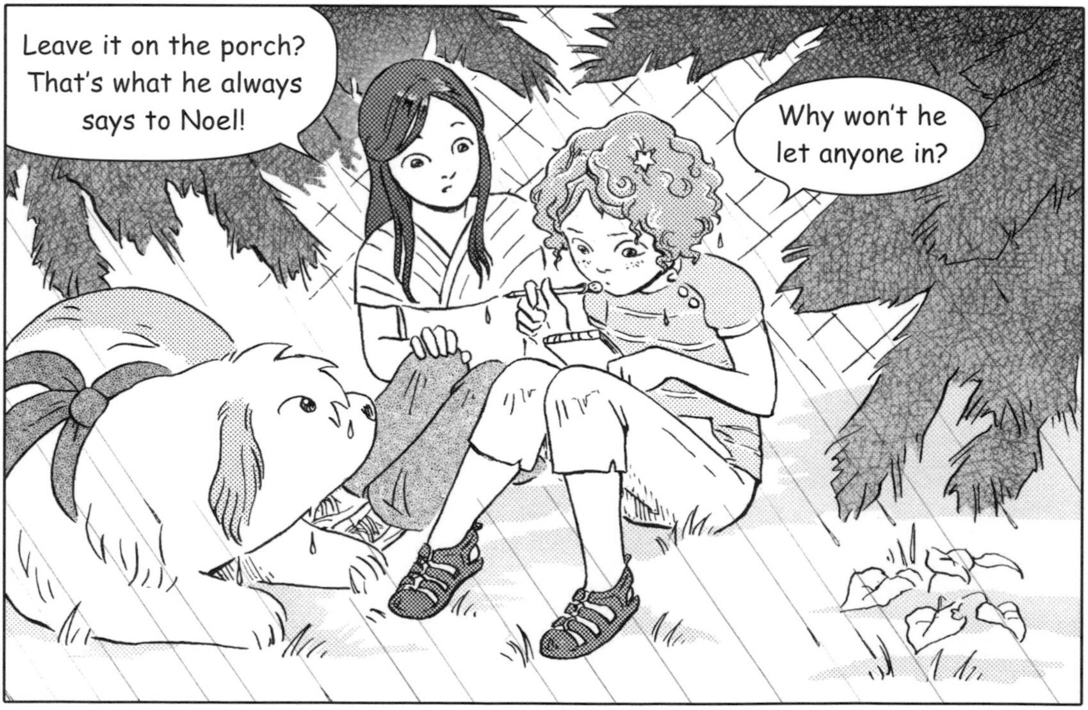
Leave it on the porch? That's what he always says to Noel!
Why won't he let anyone in?

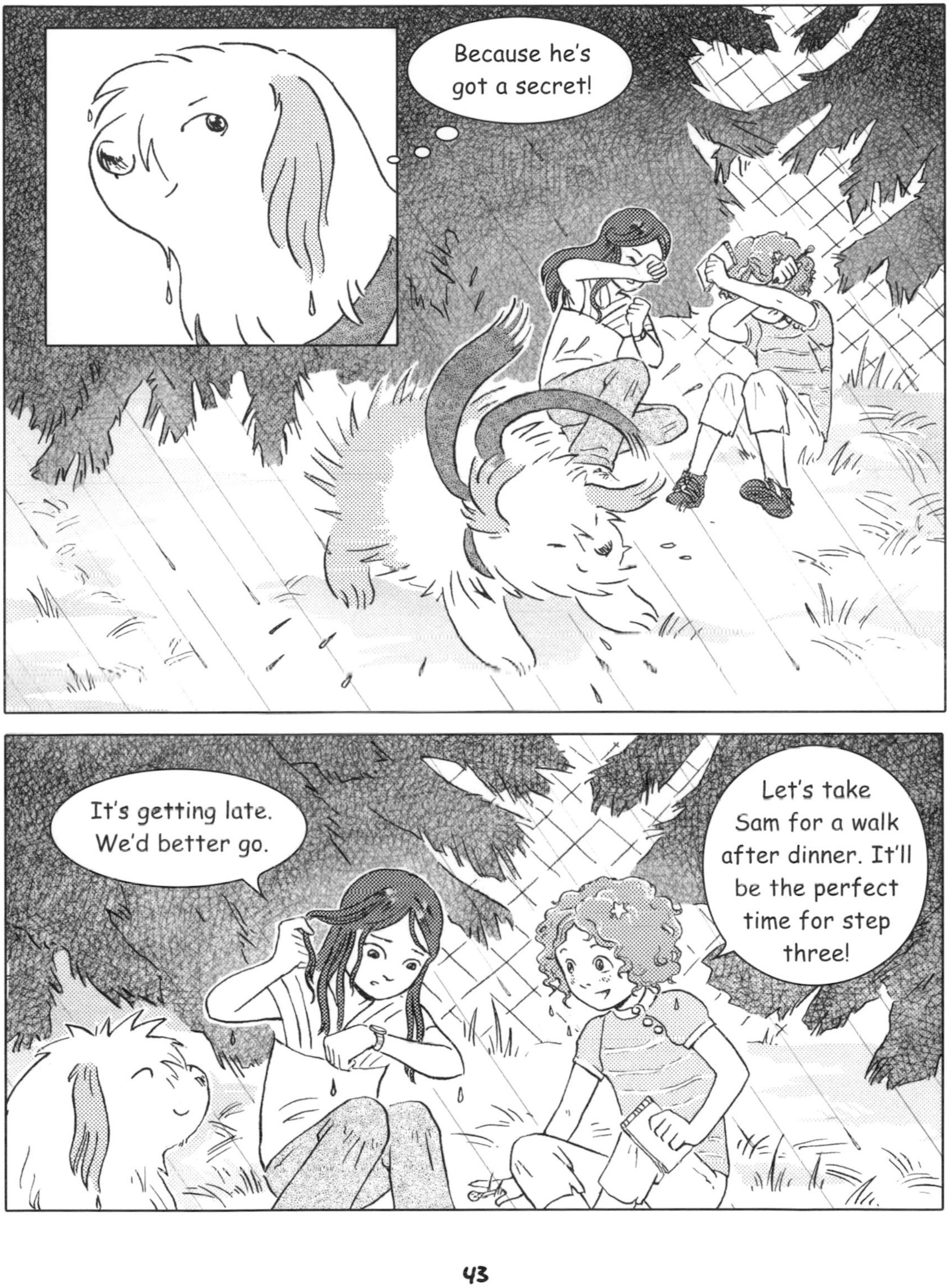
Because he's got a secret!
It's getting late. We'd better go.
Let's take Sam for a walk after dinner. It'll be the perfect time for step three!

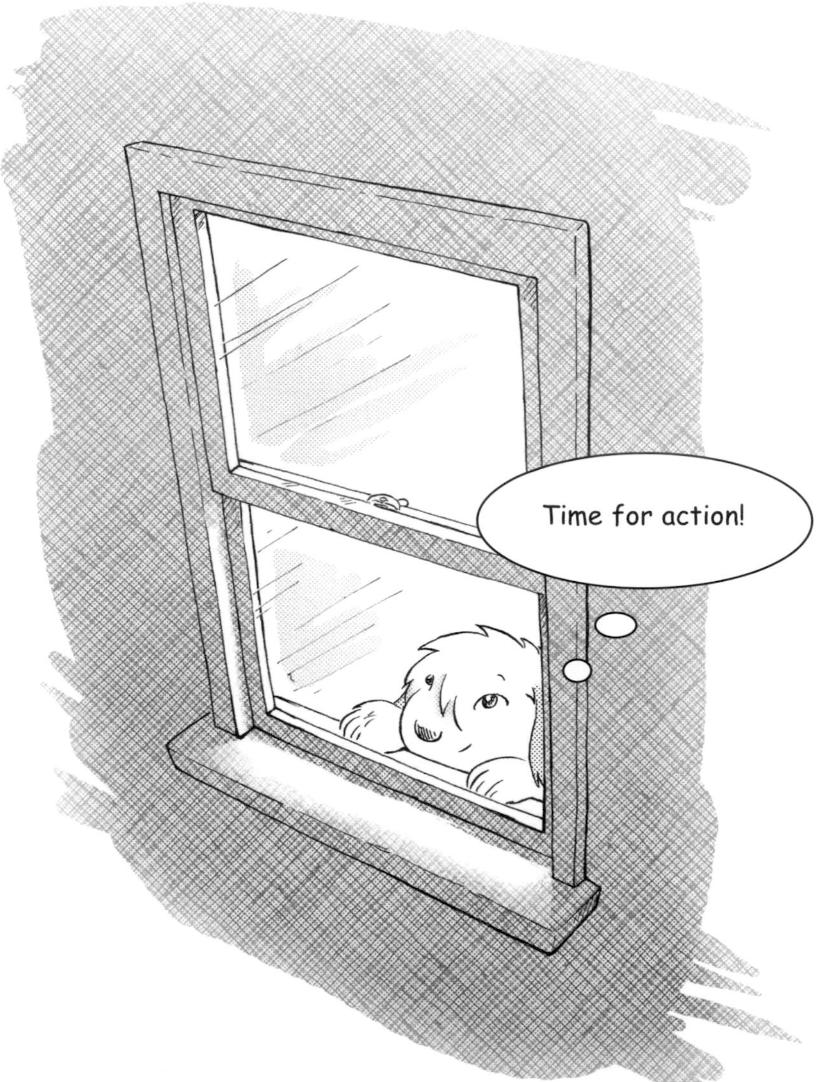
Time for action!

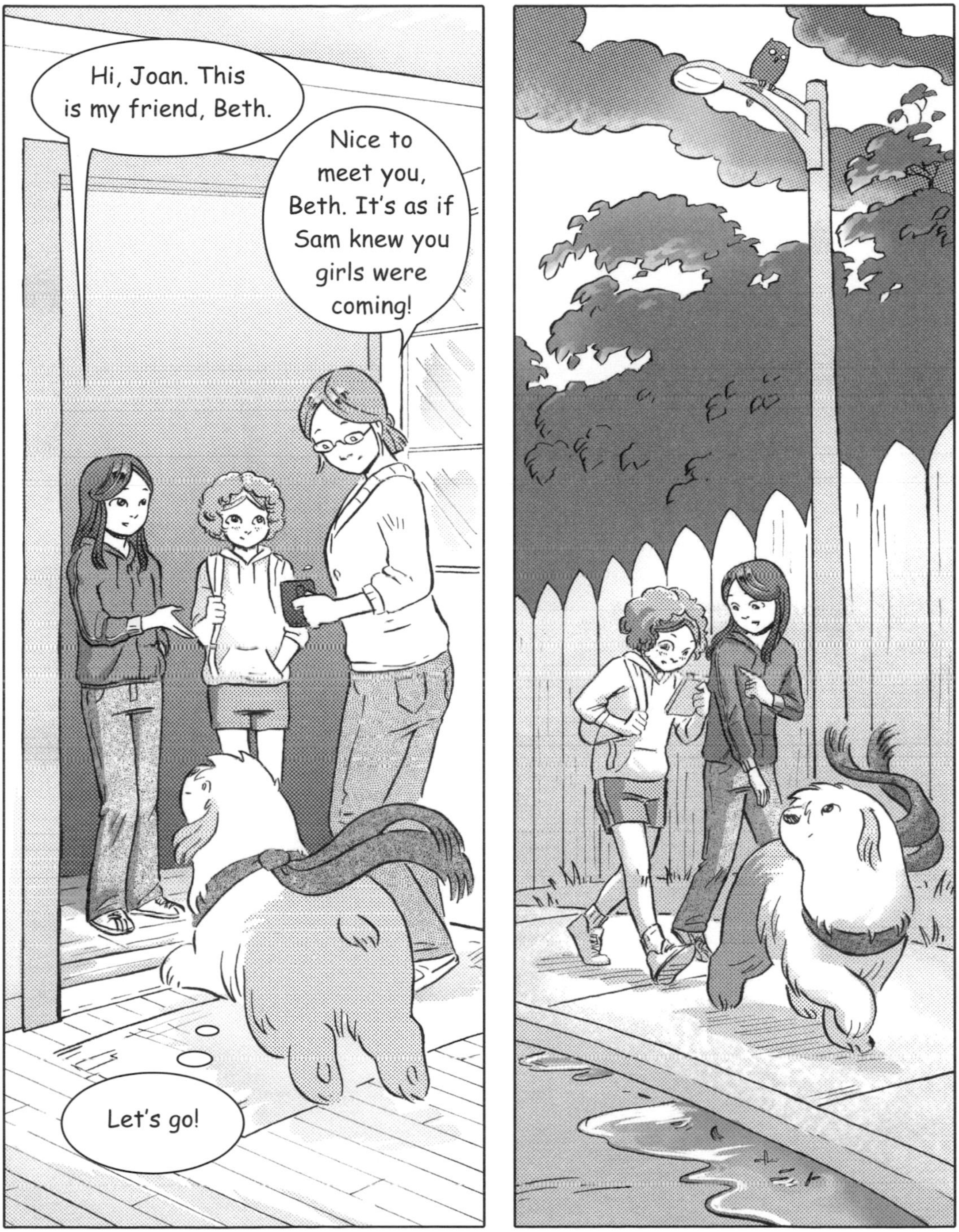
Hi, Joan. This is my friend, Beth.
Nice to meet you, Beth. It's as if Sam knew you girls were coming!
Let's go!

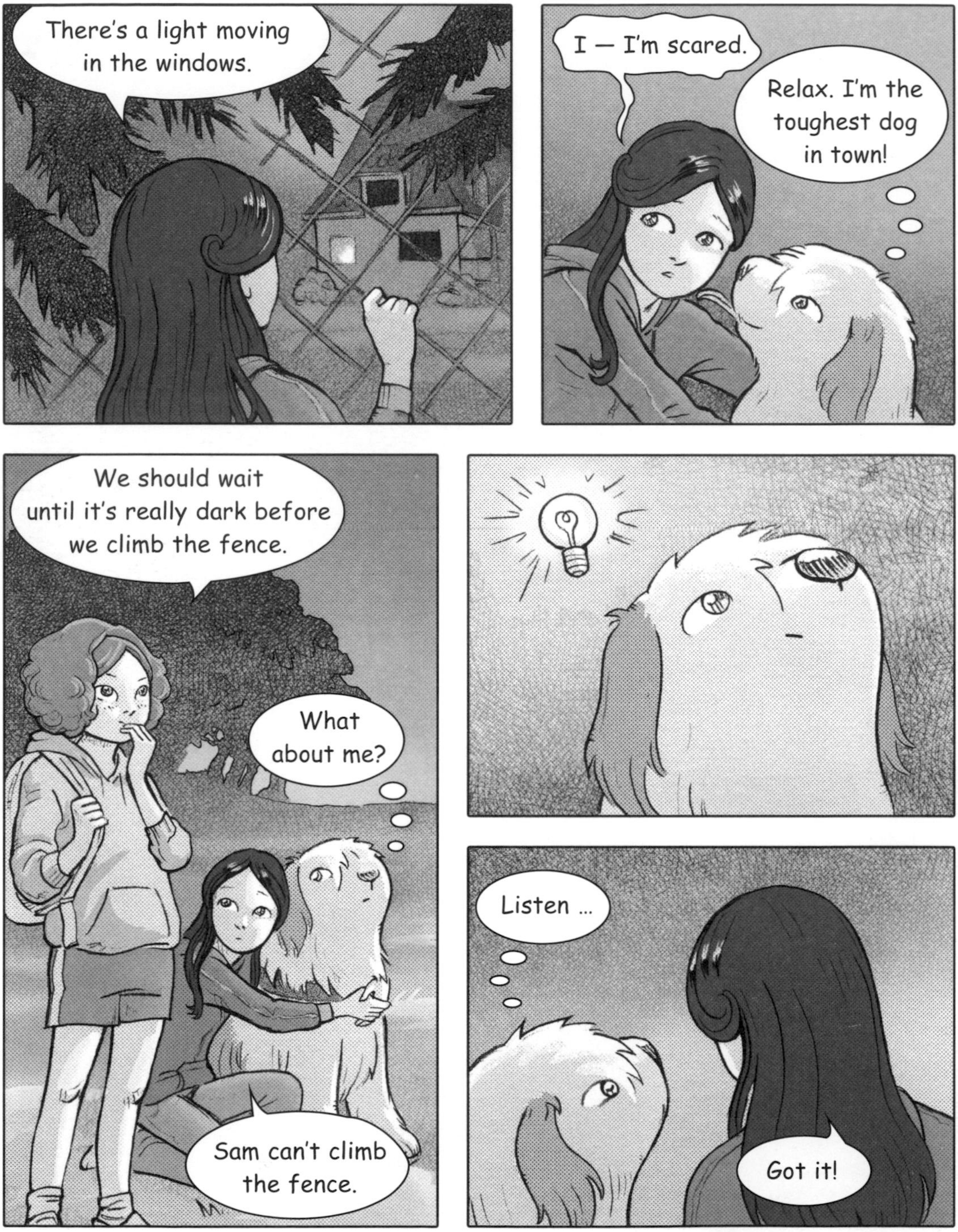
There's a light moving in the windows.
I — I'm scared.
Relax. I'm the toughest dog in town!
We should wait until it's really dark before we climb the fence.
What about me?
Sam can't climb the fence.
Listen ...
Got it!

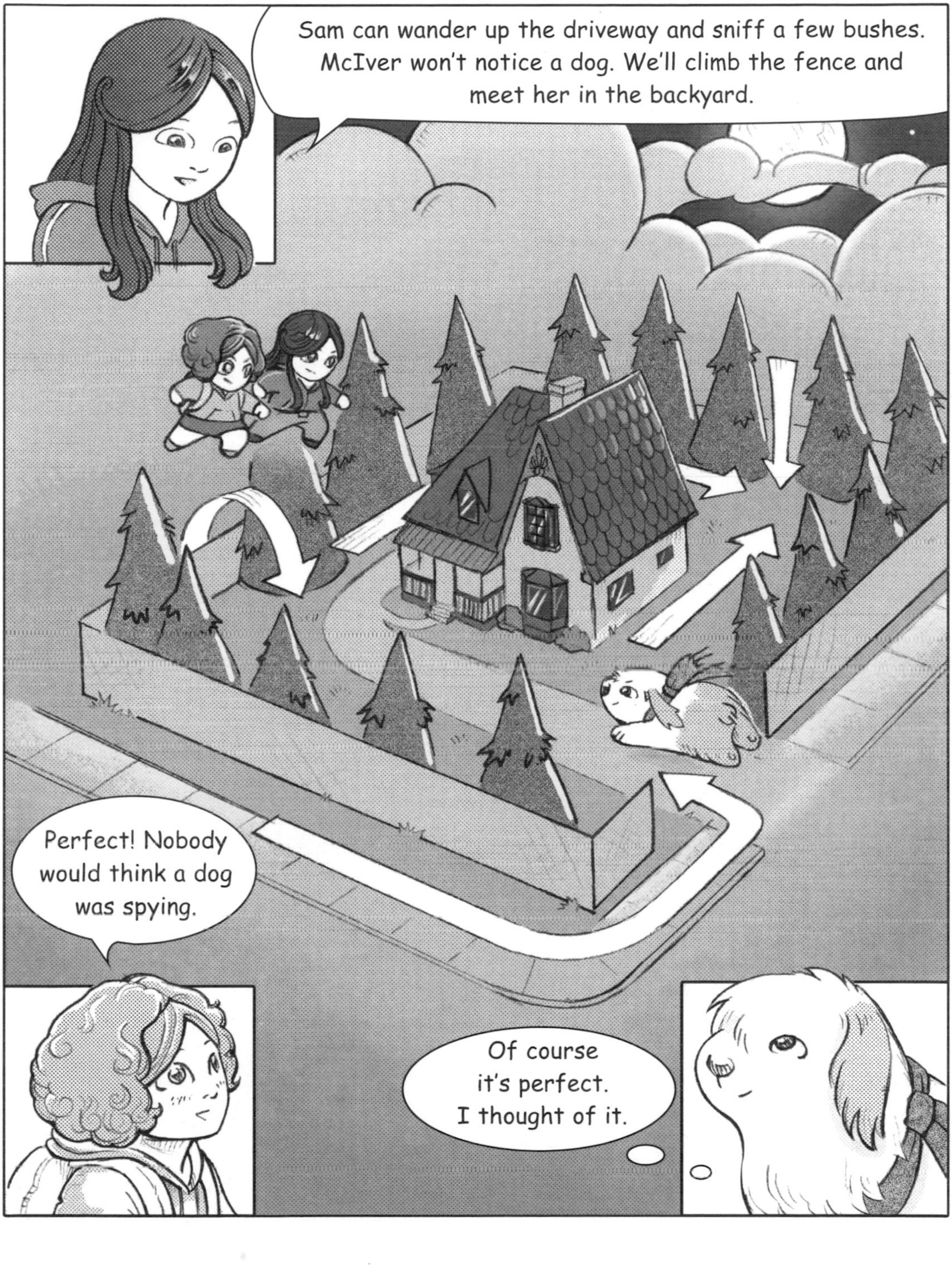

Sam can wander up the driveway and sniff a few bushes. McIver won't notice a dog. We'll climb the fence and meet her in the backyard.
Perfect! Nobody would think a dog was spying.
Of course it's perfect. I thought of it.

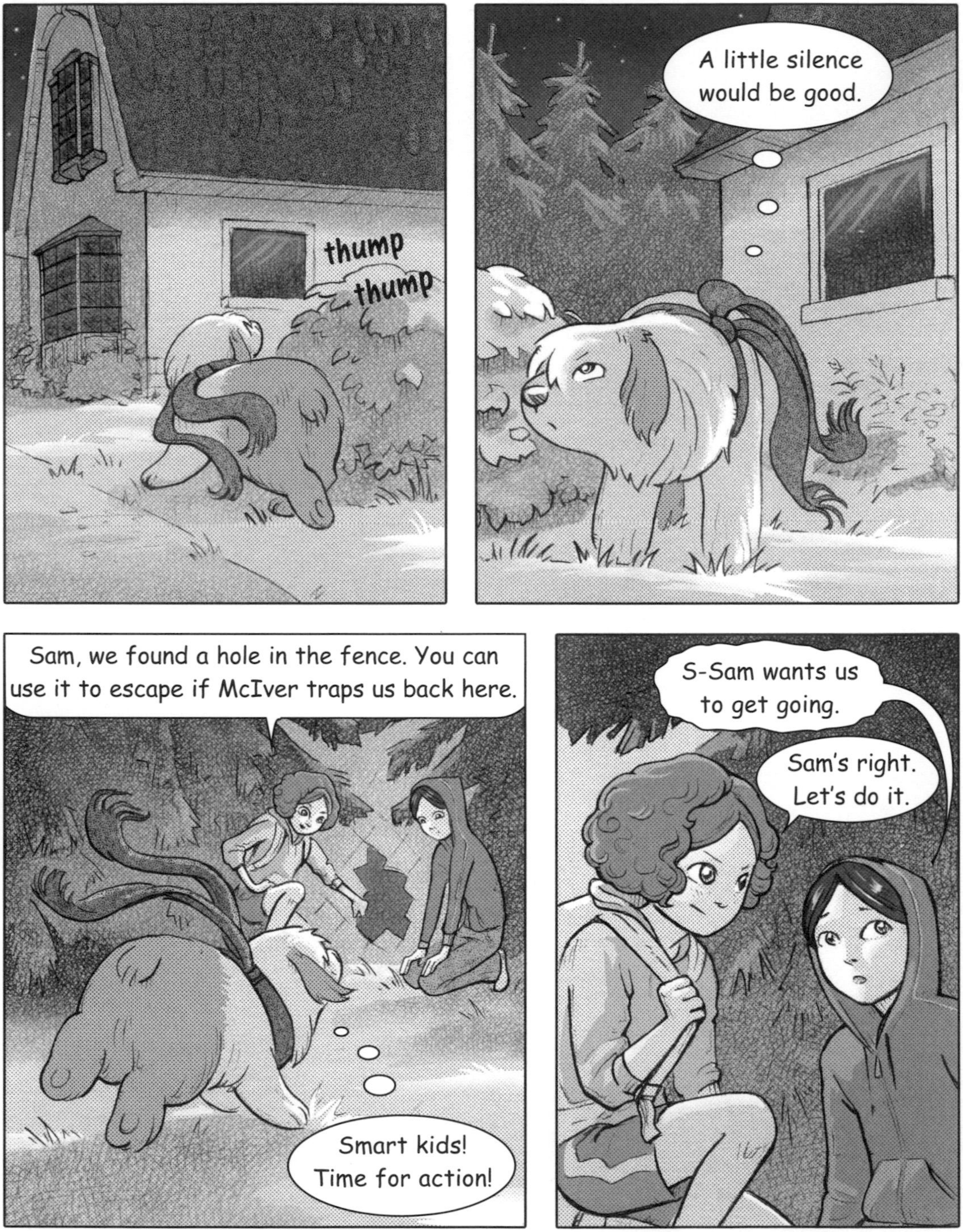
thump
thump
A little silence would be good.
Sam, we found a hole in the fence. You can use it to escape if McIver traps us back here.
Smart kids! Time for action!
S-Sam wants us to get going.
Sam's right. Let's do it.

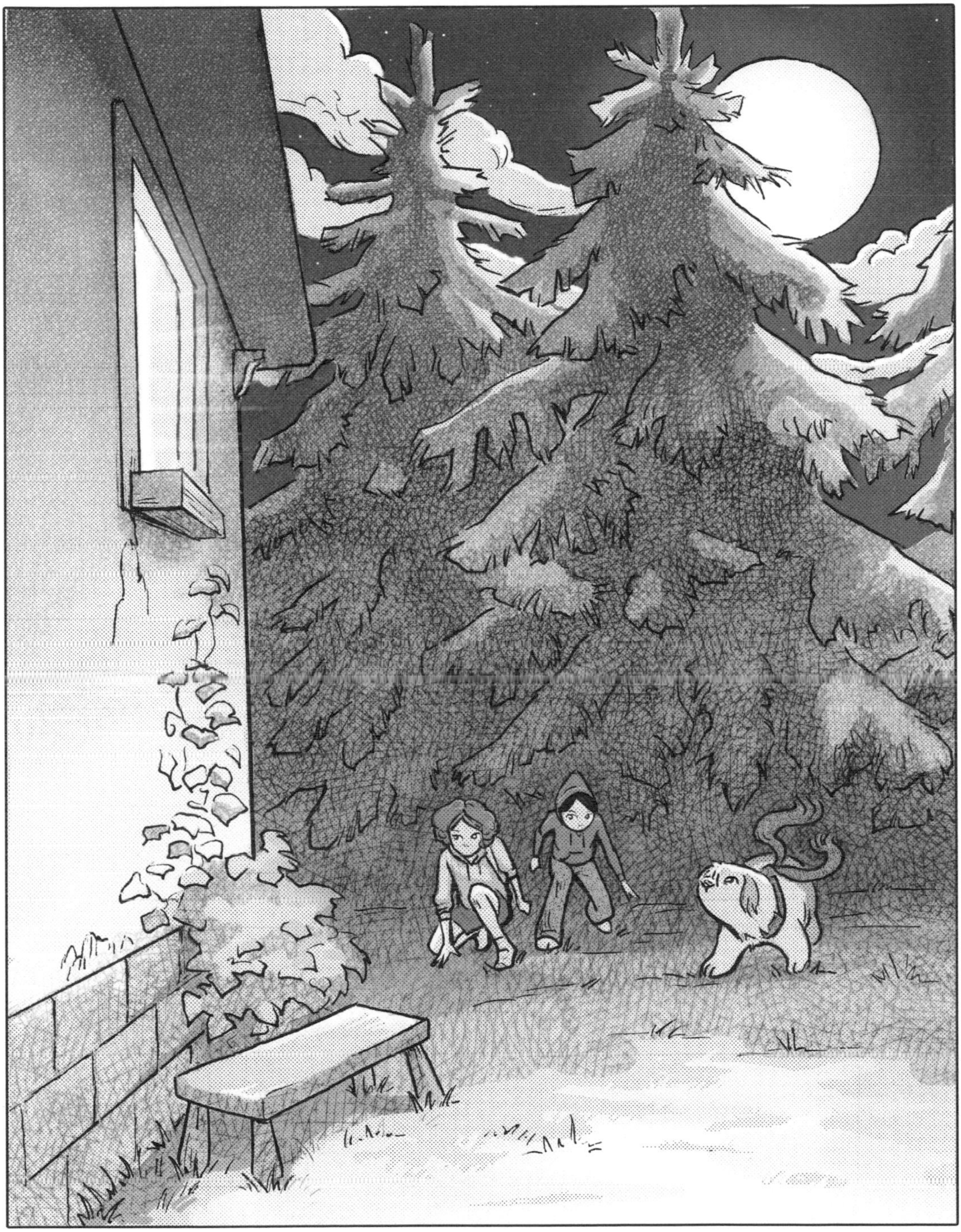

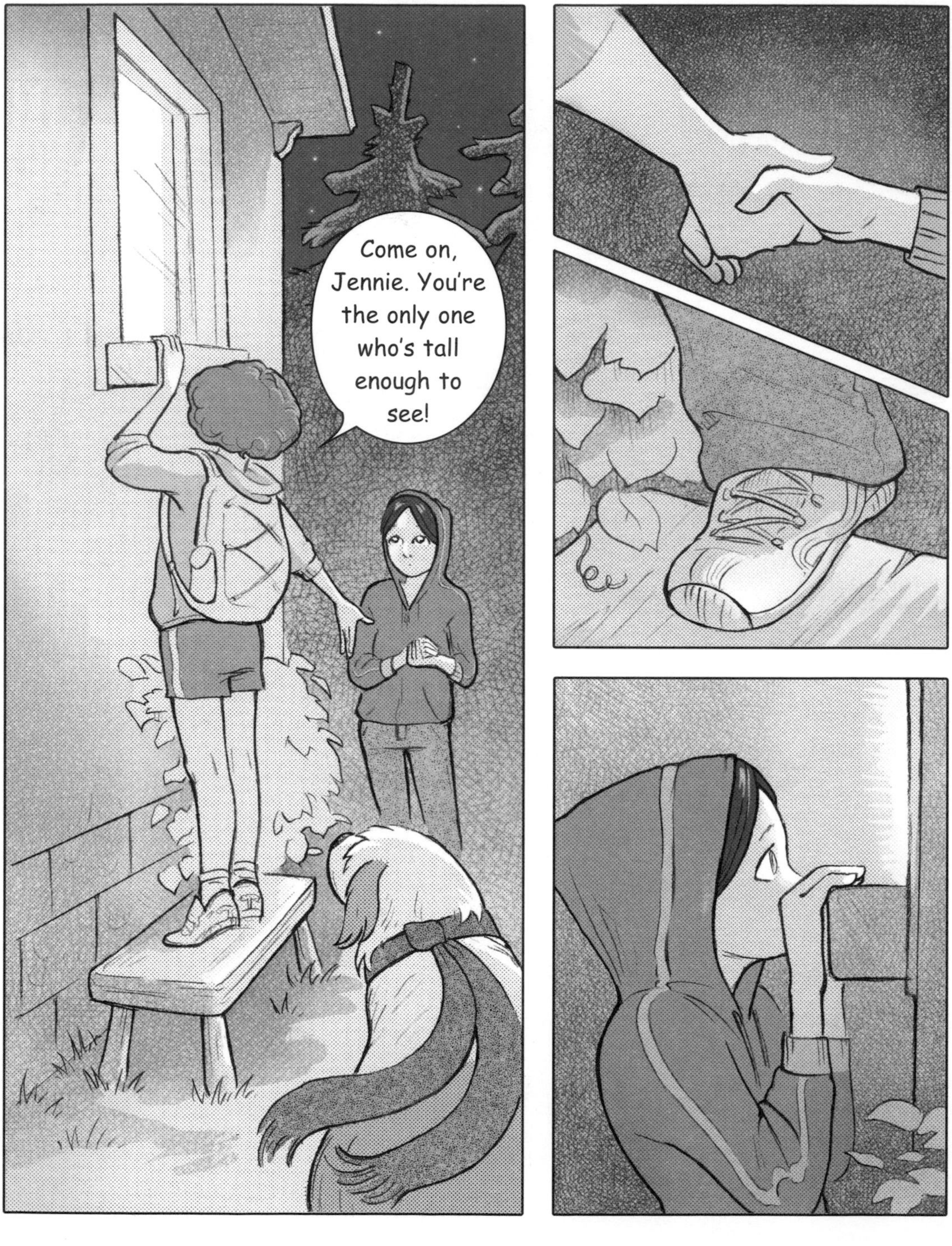
Come on, Jennie. You're the only one who's tall enough to see!

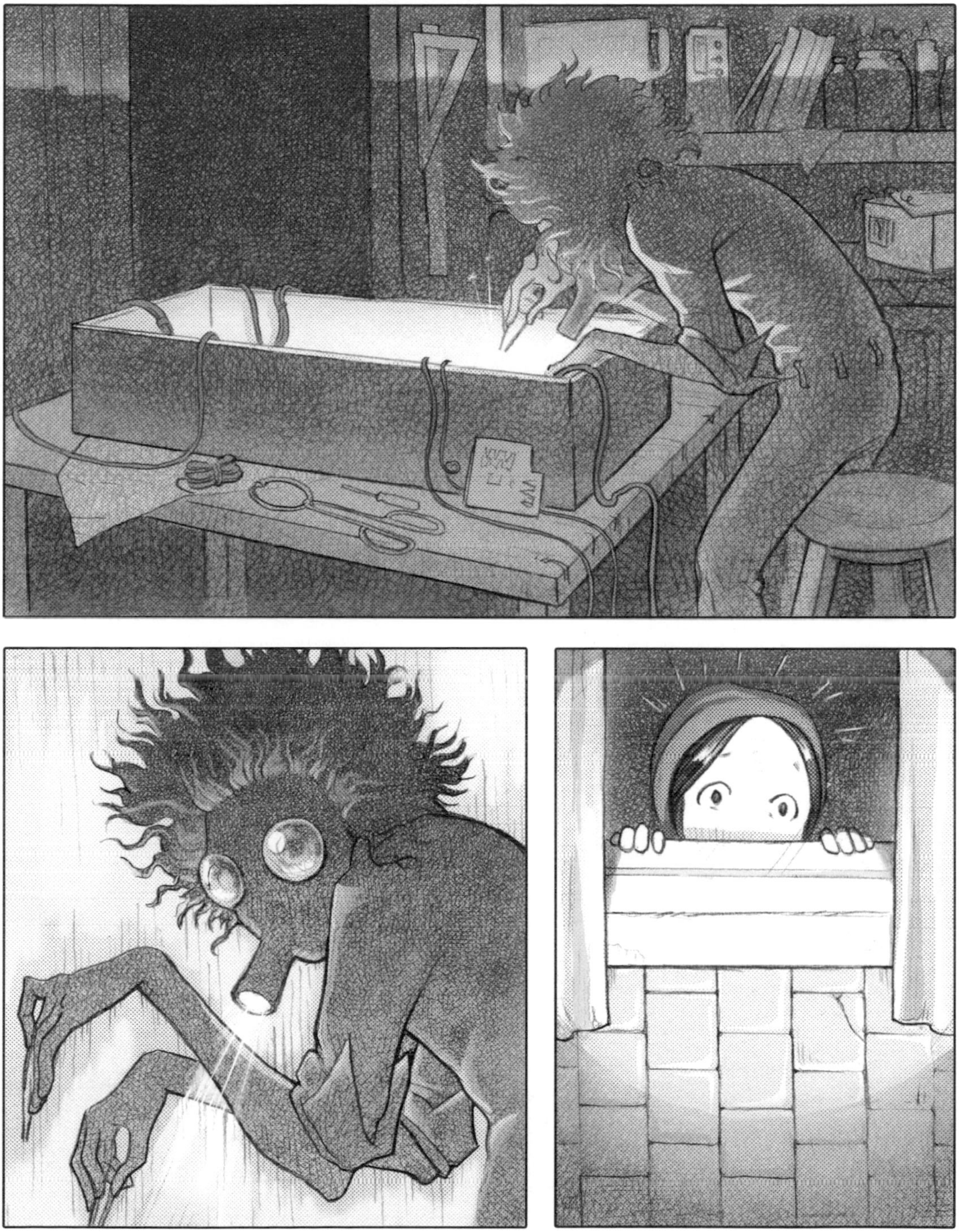

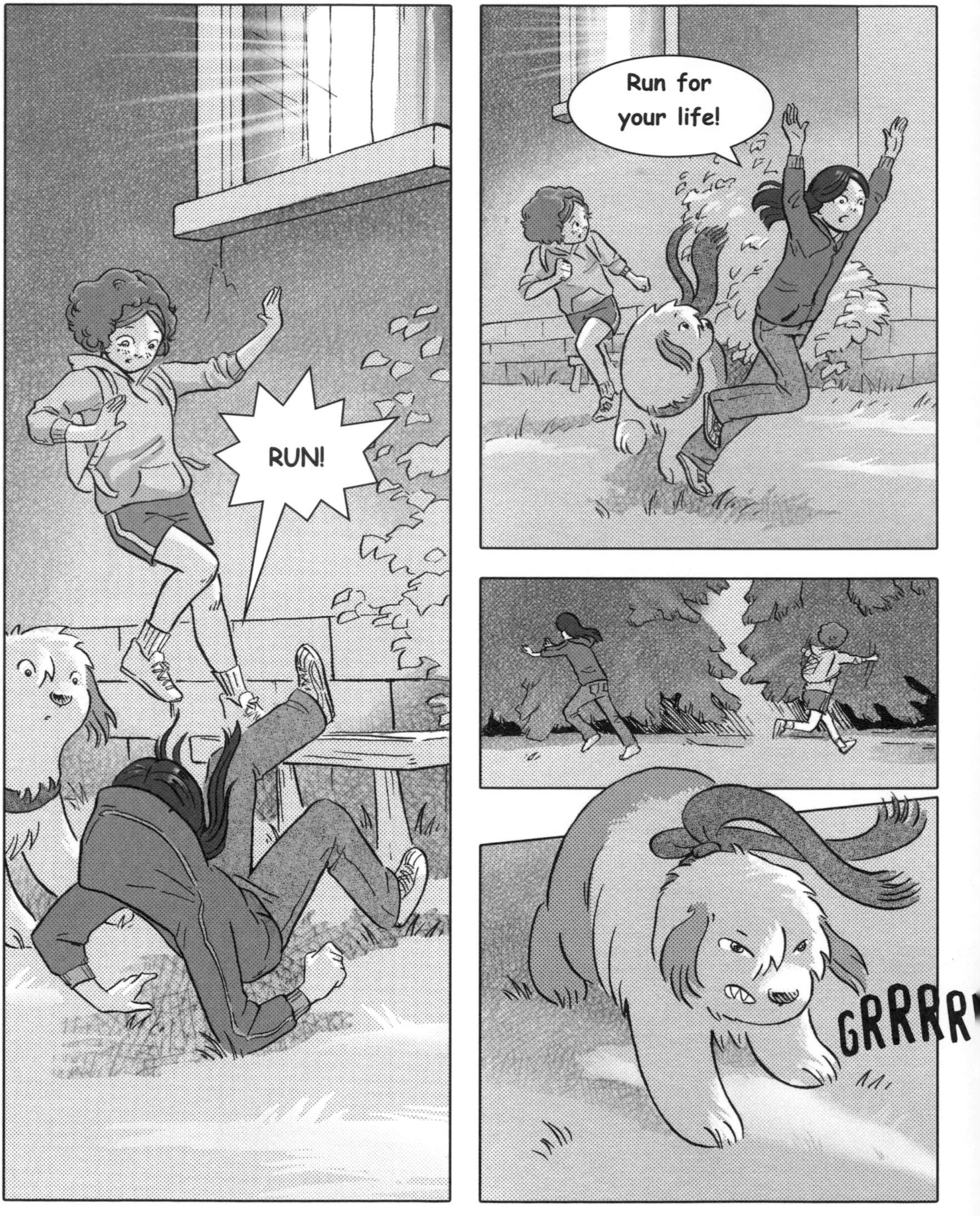
RUN!
Run for your life!
GRRRR

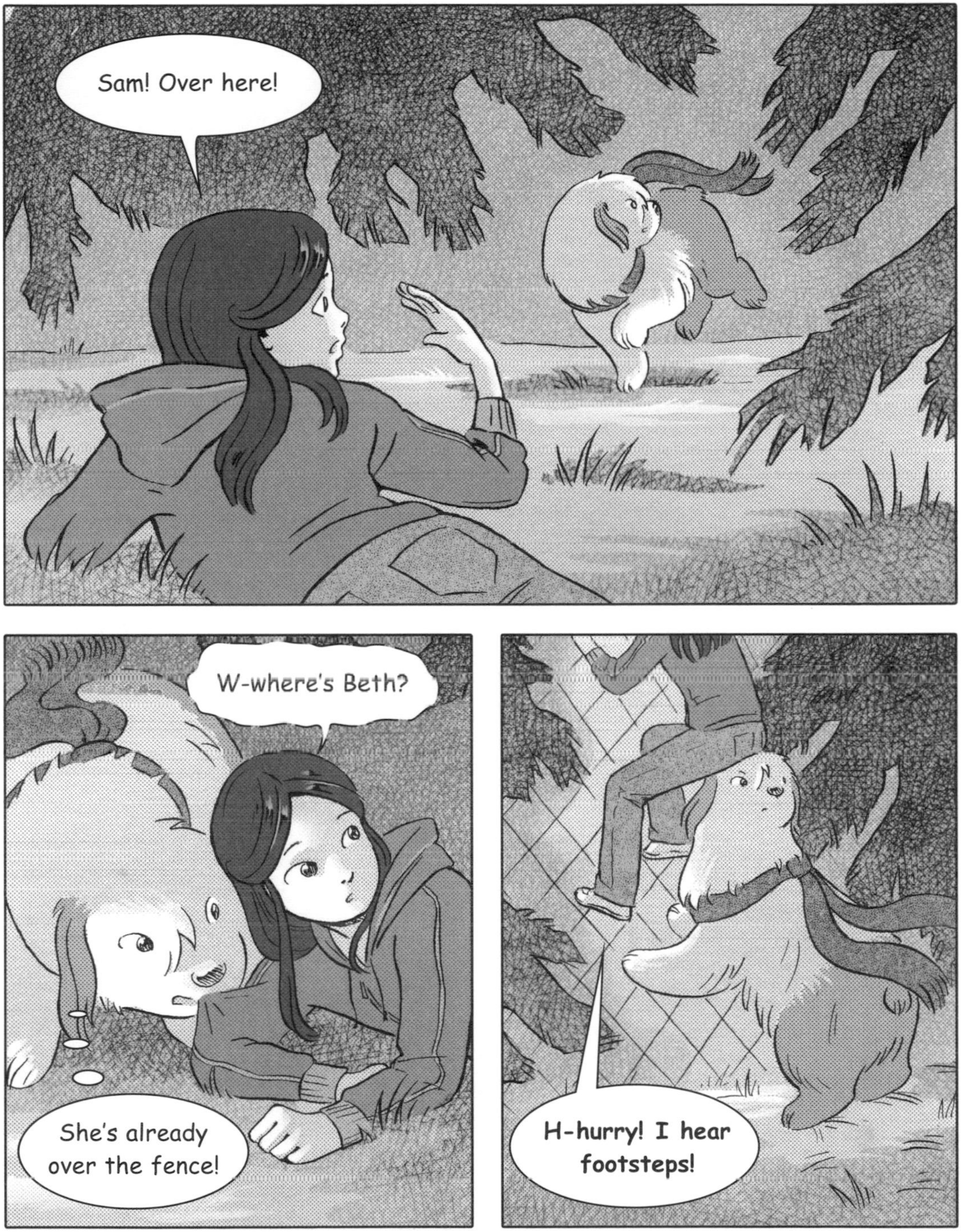
Sam! Over here!
W-where's Beth?
She's already over the fence!
H-hurry! I hear footsteps!

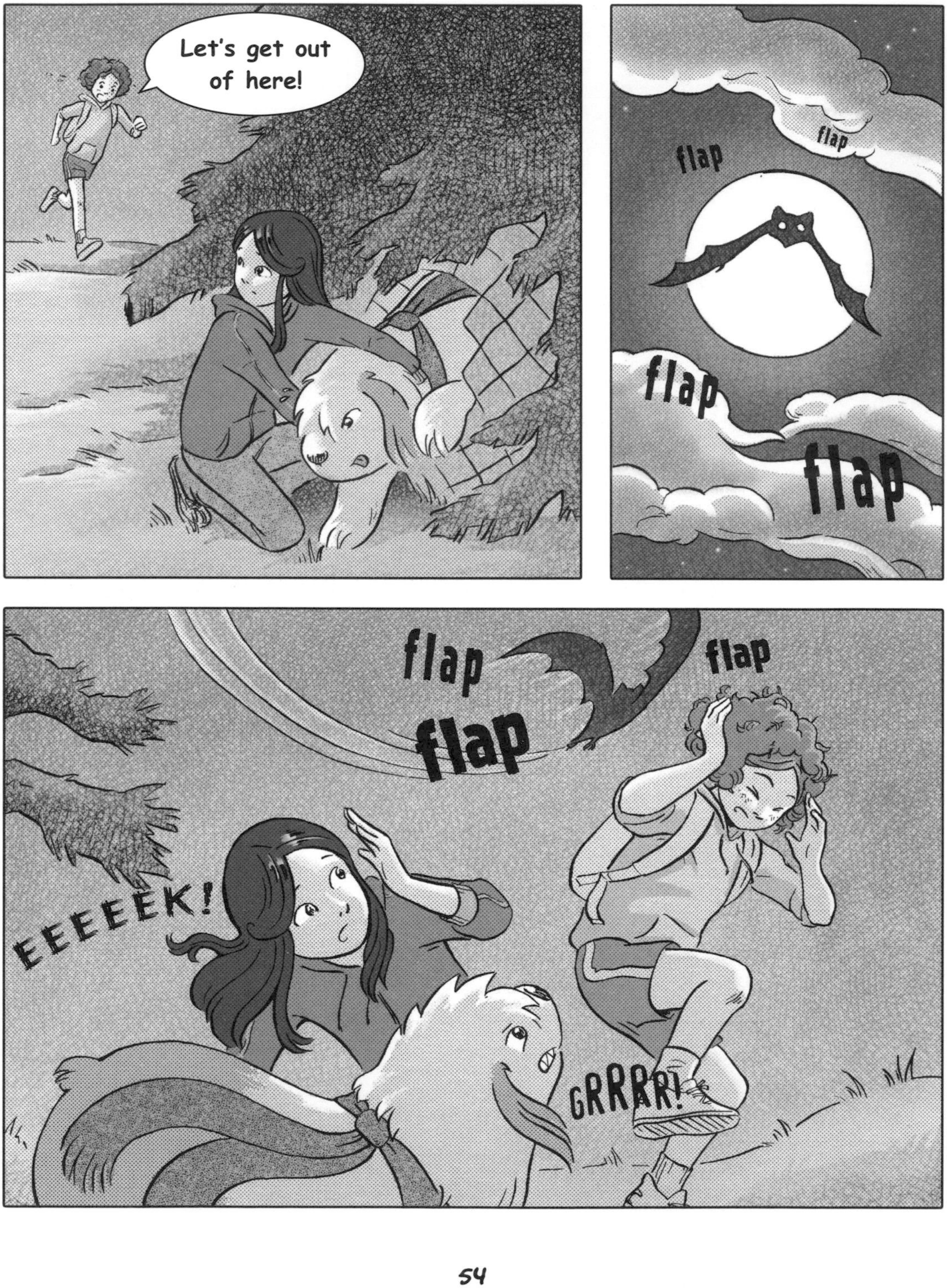

Let's get out of here!
flap
flap
flap
flap
flap
flap
flap
EEEEEK!
GRRRR!

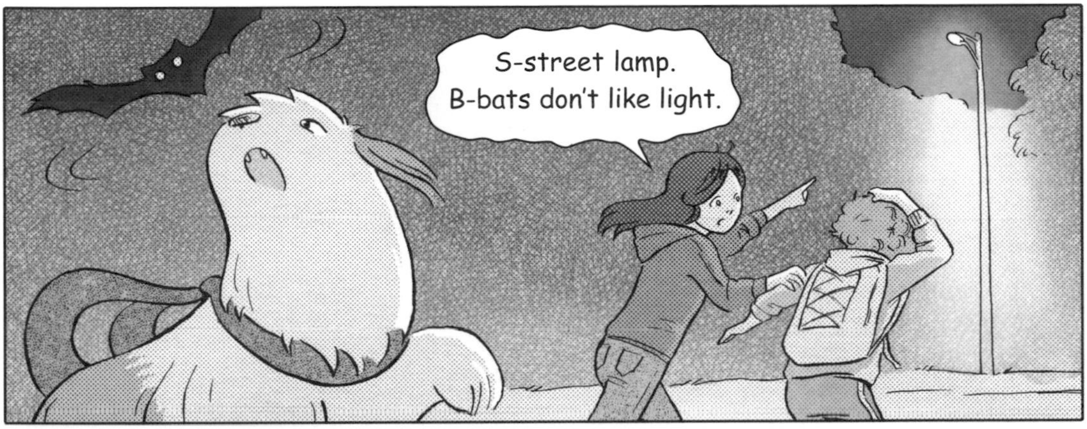
S-street lamp.
B-bats don't like light.

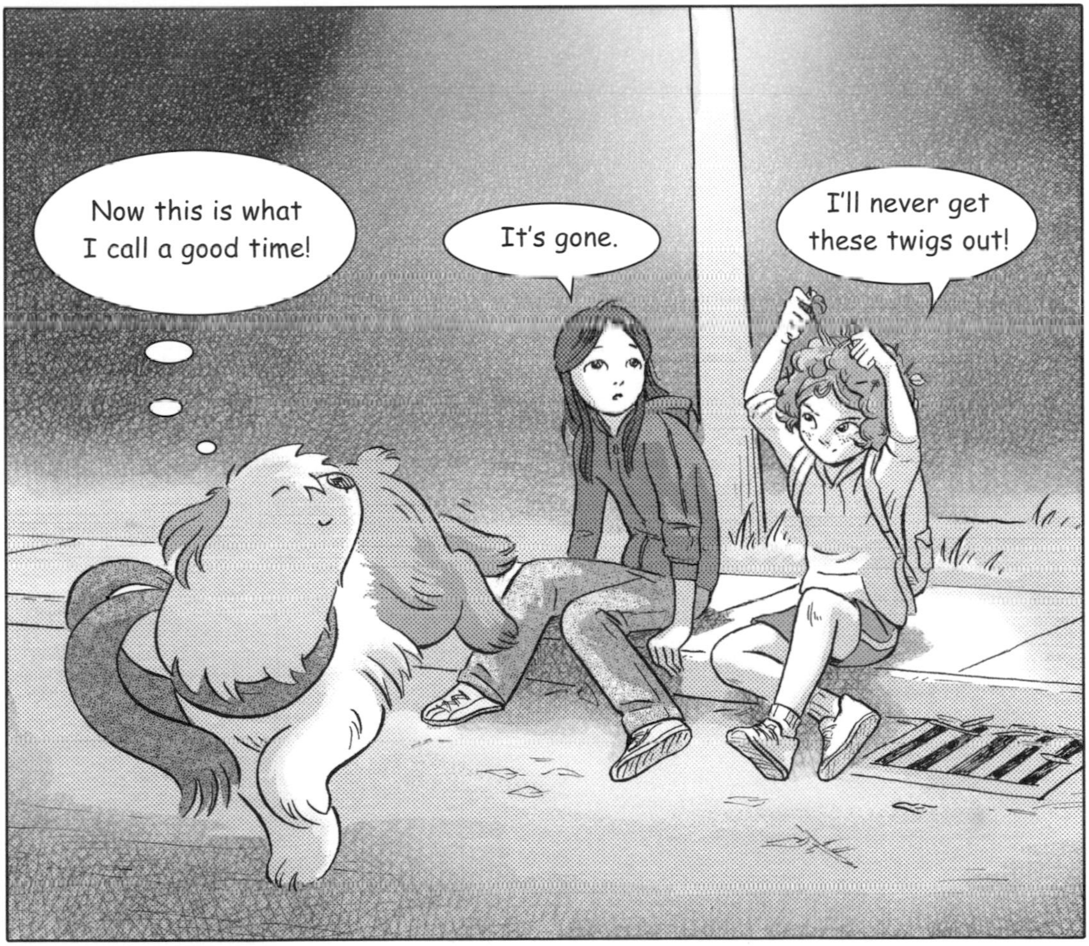
Now this is what
I call a good time!
It's gone.
I'll never get
these twigs out!

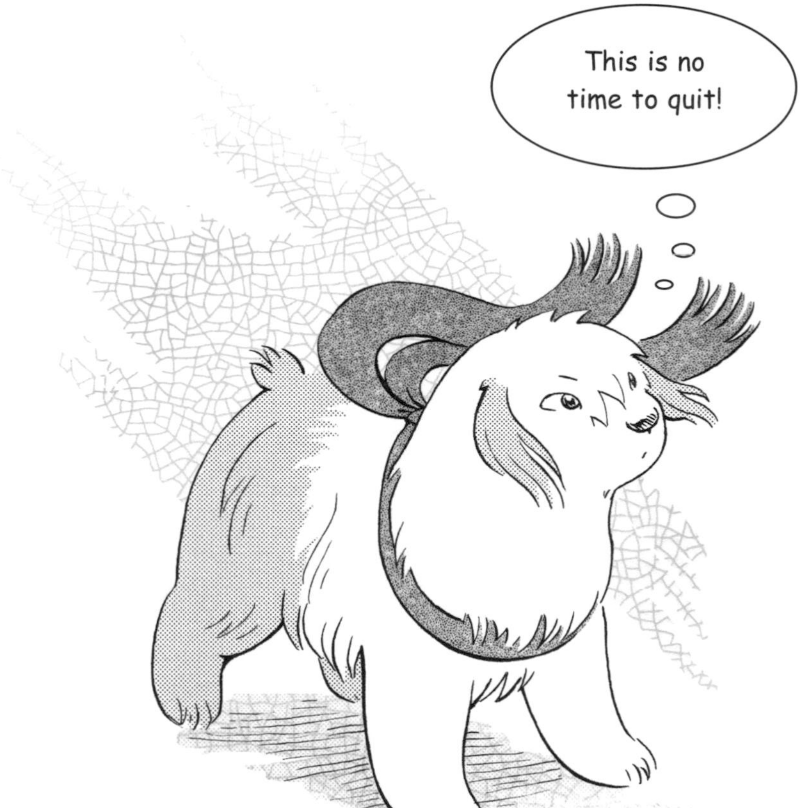
This is no
time to quit!

The next morning ...

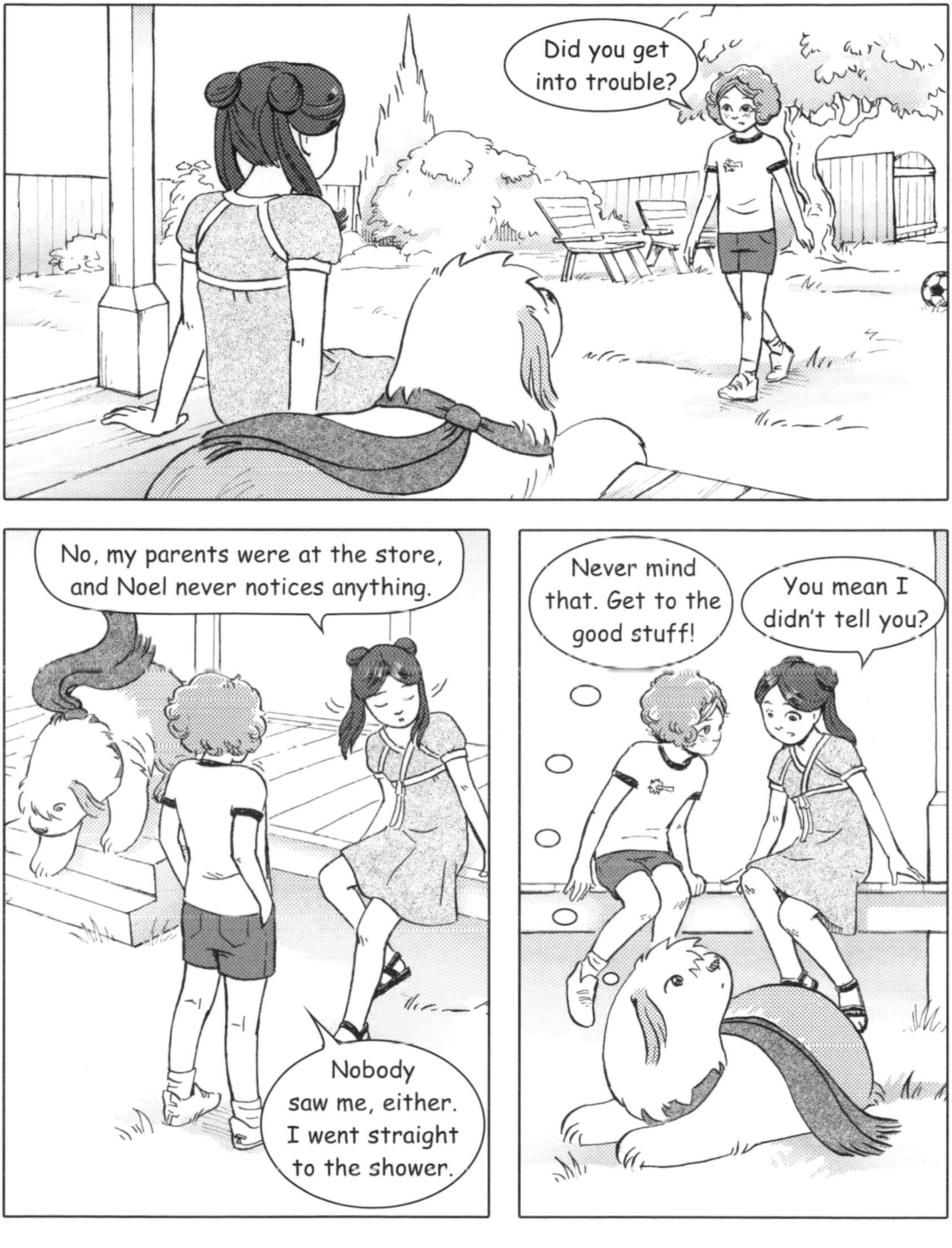

Did you get into trouble?
No, my parents were at the store, and Noel never notices anything.
Nobody saw me, either. I went straight to the shower.
Never mind that. Get to the good stuff!
You mean I didn't tell you?

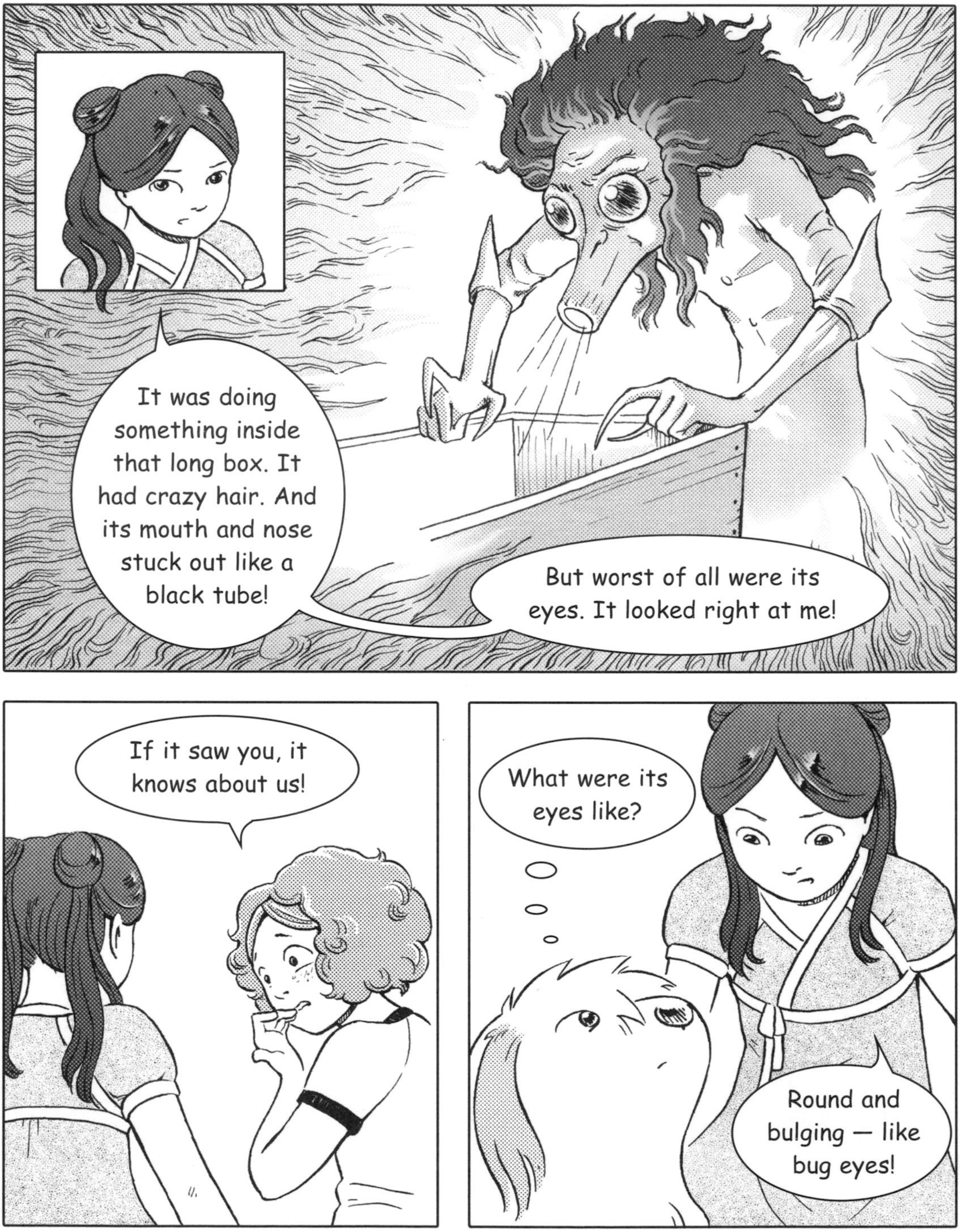
It was doing something inside that long box. It had crazy hair. And its mouth and nose stuck out like a black tube!
But worst of all were its eyes. It looked right at me!
If it saw you, it knows about us!
What were its eyes like?
Round and bulging — like bug eyes!

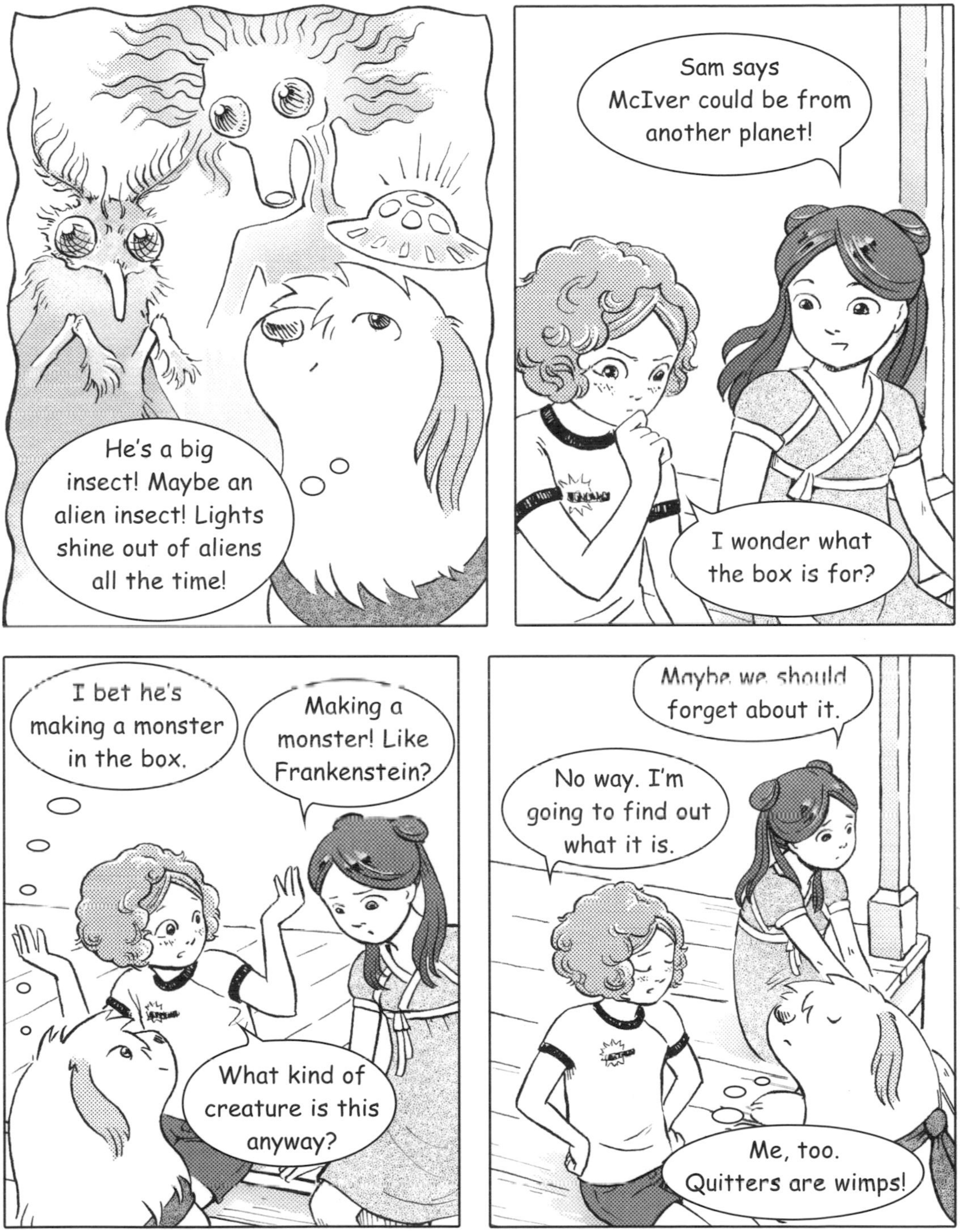
He's a big insect! Maybe an alien insect! Lights shine out of aliens all the time!
Sam says McIver could be from another planet!
I wonder what the box is for?
I bet he's making a monster in the box.
Making a monster! Like Frankenstein?
What kind of creature is this anyway?
Maybe we should forget about it.
No way. I'm going to find out what it is.
Me, too. Quitters are wimps!

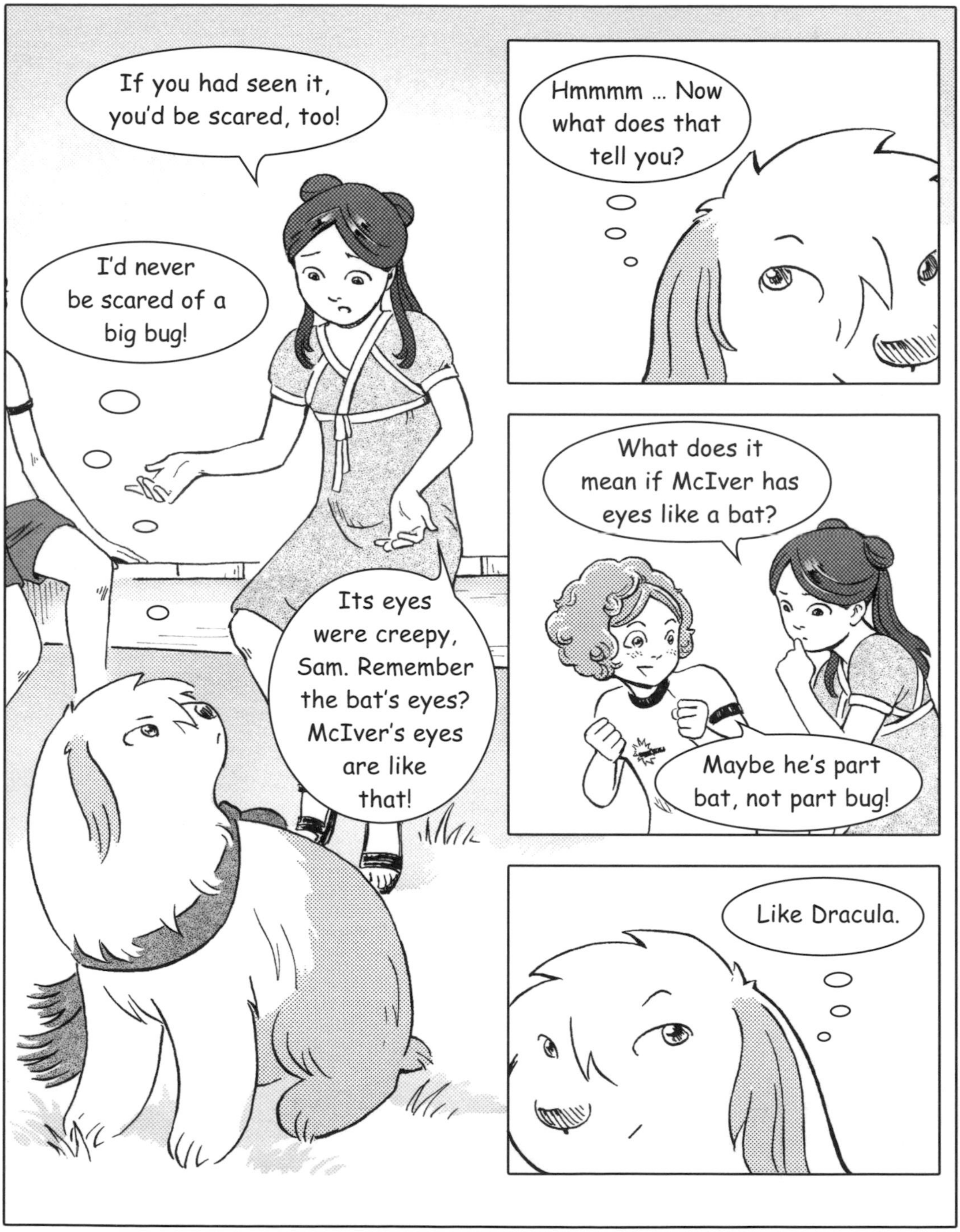
If you had seen it, you'd be scared, too!
I'd never be scared of a big bug!
Its eyes were creepy, Sam. Remember the bat's eyes? McIver's eyes are like that!
Hmmmm ... Now what does that tell you?
What does it mean if McIver has eyes like a bat?
Maybe he's part bat, not part bug!
Like Dracula.

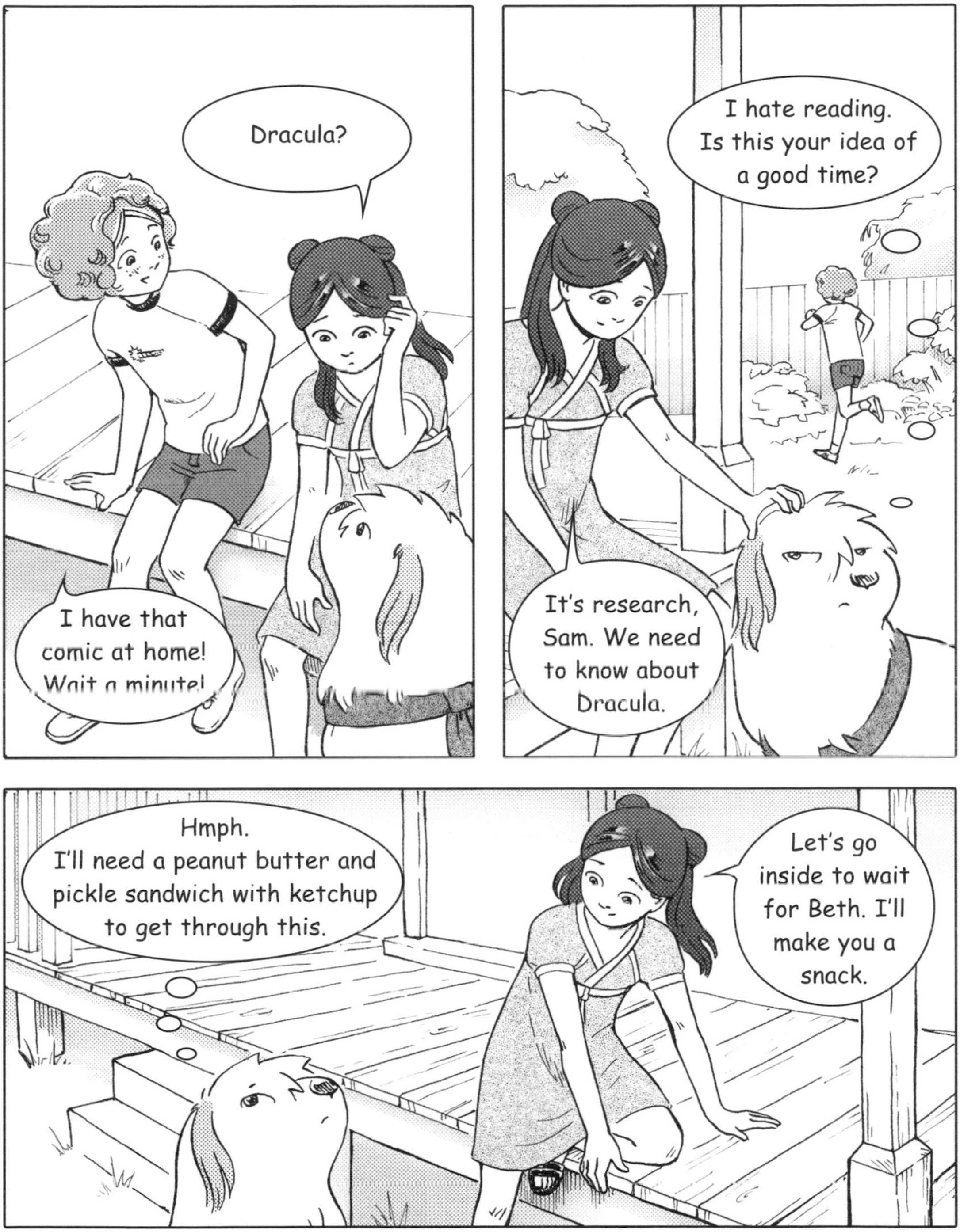
Dracula?
I have that comic at home! Wait a minute!
I hate reading. Is this your idea of a good time?
It's research, Sam. We need to know about Dracula.
Hmph. I'll need a peanut butter and pickle sandwich with ketchup to get through this.
Let's go inside to wait for Beth. I'll make you a snack.

Later ...

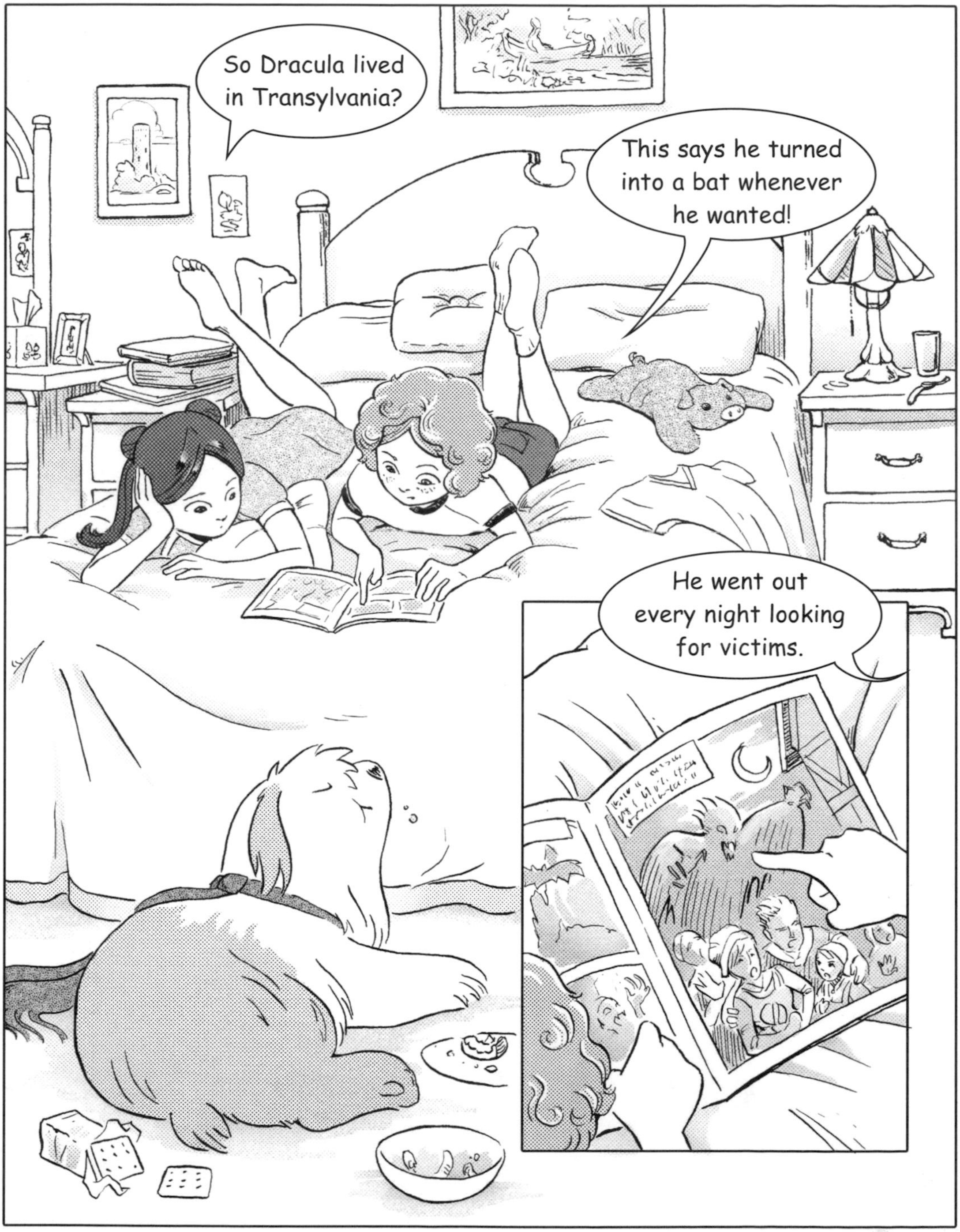
So Dracula lived in Transylvania?
This says he turned into a bat whenever he wanted!
He went out every night looking for victims.

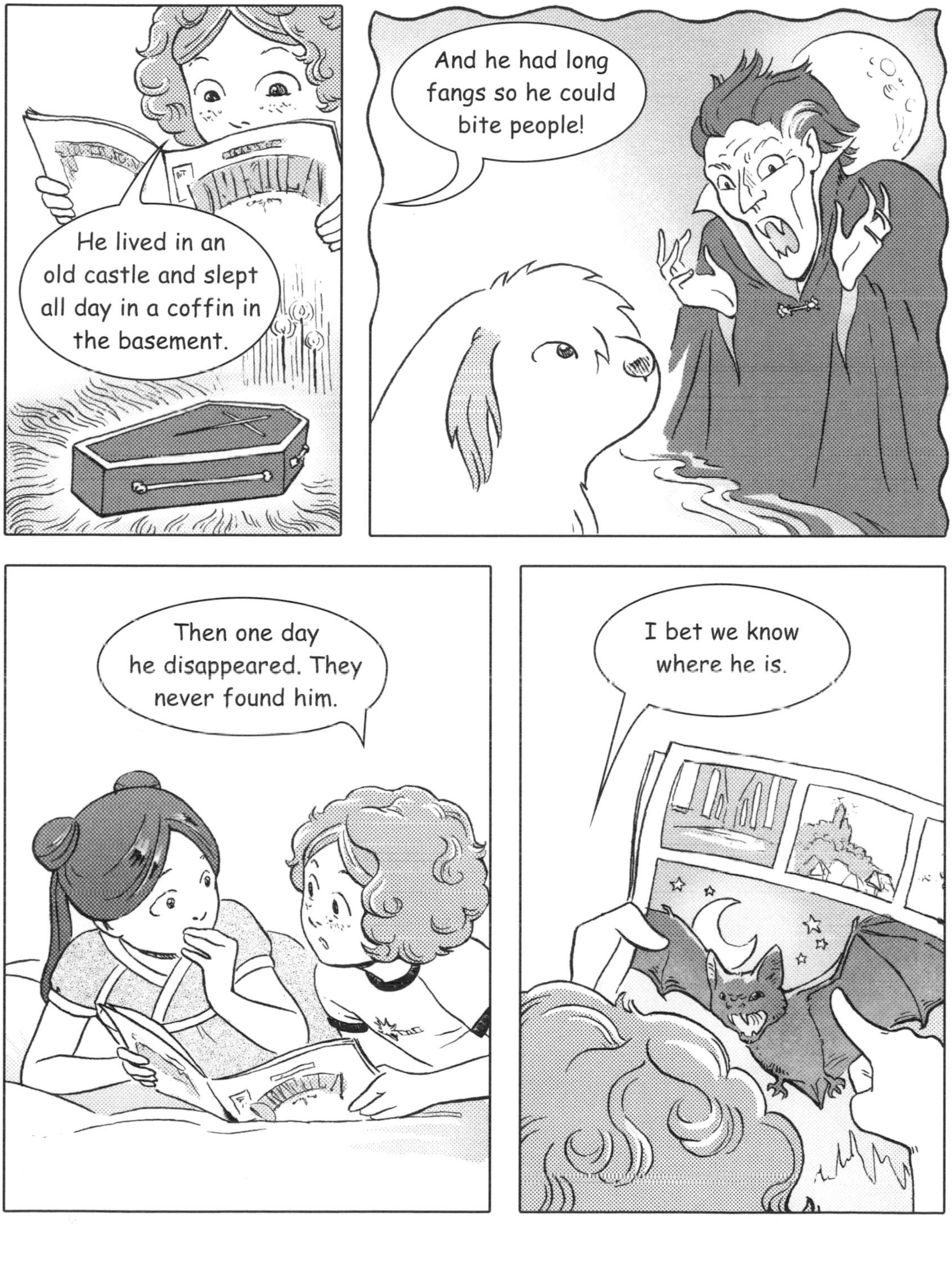
He lived in an old castle and slept all day in a coffin in the basement.
And he had long fangs so he could bite people!
Then one day he disappeared. They never found him.
I bet we know where he is.

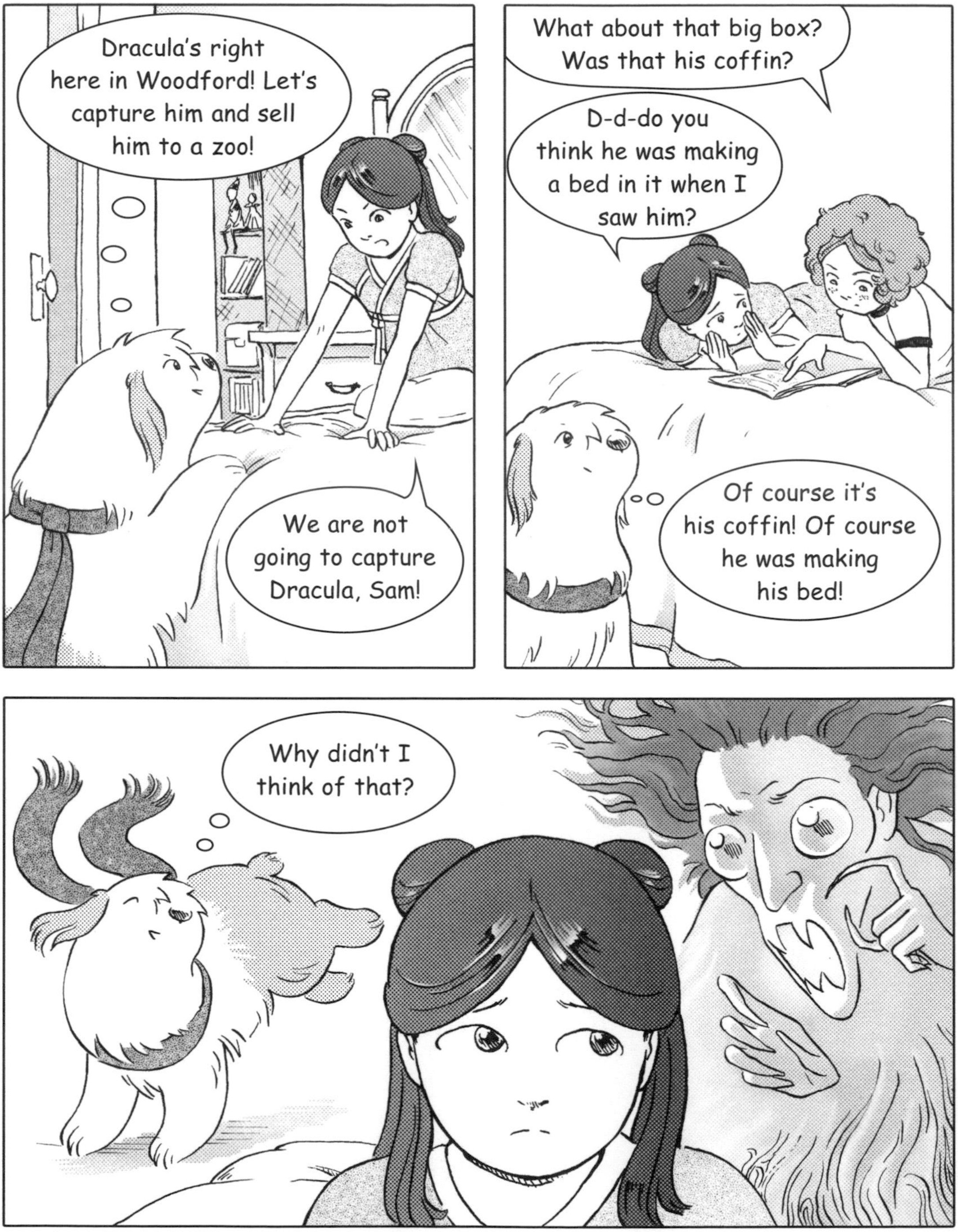
Dracula's right here in Woodford! Let's capture him and sell him to a zoo!
We are not going to capture Dracula, Sam!
What about that big box? Was that his coffin?
D-d-do you think he was making a bed in it when I saw him?
Of course it's his coffin! Of course he was making his bed!
Why didn't I think of that?

Later that evening ...

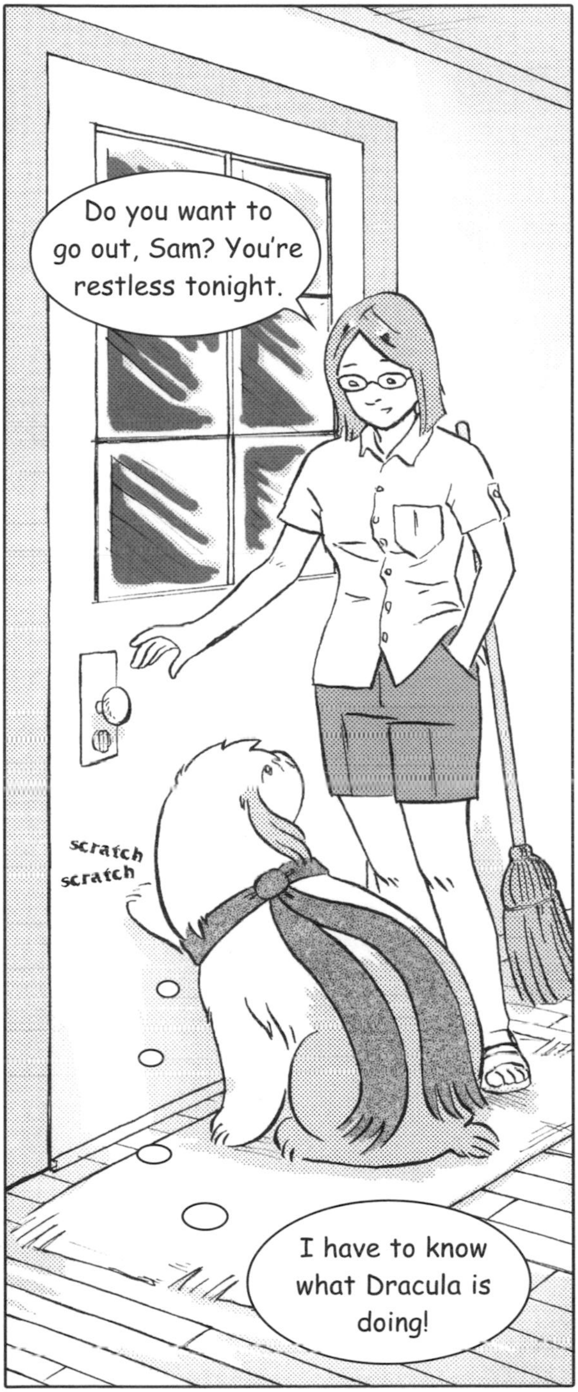
Do you want to go out, Sam? You're restless tonight.
scratch scratch
I have to know what Dracula is doing!

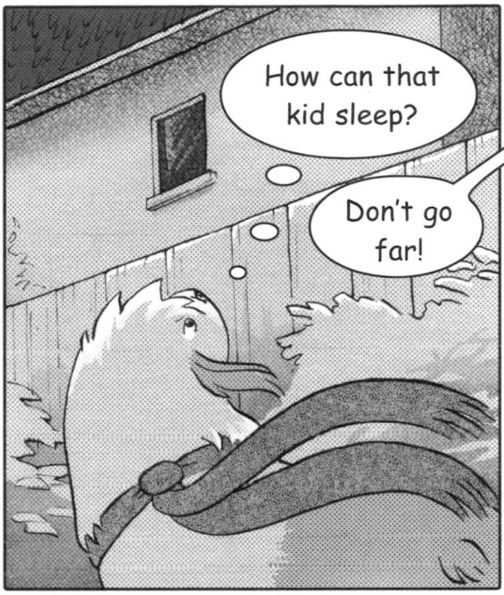
How can that kid sleep?
Don't go far!

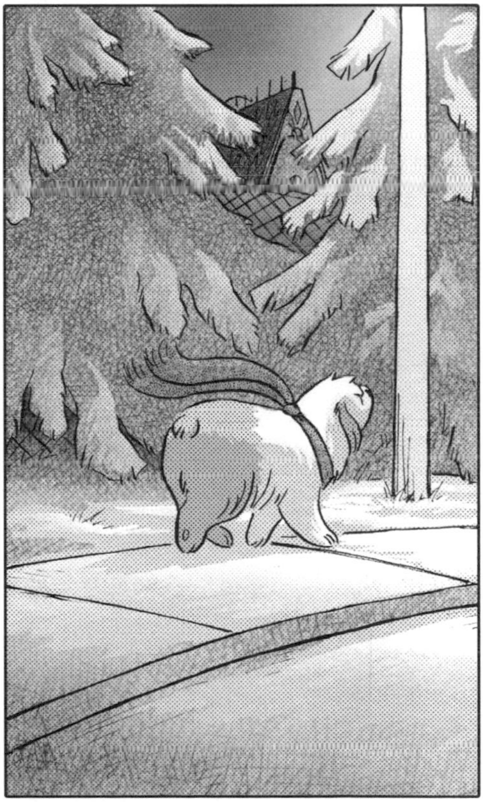

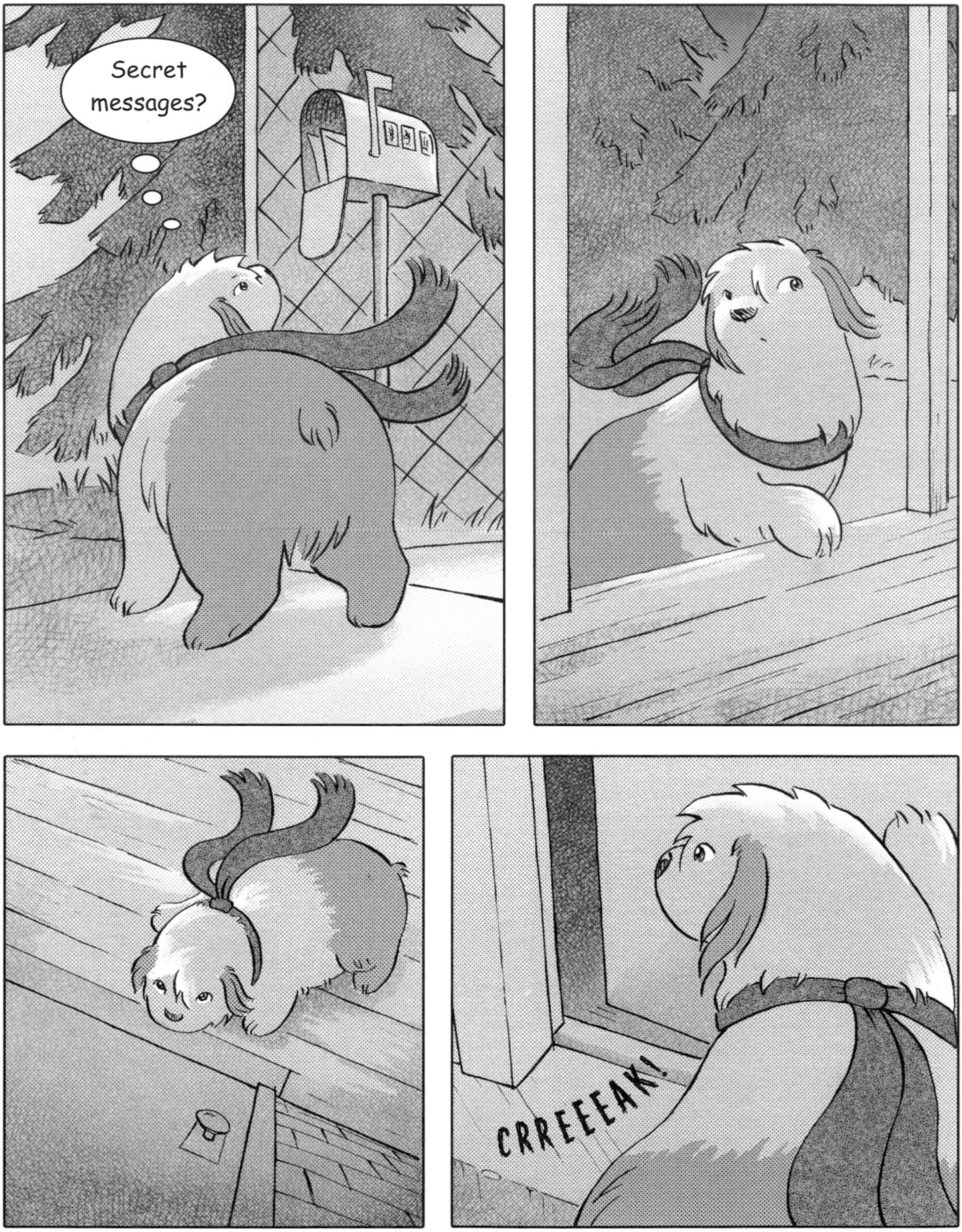
Secret messages?
CRREEEAK!

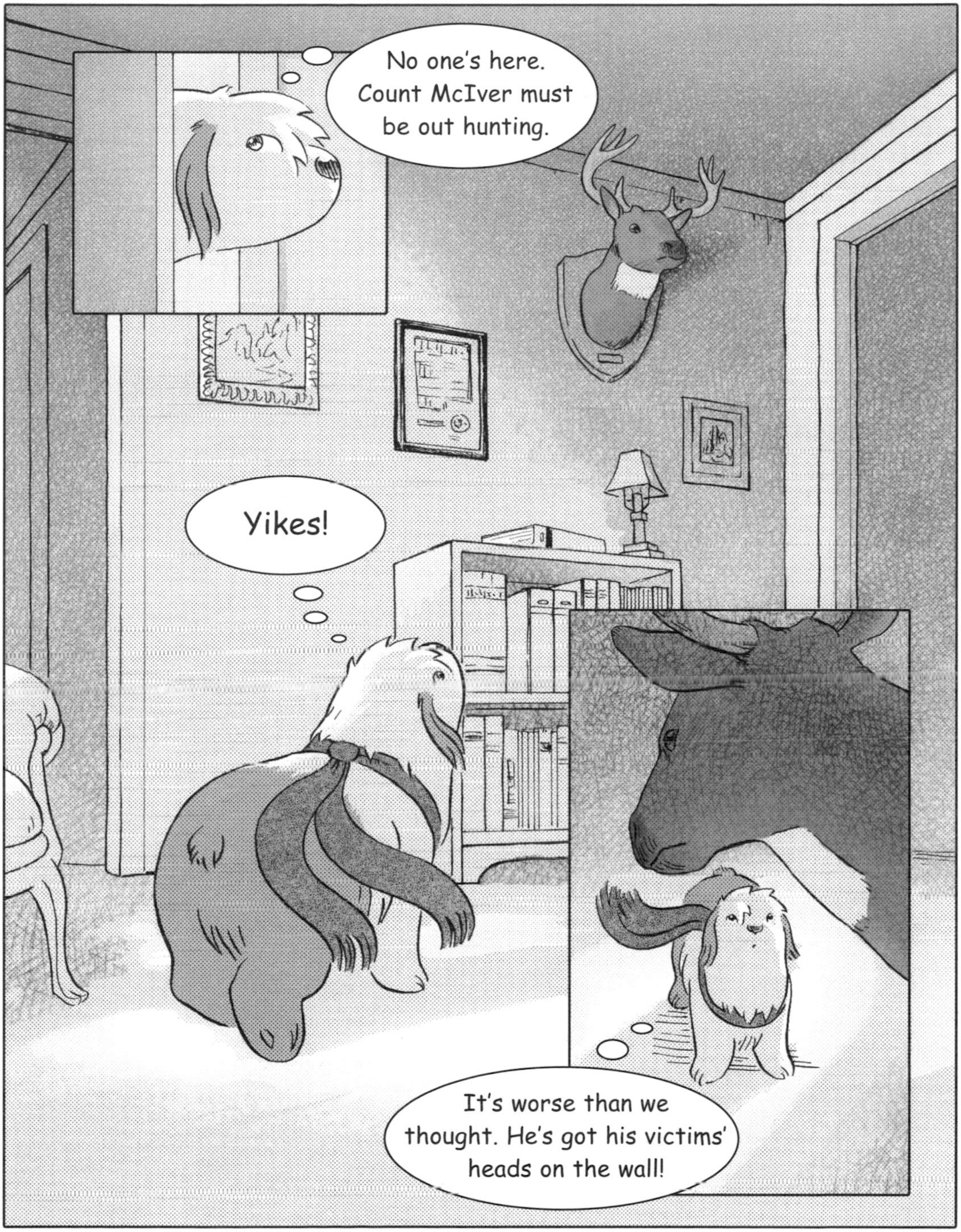
No one's here. Count McIver must be out hunting.
Yikes!
It's worse than we thought. He's got his victims' heads on the wall!

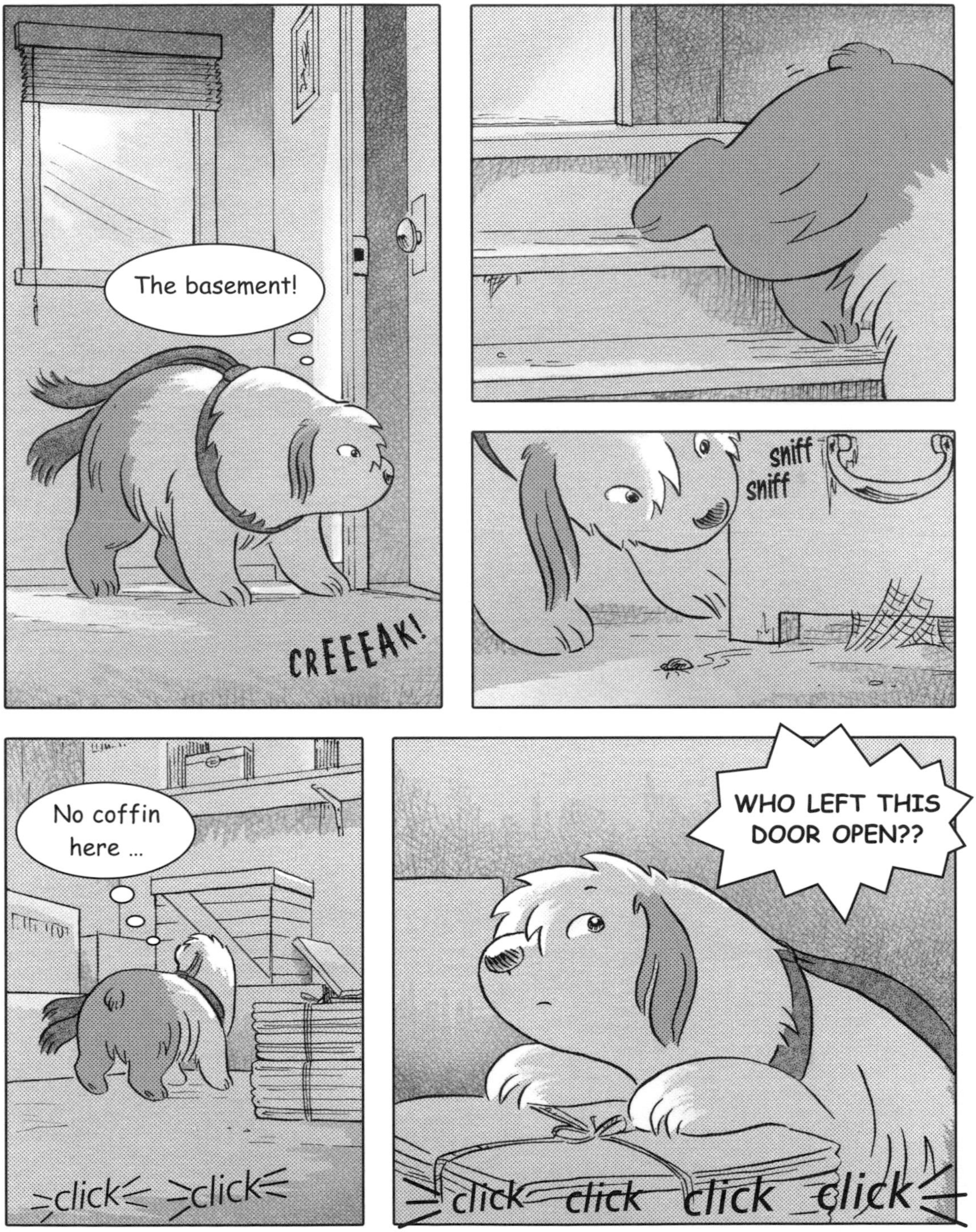

The basement!
CREEEAK!
sniff
sniff
No coffin here ...
click click
WHO LEFT THIS DOOR OPEN??
click click click click

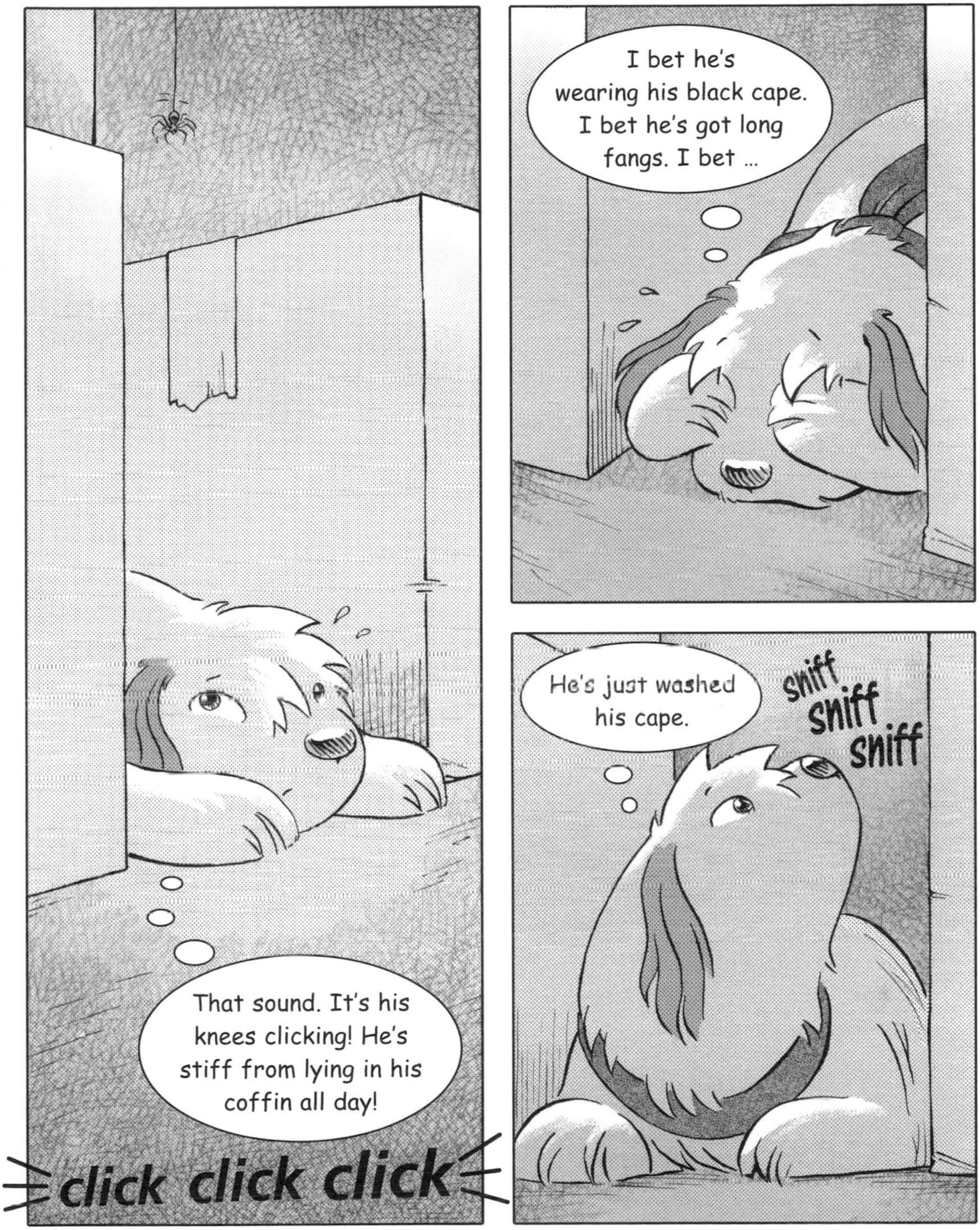
That sound. It's his knees clicking! He's stiff from lying in his coffin all day!
click click click
I bet he's wearing his black cape. I bet he's got long fangs. I bet ...
He's just washed his cape.
sniff sniff sniff

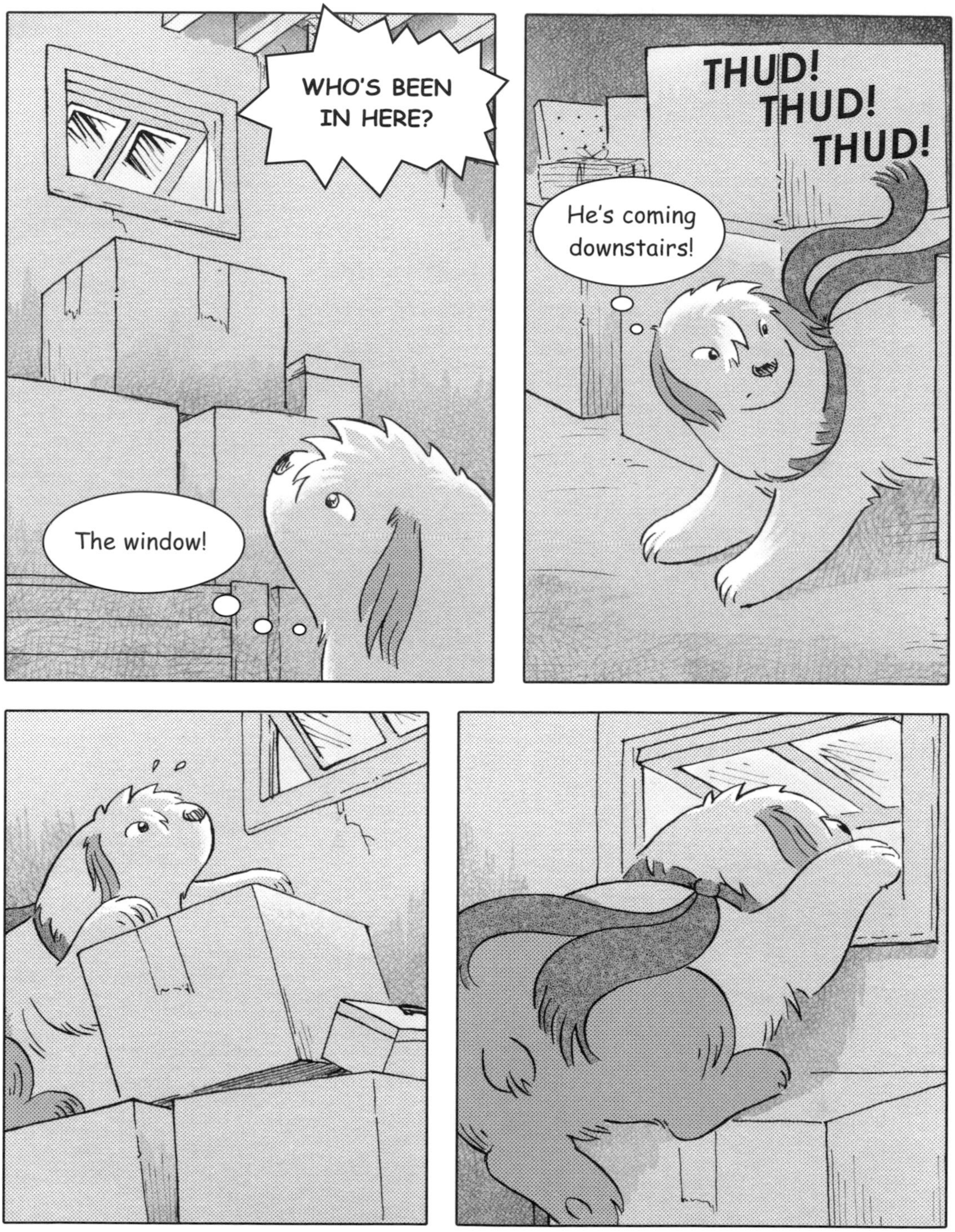
WHO'S BEEN IN HERE?
The window!
THUD! THUD! THUD!
He's coming downstairs!

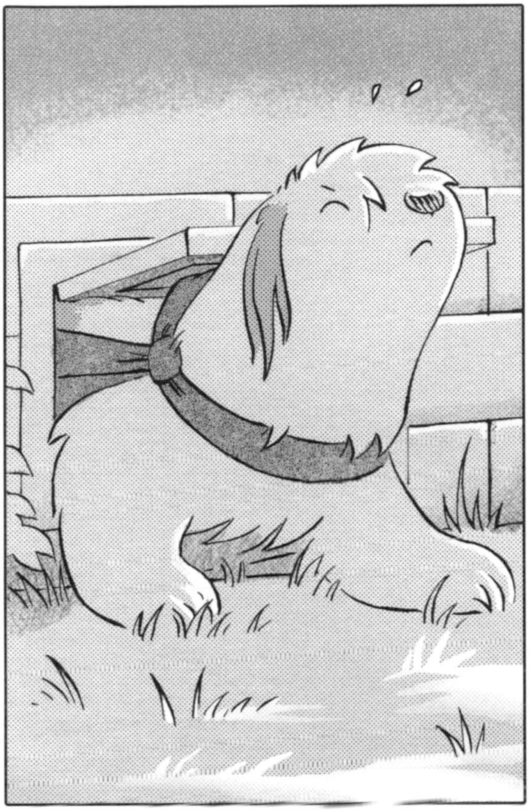

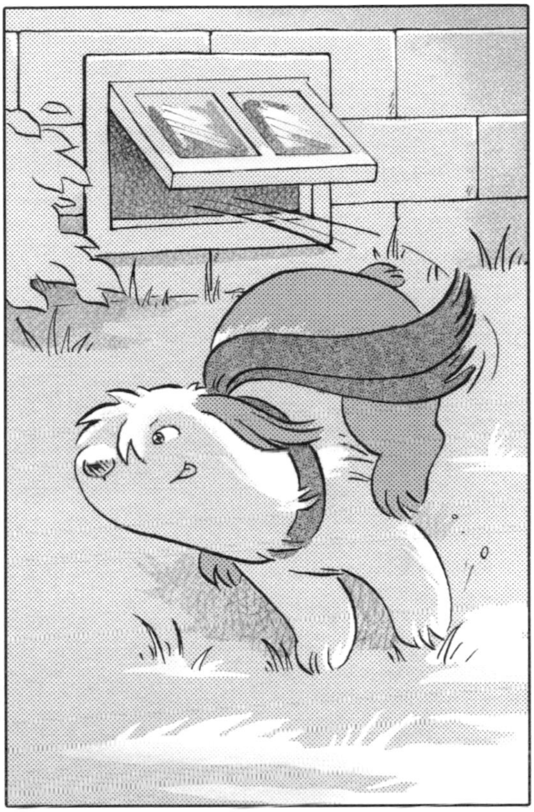

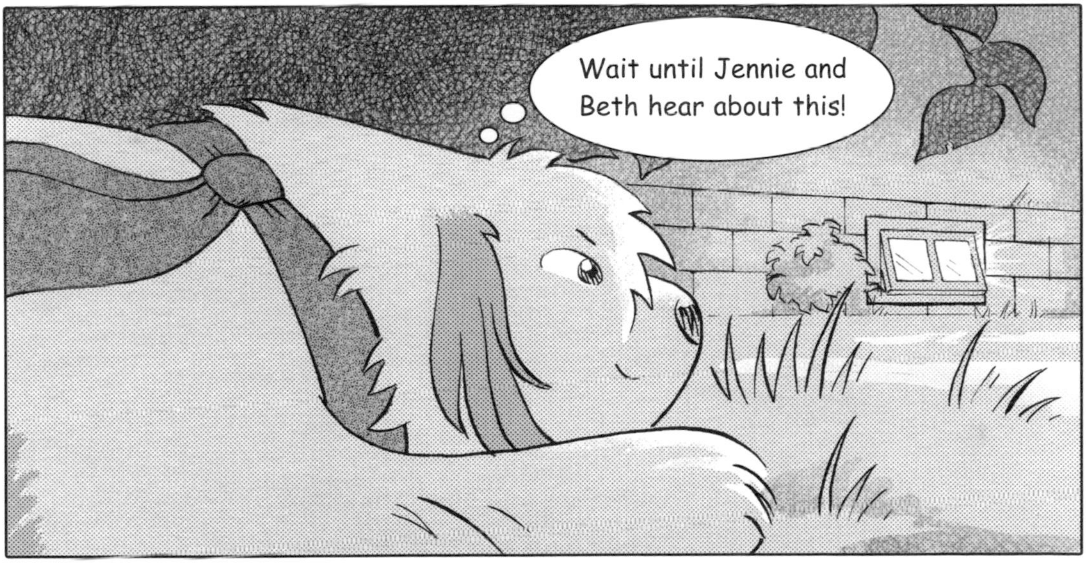
Wait until Jennie and Beth hear about this!

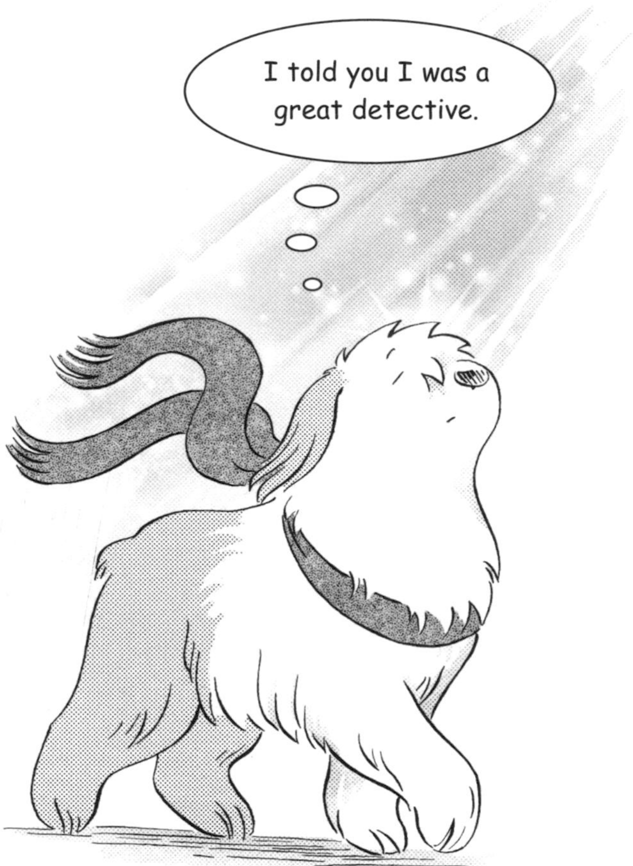
I told you I was a great detective.

The next morning ...

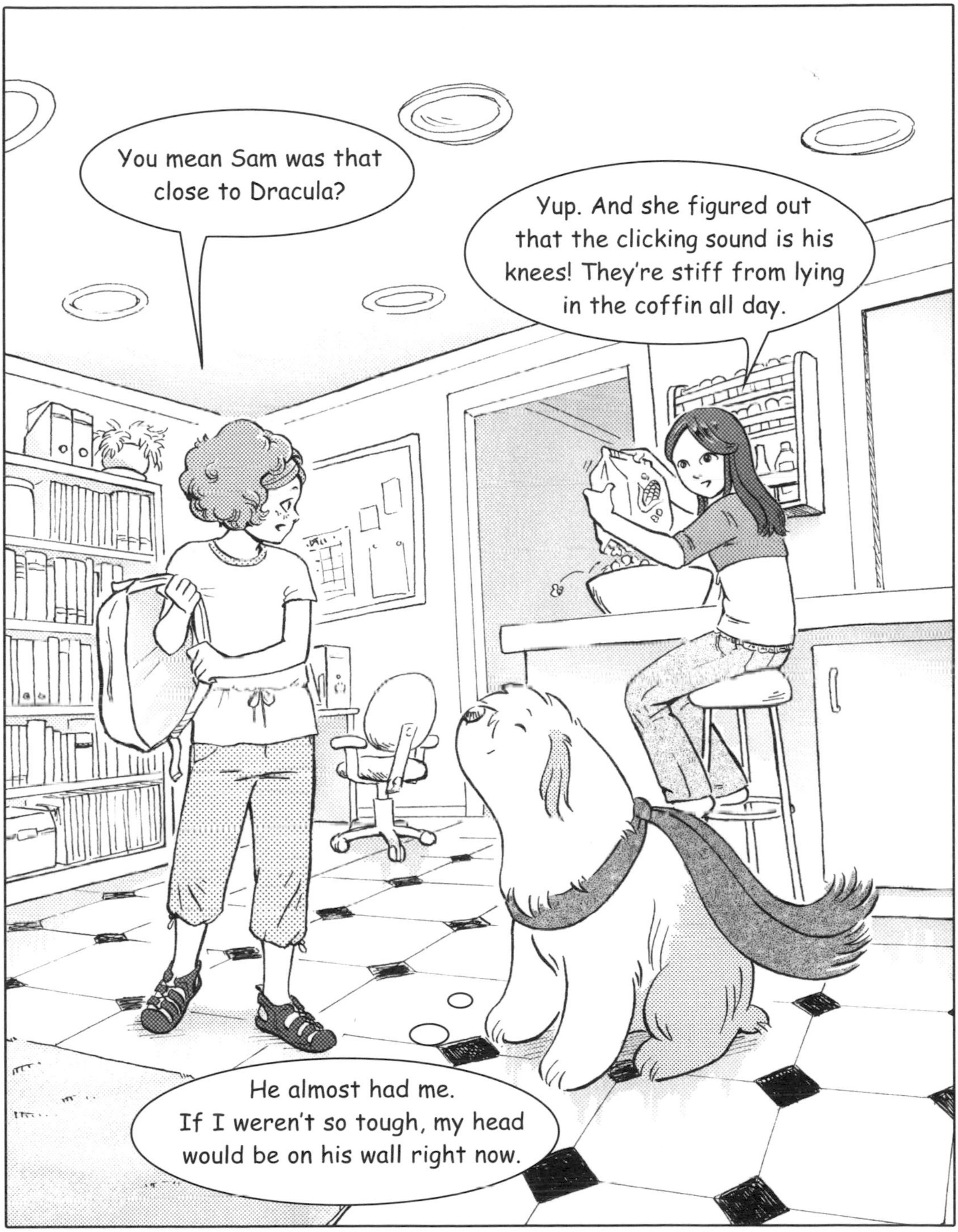
You mean Sam was that close to Dracula?
Yup. And she figured out that the clicking sound is his knees! They're stiff from lying in the coffin all day.
He almost had me. If I weren't so tough, my head would be on his wall right now.

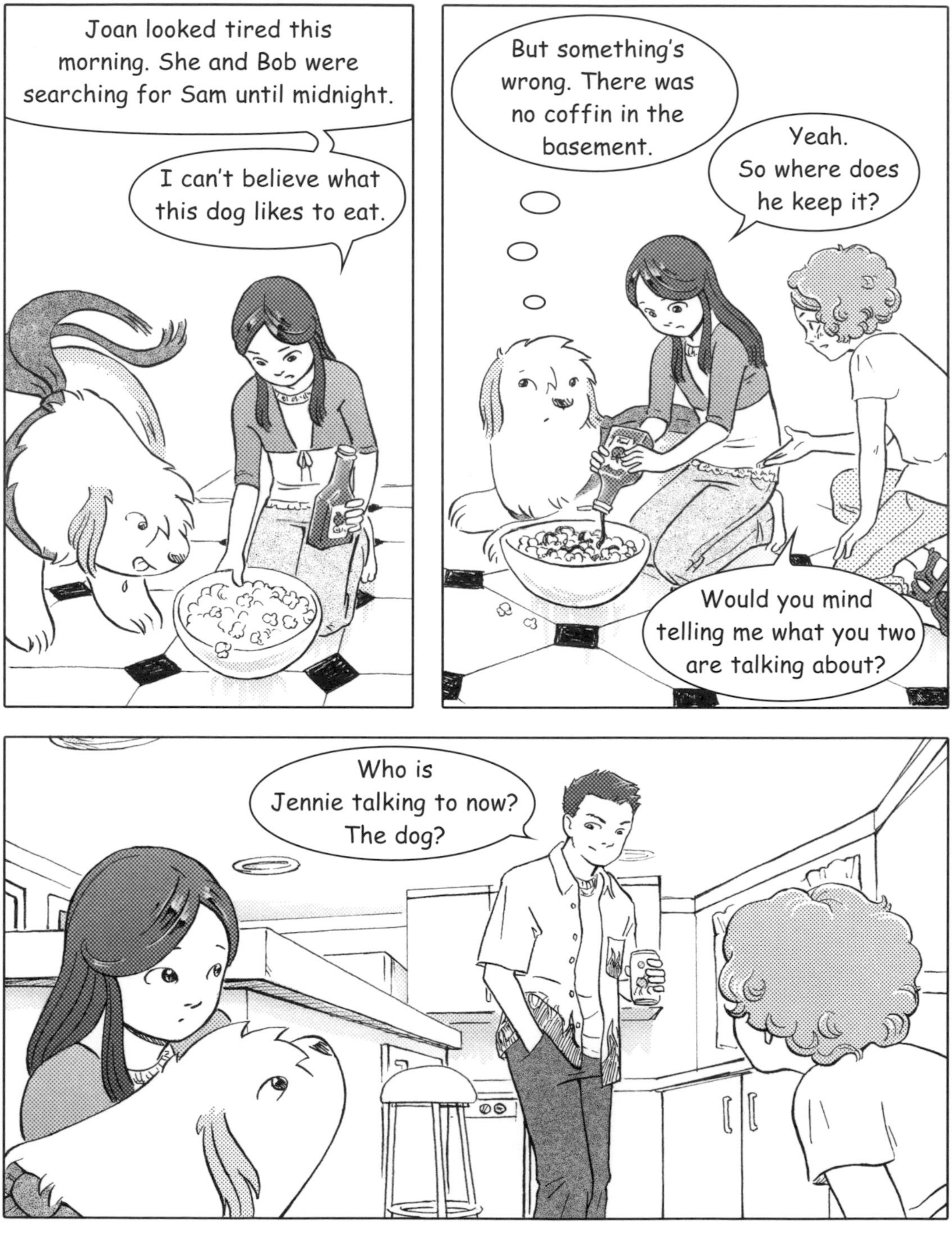
Joan looked tired this morning. She and Bob were searching for Sam until midnight.
I can't believe what this dog likes to eat.
But something's wrong. There was no coffin in the basement.
Yeah. So where does he keep it?
Would you mind telling me what you two are talking about?
Who is Jennie talking to now? The dog?

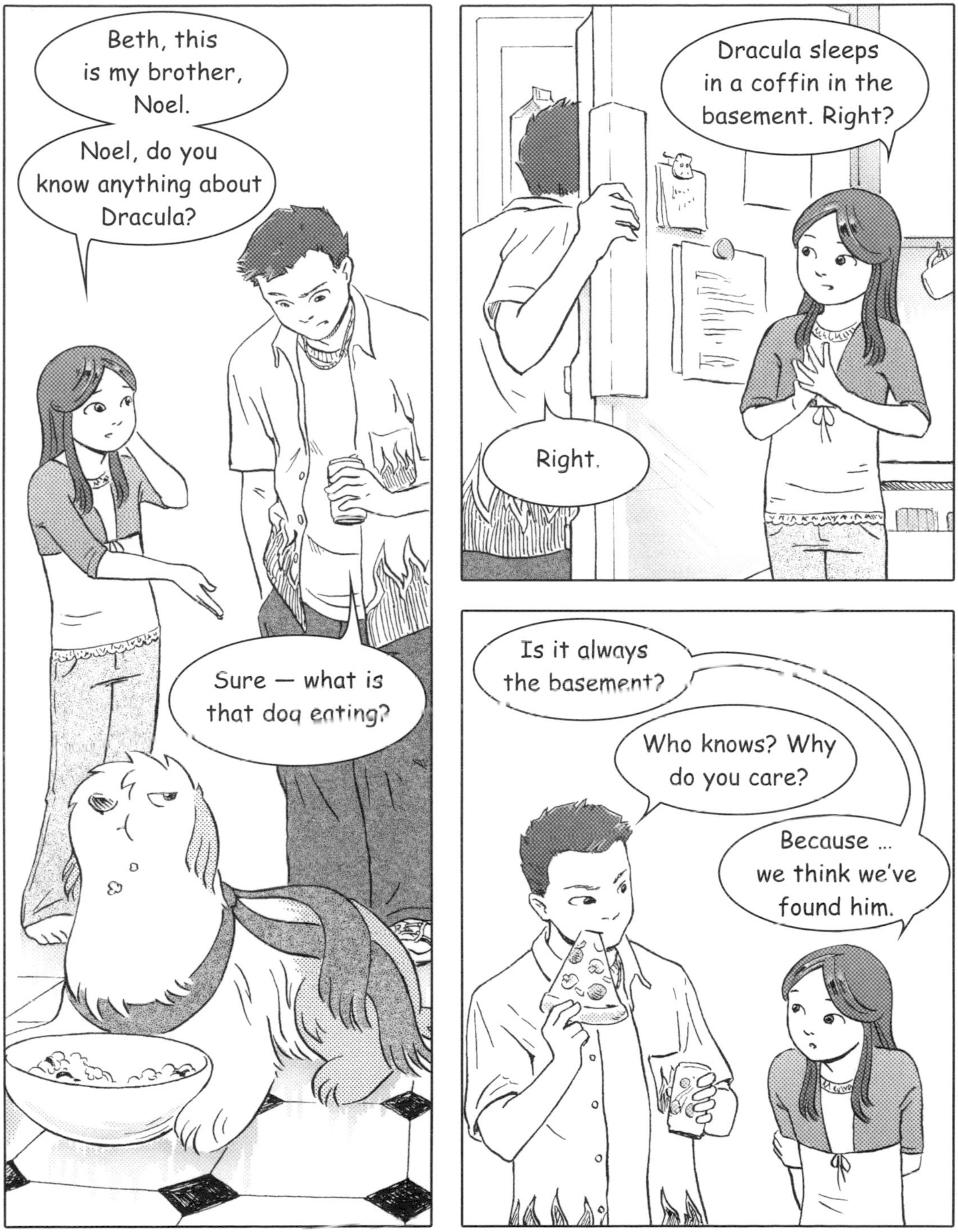
Beth, this is my brother, Noel.
Noel, do you know anything about Dracula?
Sure — what is that dog eating?
Dracula sleeps in a coffin in the basement. Right?
Right.
Is it always the basement?
Who knows? Why do you care?
Because ... we think we've found him.

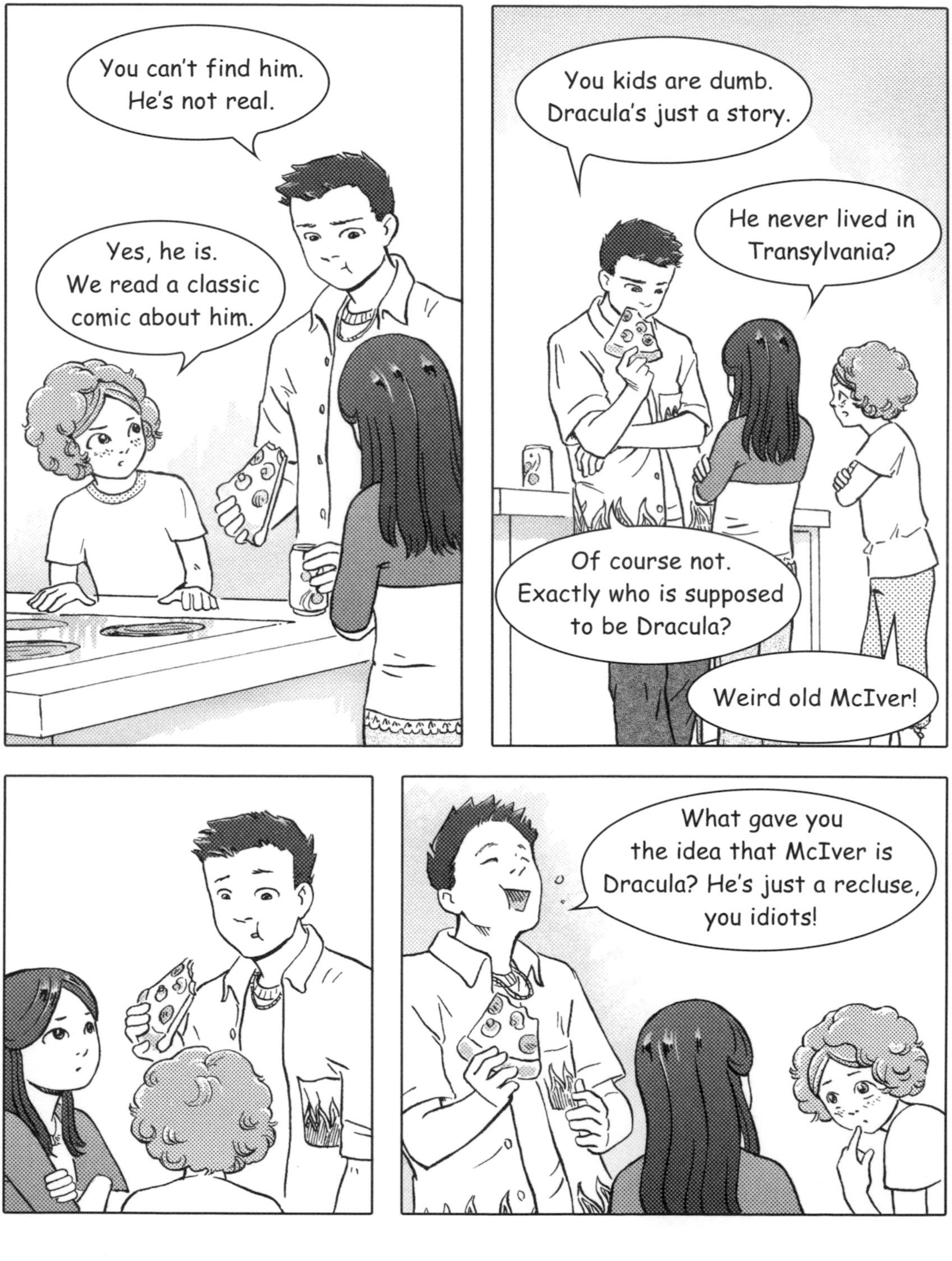

You can't find him. He's not real.
Yes, he is. We read a classic comic about him.
You kids are dumb. Dracula's just a story.
He never lived in Transylvania?
Of course not. Exactly who is supposed to be Dracula?
Weird old McIver!
What gave you the idea that McIver is Dracula? He's just a recluse, you idiots!

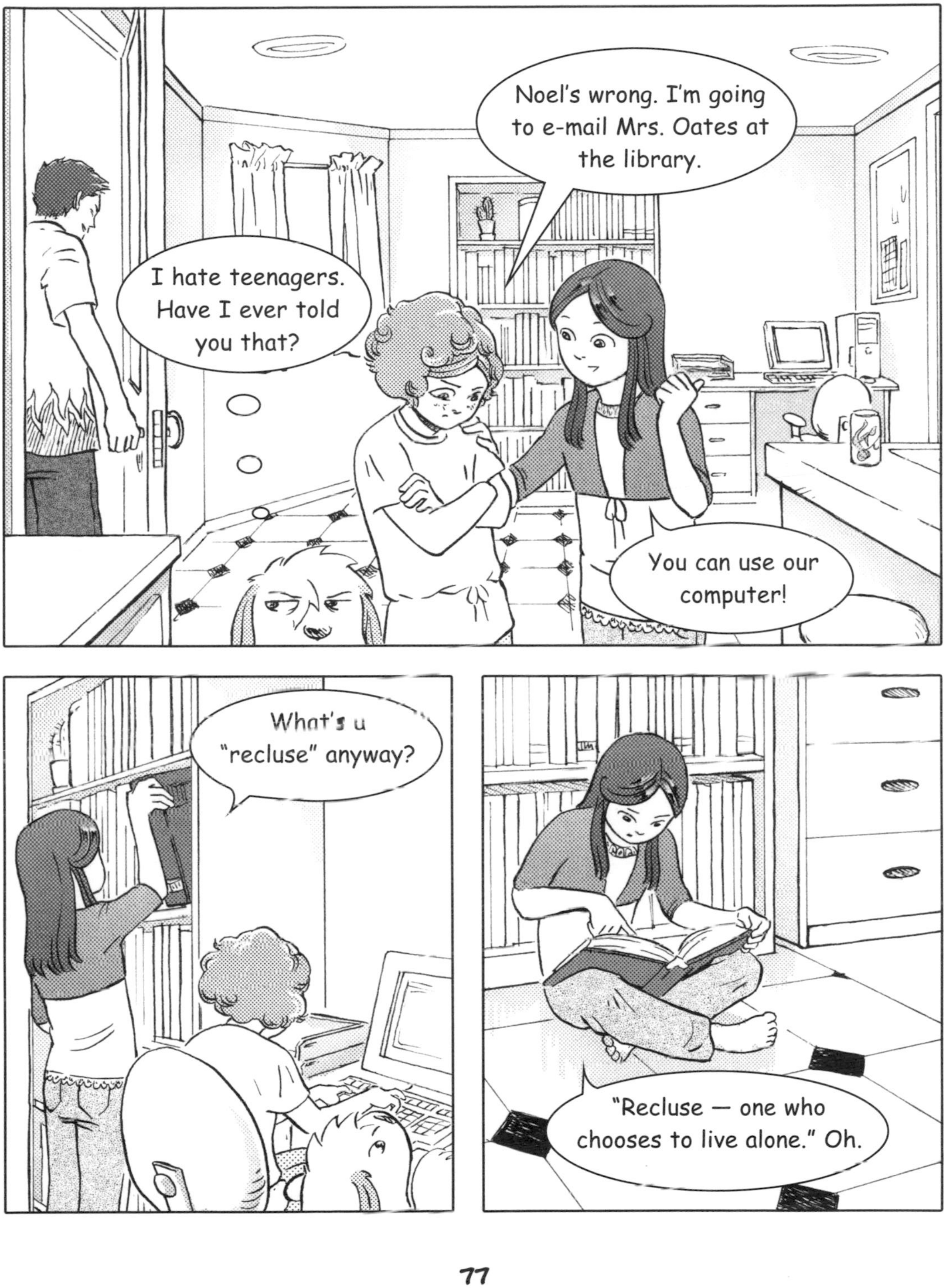

I hate teenagers. Have I ever told you that?
Noel's wrong. I'm going to e-mail Mrs. Oates at the library.
You can use our computer!
What's a "recluse" anyway?
"Recluse — one who chooses to live alone." Oh.

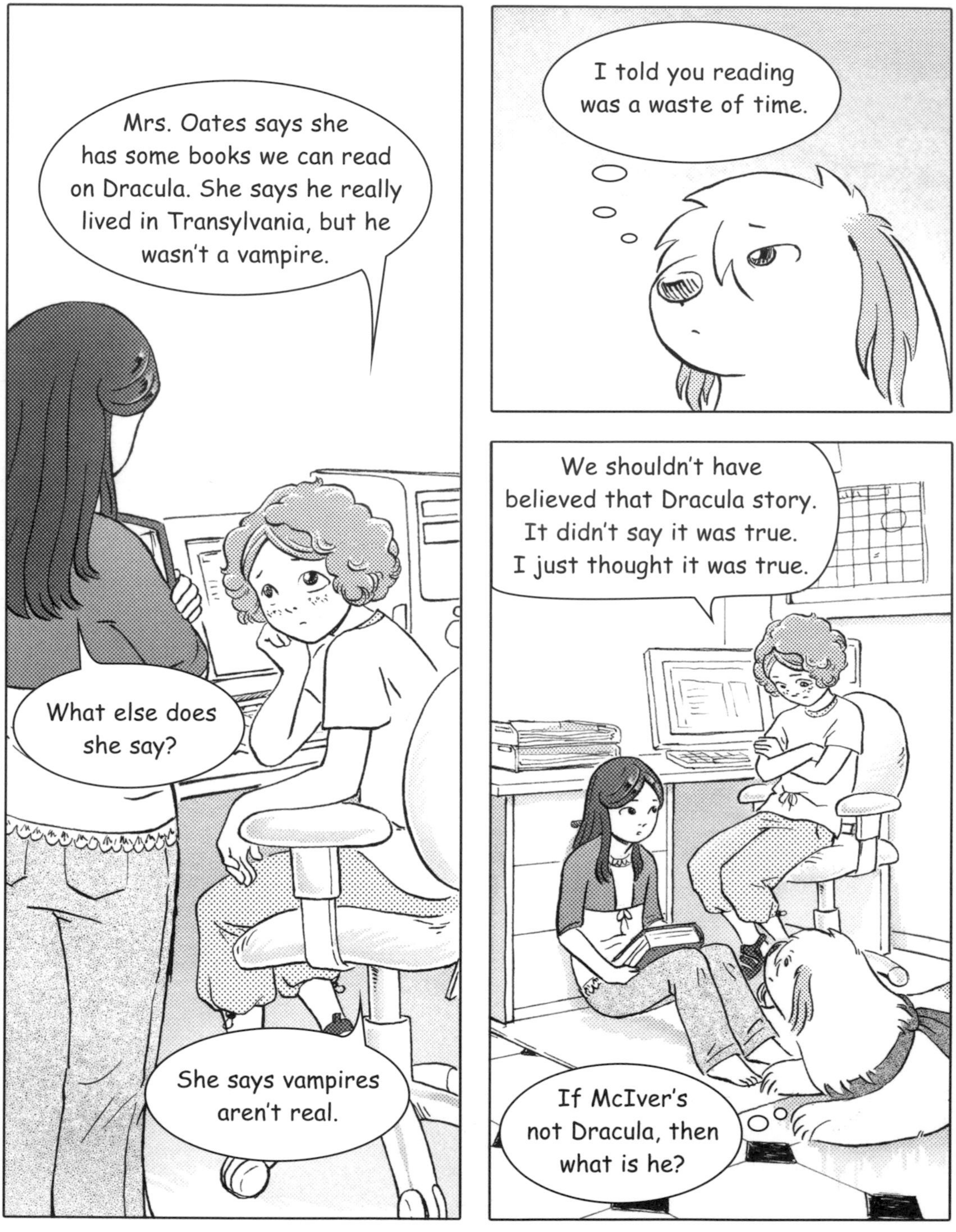
Mrs. Oates says she has some books we can read on Dracula. She says he really lived in Transylvania, but he wasn't a vampire.
What else does she say?
She says vampires aren't real.
I told you reading was a waste of time.
We shouldn't have believed that Dracula story. It didn't say it was true. I just thought it was true.
If McIver's not Dracula, then what is he?

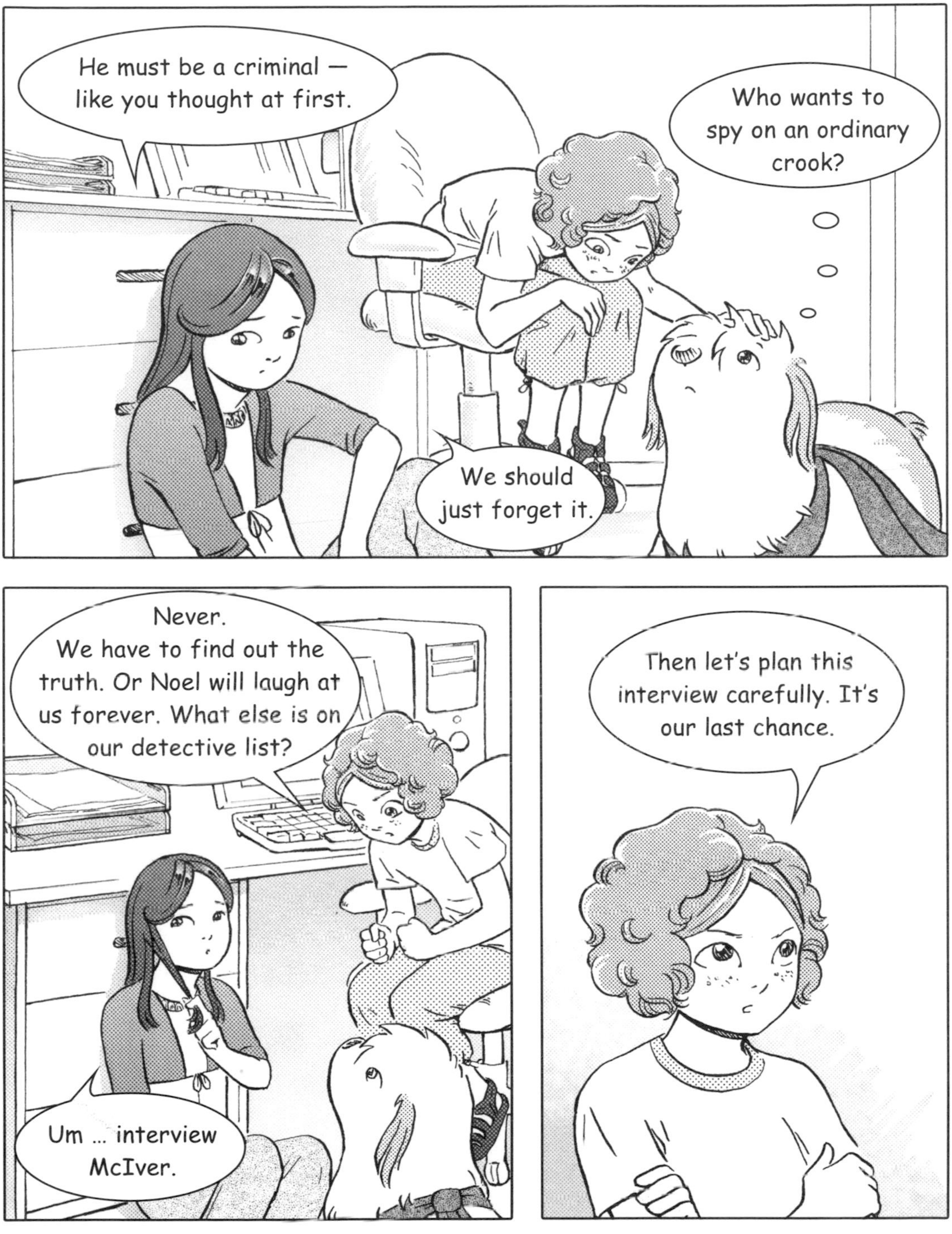
He must be a criminal — like you thought at first.
Who wants to spy on an ordinary crook?
We should just forget it.
Never. We have to find out the truth. Or Noel will laugh at us forever. What else is on our detective list?
Um ... interview McIver.
Then let's plan this interview carefully. It's our last chance.

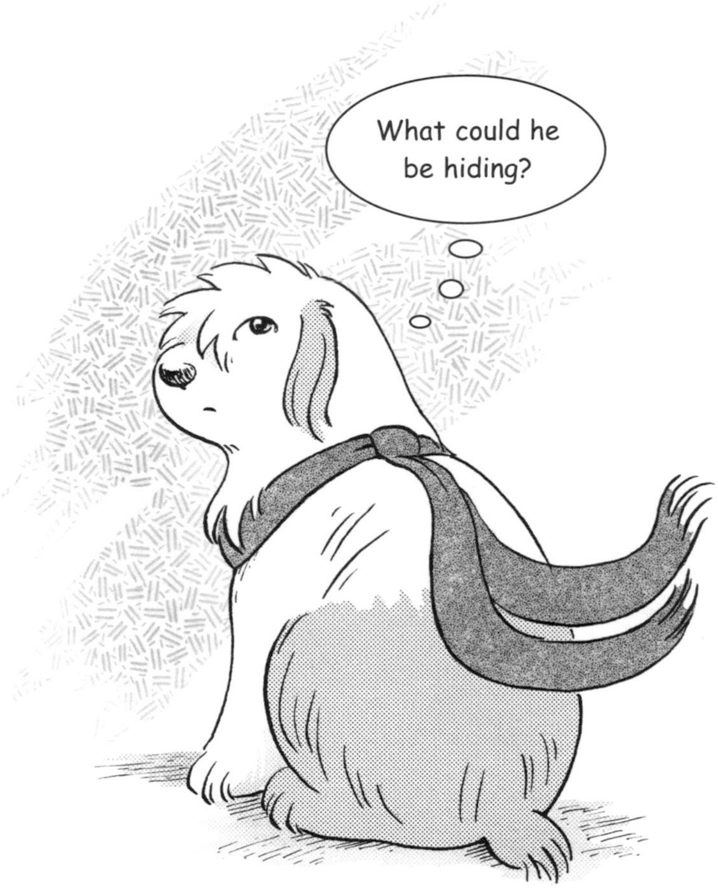
What could he be hiding?

The next day ...

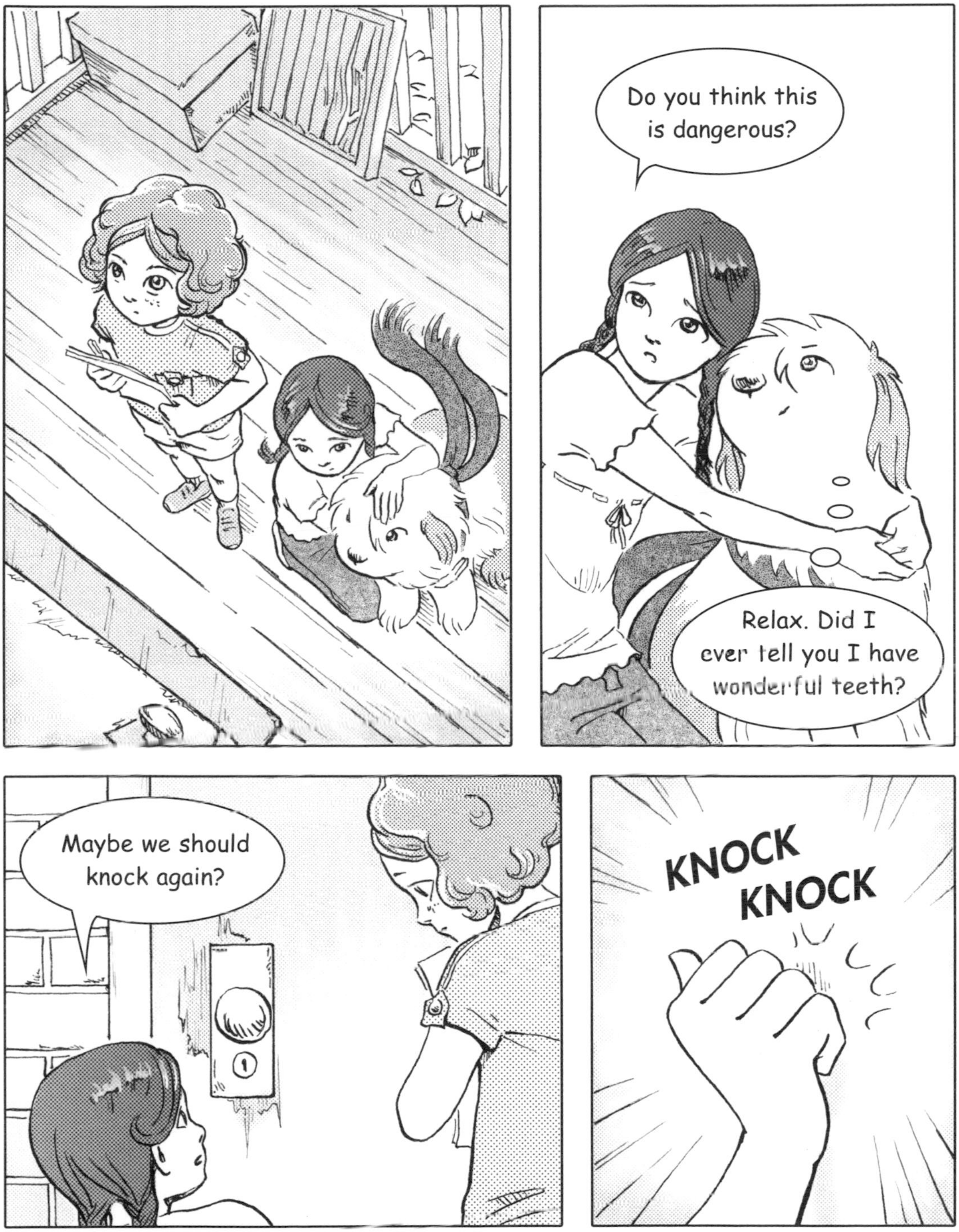
Do you think this is dangerous?
Relax. Did I ever tell you I have wonderful teeth?
Maybe we should knock again?
KNOCK KNOCK

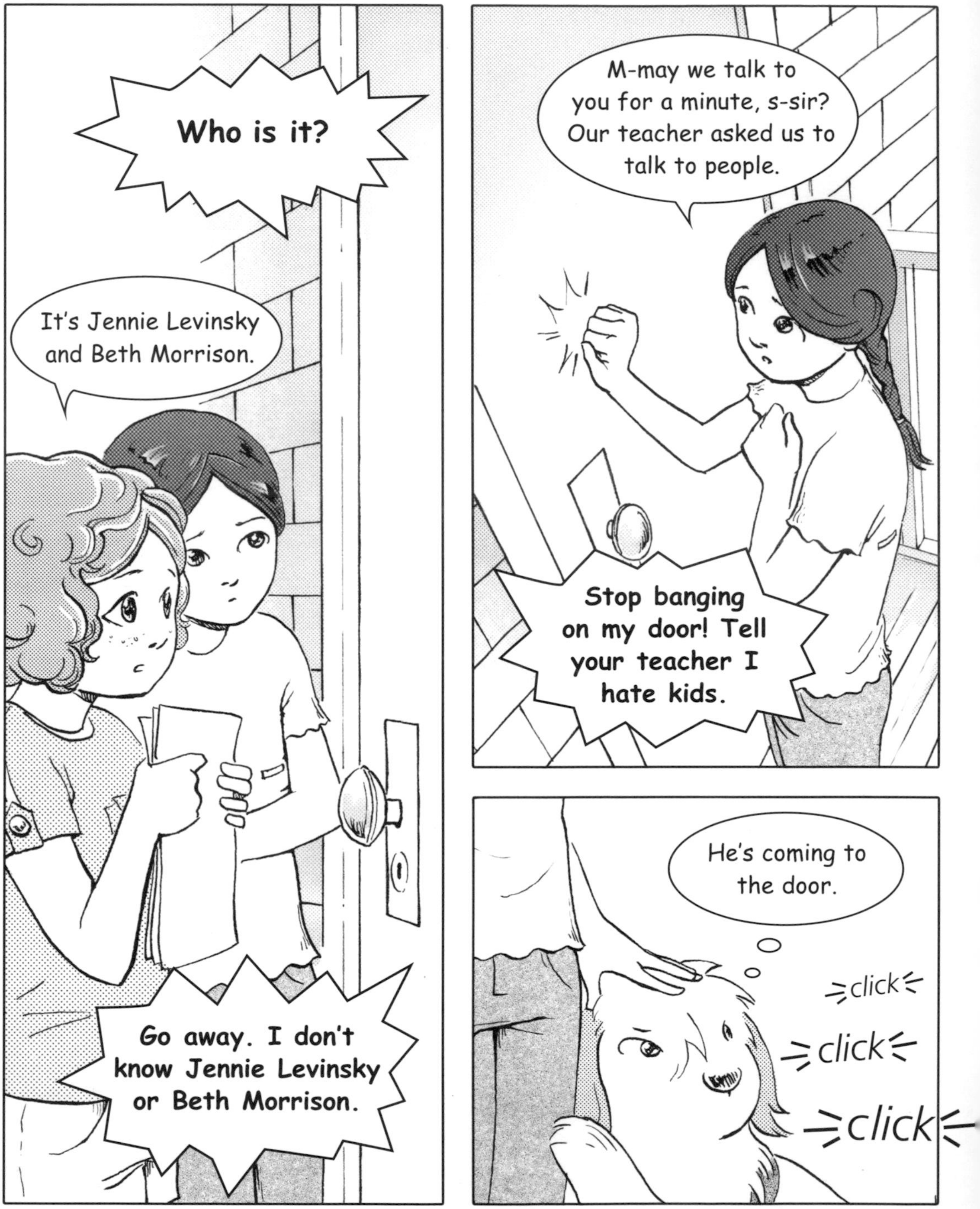
Who is it?
It's Jennie Levinsky and Beth Morrison.
Go away. I don't know Jennie Levinsky or Beth Morrison.
M-may we talk to you for a minute, s-sir? Our teacher asked us to talk to people.
Stop banging on my door! Tell your teacher I hate kids.
He's coming to the door.
click
click
click

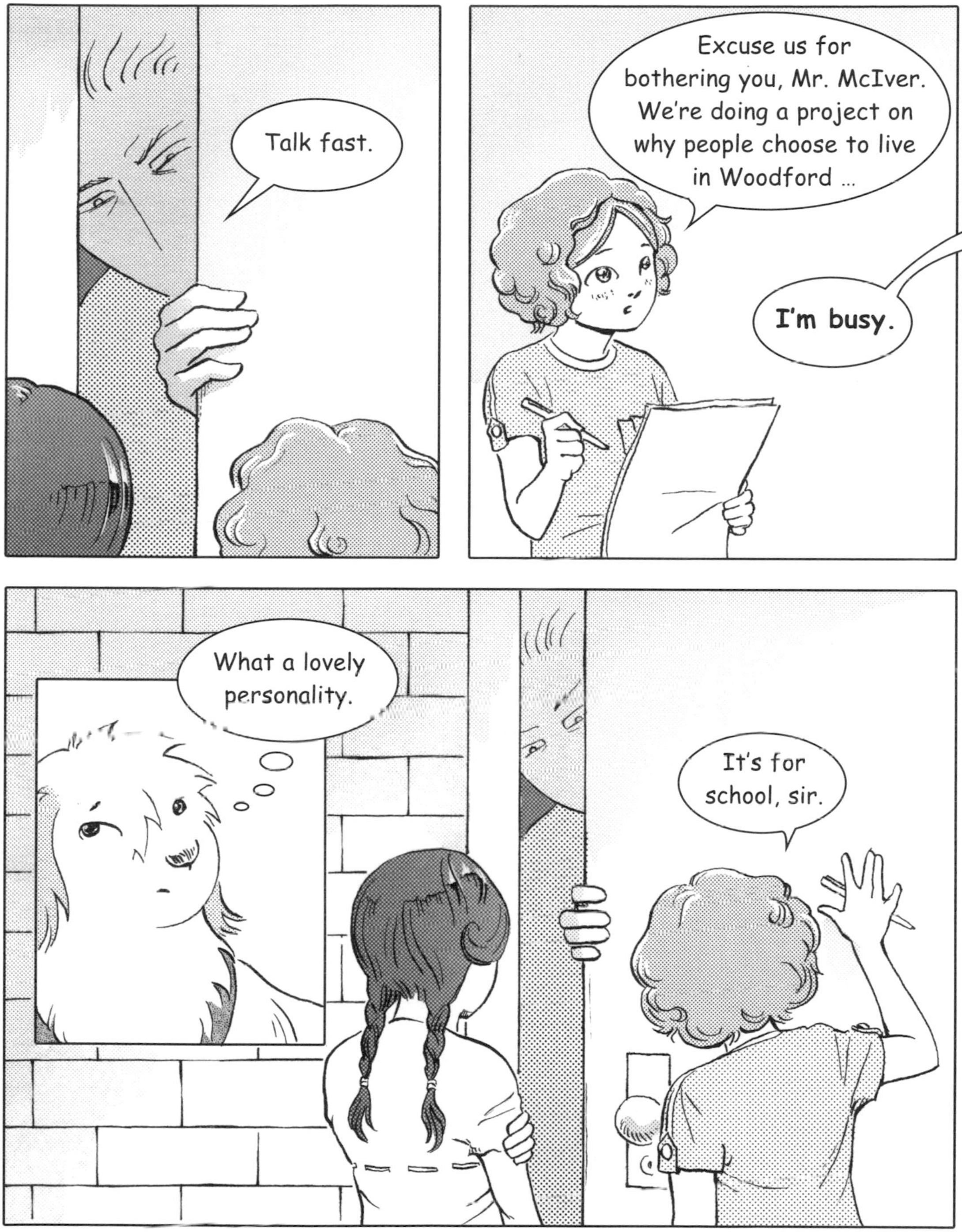
Talk fast.
Excuse us for bothering you, Mr. McIver. We're doing a project on why people choose to live in Woodford ...
I'm busy.
What a lovely personality.
It's for school, sir.

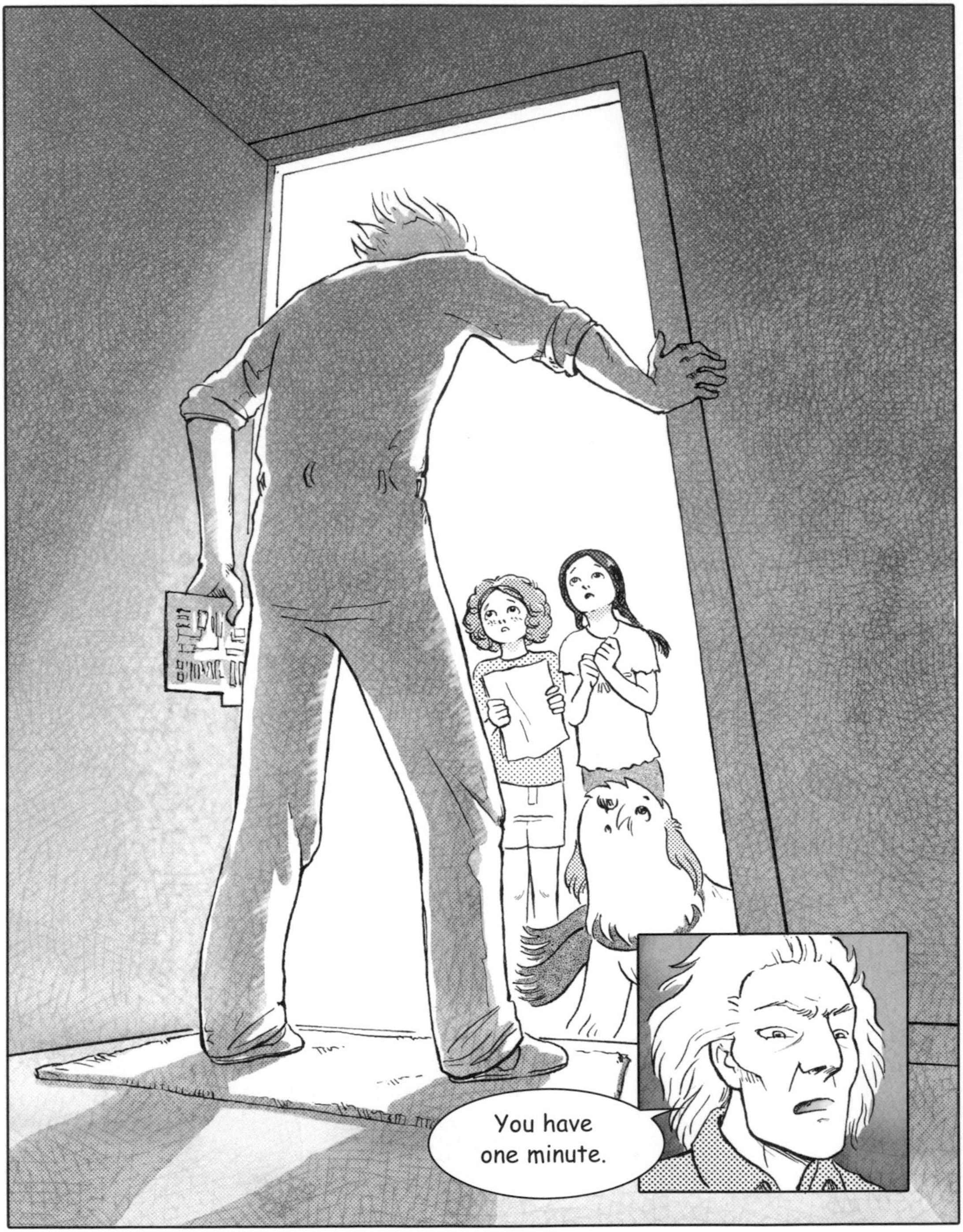
You have one minute.

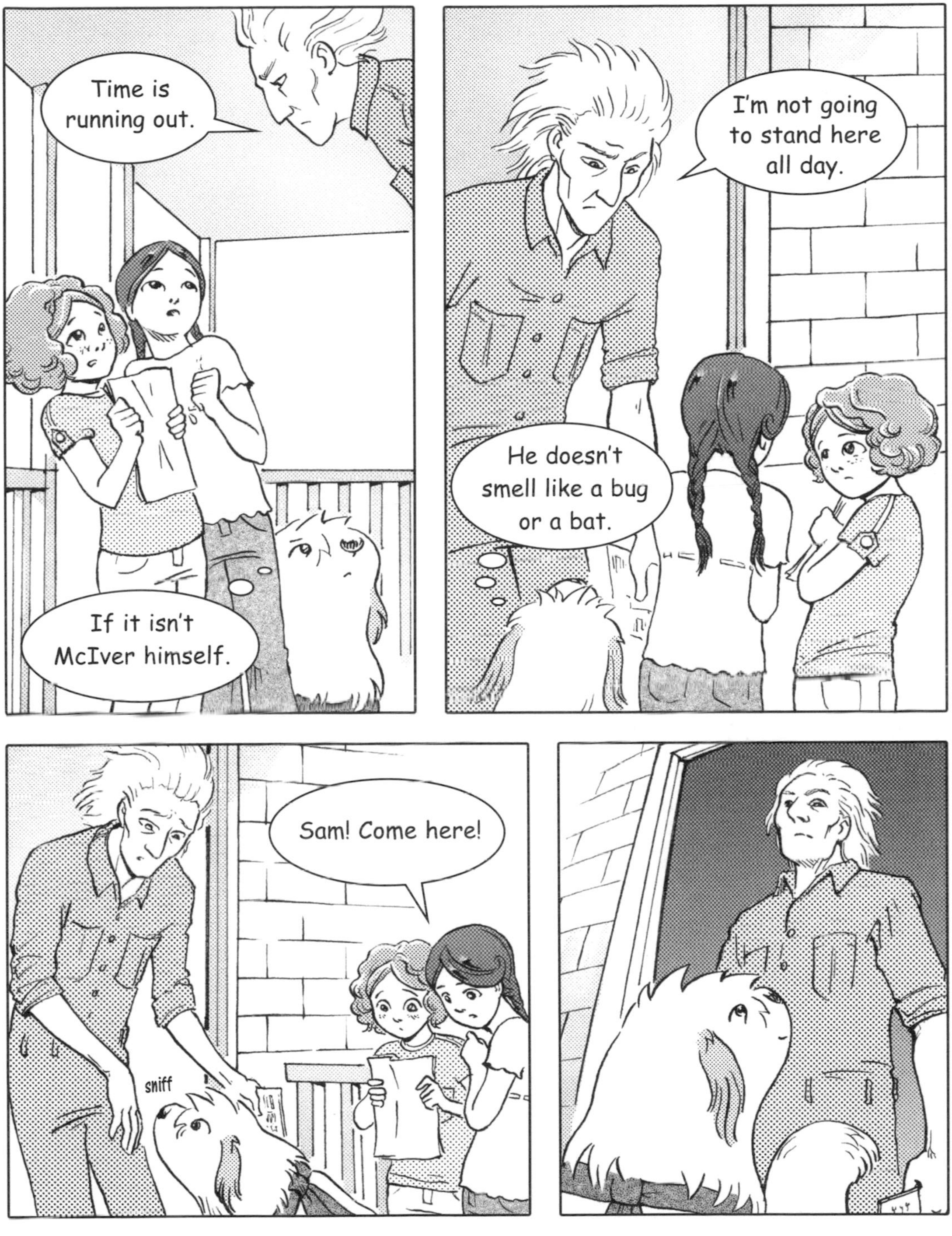
Time is running out.
If it isn't McIver himself.
I'm not going to stand here all day.
He doesn't smell like a bug or a bat.
Sam! Come here!
sniff

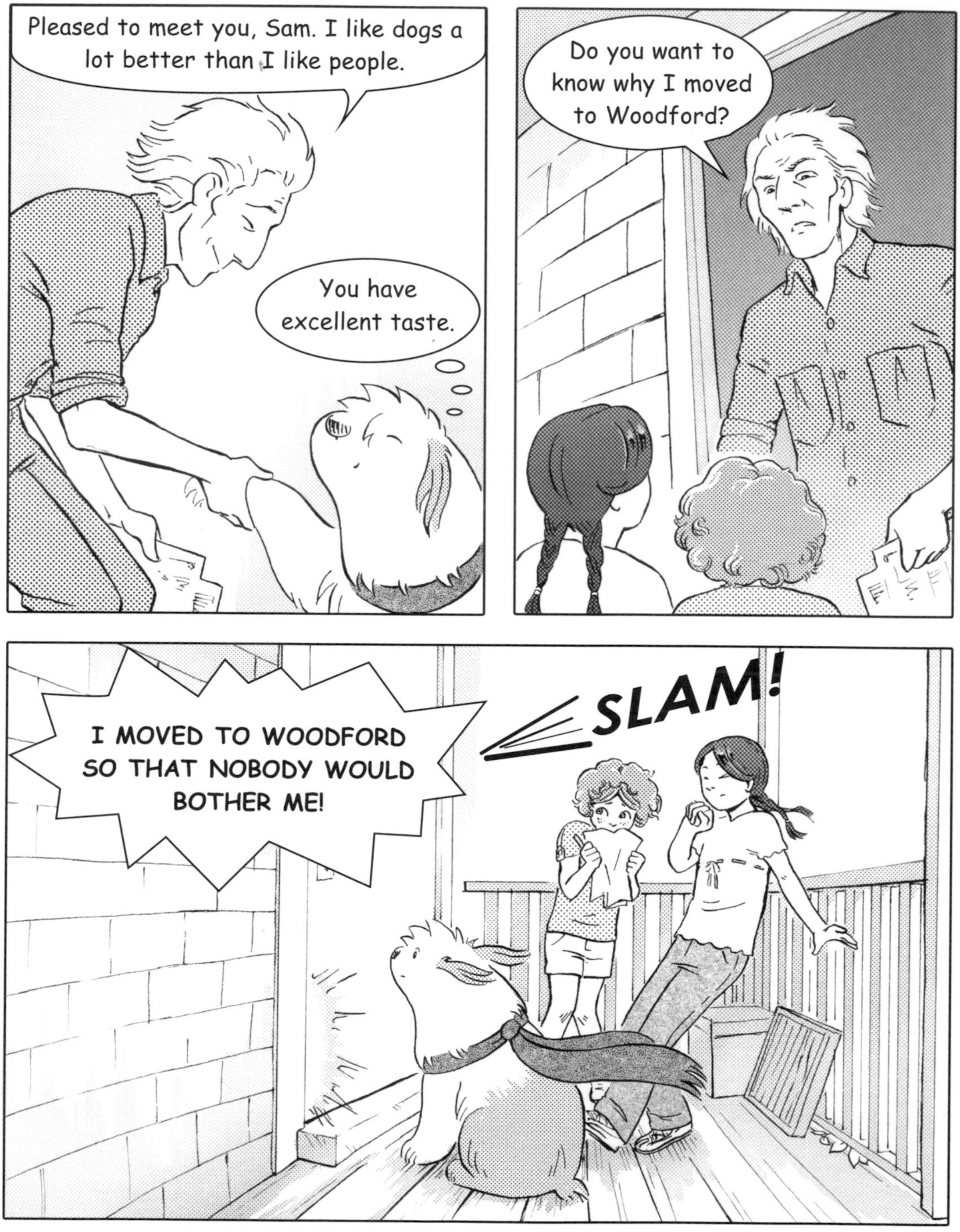
Pleased to meet you, Sam. I like dogs a lot better than I like people.
You have excellent taste.
Do you want to know why I moved to Woodford?
I MOVED TO WOODFORD SO THAT NOBODY WOULD BOTHER ME!
SLAM!

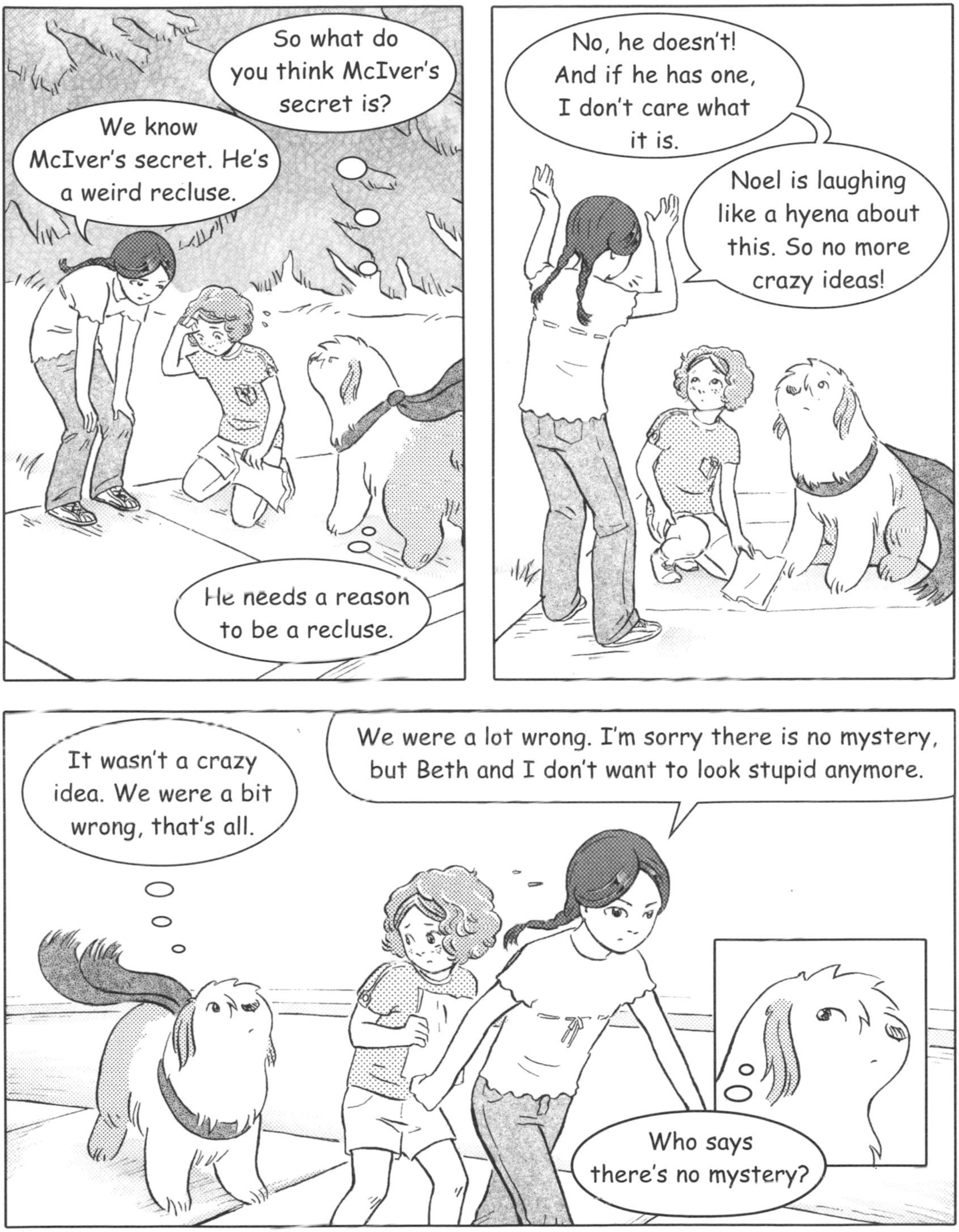
So what do you think McIver's secret is?
We know McIver's secret. He's a weird recluse.
He needs a reason to be a recluse.
No, he doesn't! And if he has one, I don't care what it is.
Noel is laughing like a hyena about this. So no more crazy ideas!
It wasn't a crazy idea. We were a bit wrong, that's all.
We were a lot wrong. I'm sorry there is no mystery, but Beth and I don't want to look stupid anymore.
Who says there's no mystery?

Later that afternoon ...

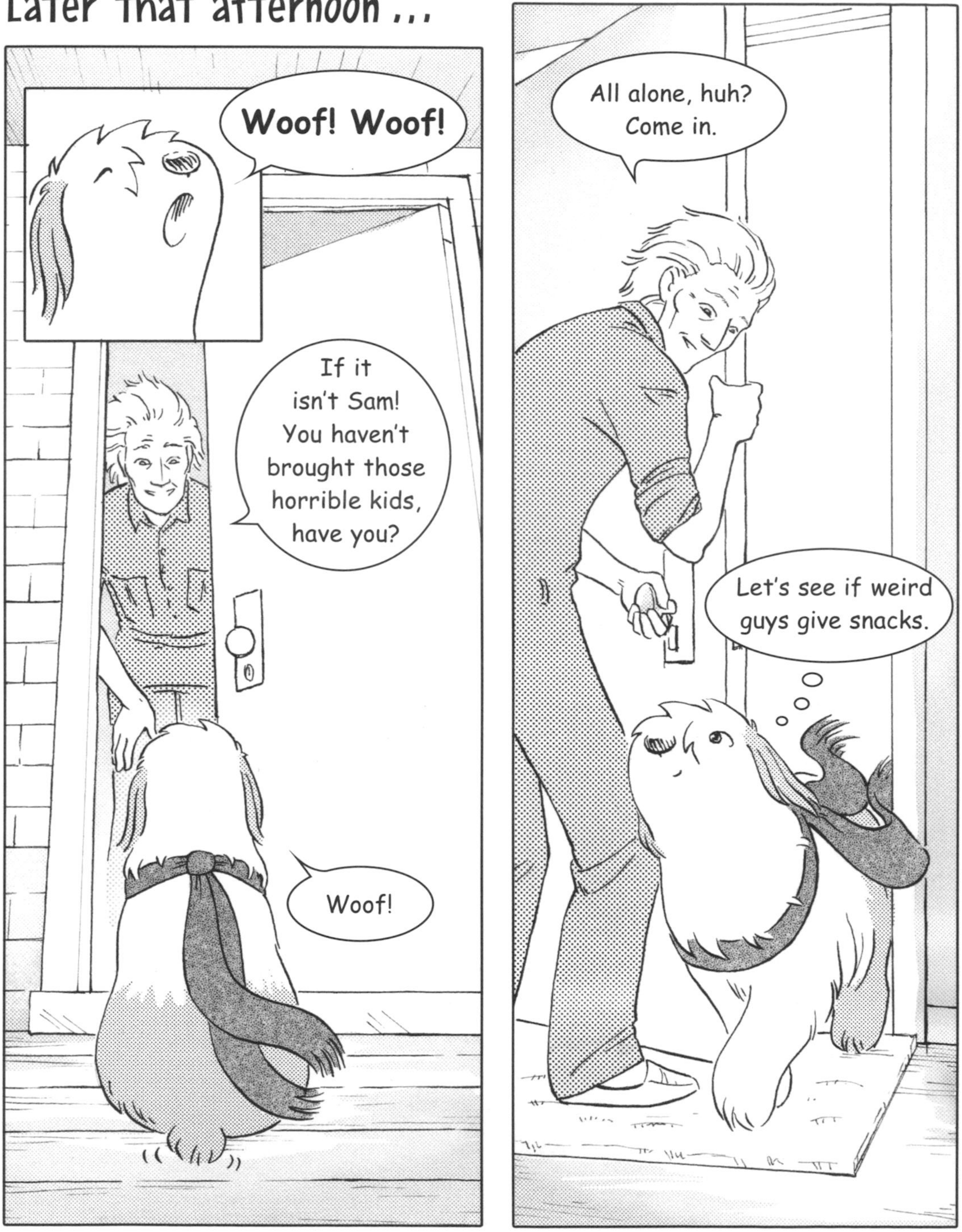
Woof! Woof!
If it isn't Sam! You haven't brought those horrible kids, have you?
Woof!
All alone, huh? Come in.
Let's see if weird guys give snacks.

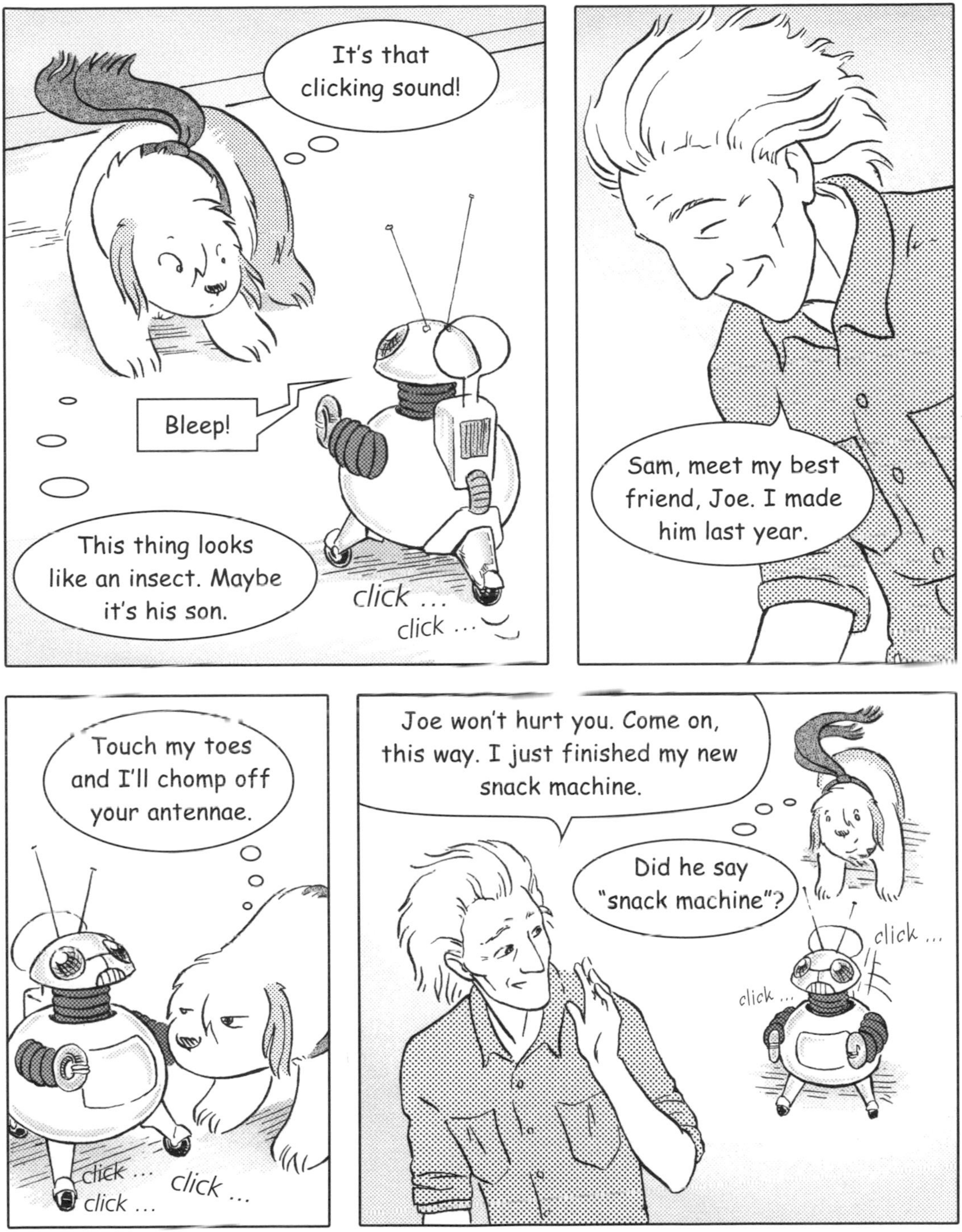
It's that clicking sound!
Bleep!
This thing looks like an insect. Maybe it's his son.
click ...
click ...
Sam, meet my best friend, Joe. I made him last year.
Touch my toes and I'll chomp off your antennae.
click ...
click ...
click ...
Joe won't hurt you. Come on, this way. I just finished my new snack machine.
Did he say "snack machine"?
click ...
click ...

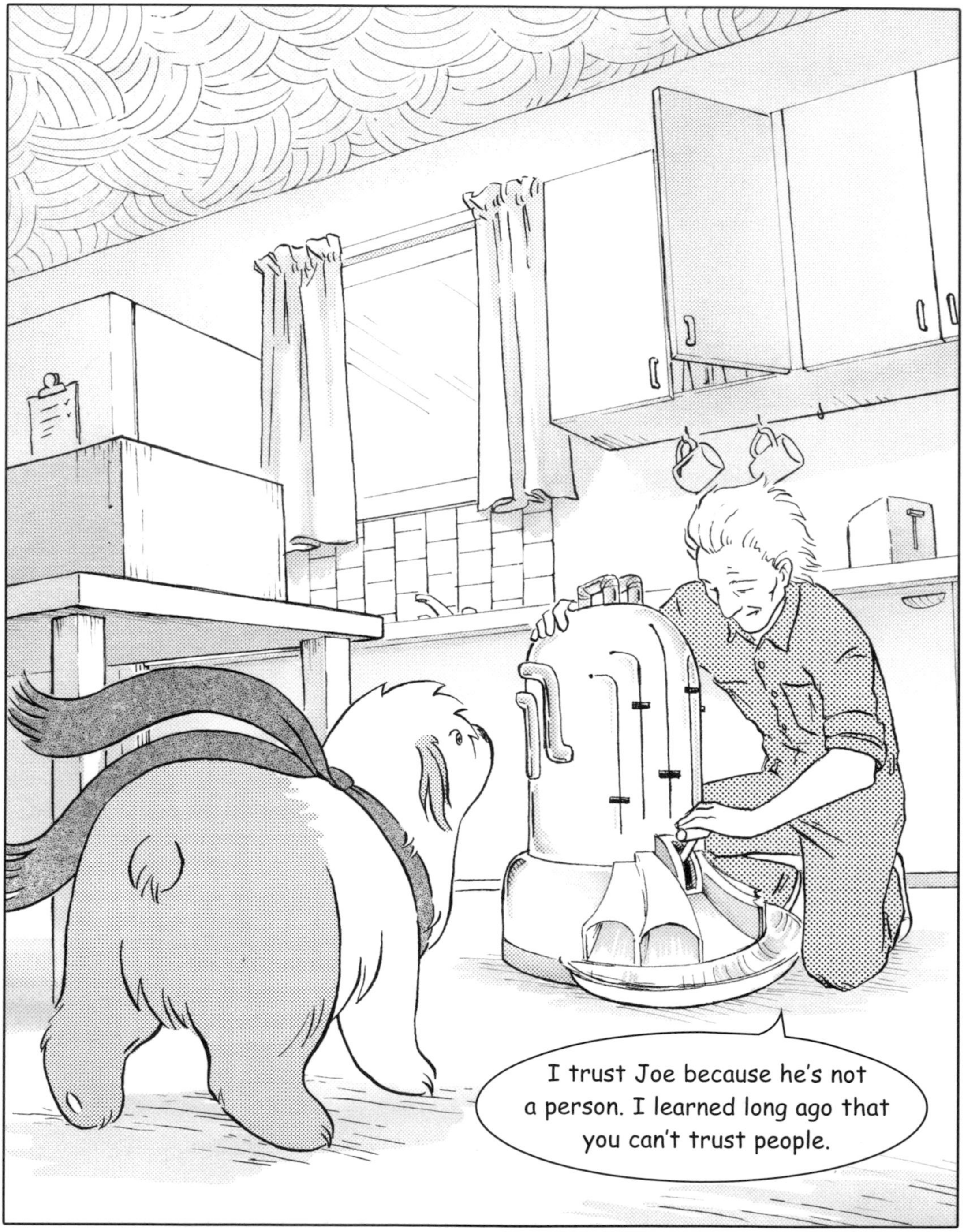
I trust Joe because he's not a person. I learned long ago that you can't trust people.

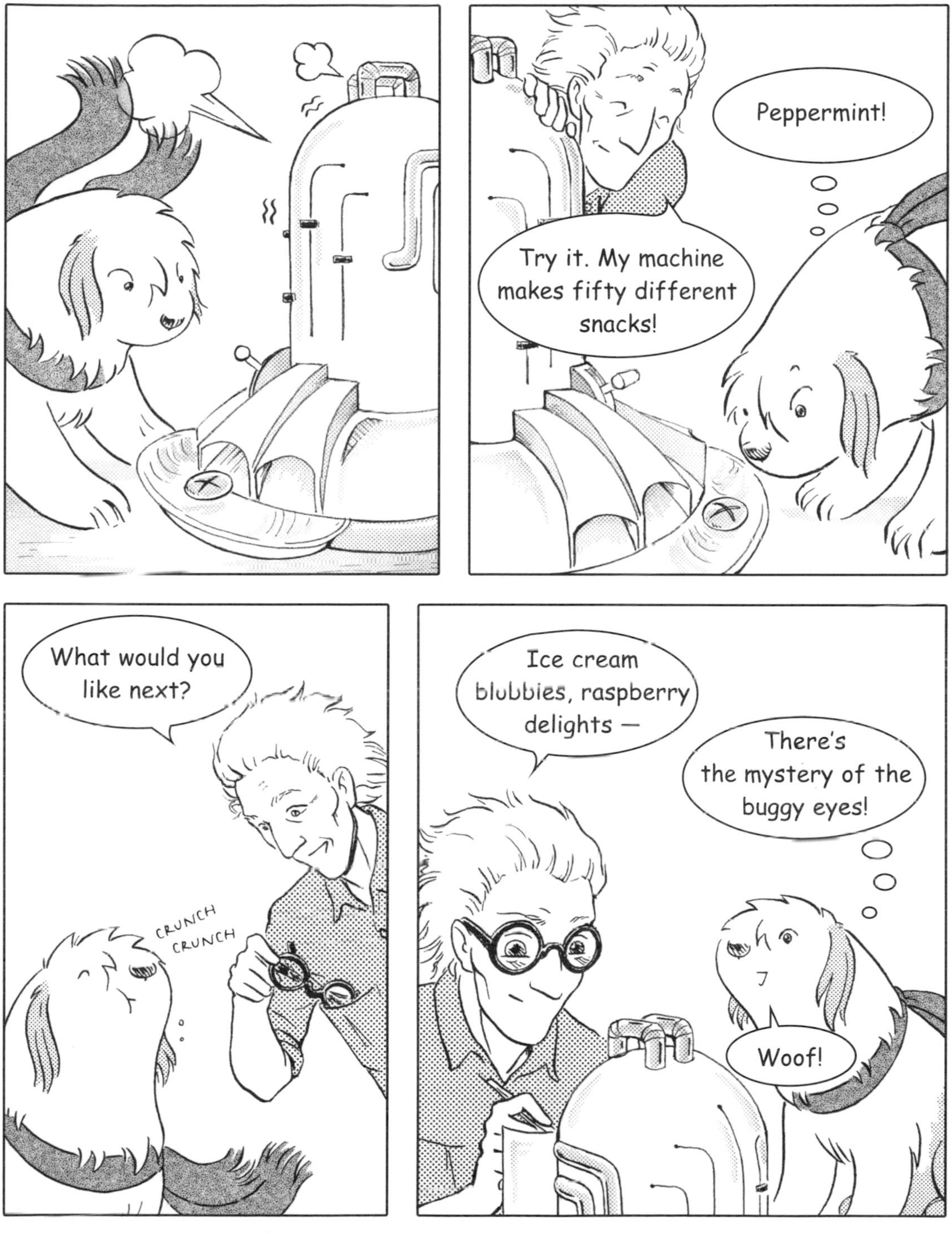
Peppermint!
Try it. My machine makes fifty different snacks!
What would you like next?
CRUNCH CRUNCH
Ice cream blubbies, raspberry delights —
There's the mystery of the buggy eyes!
Woof!

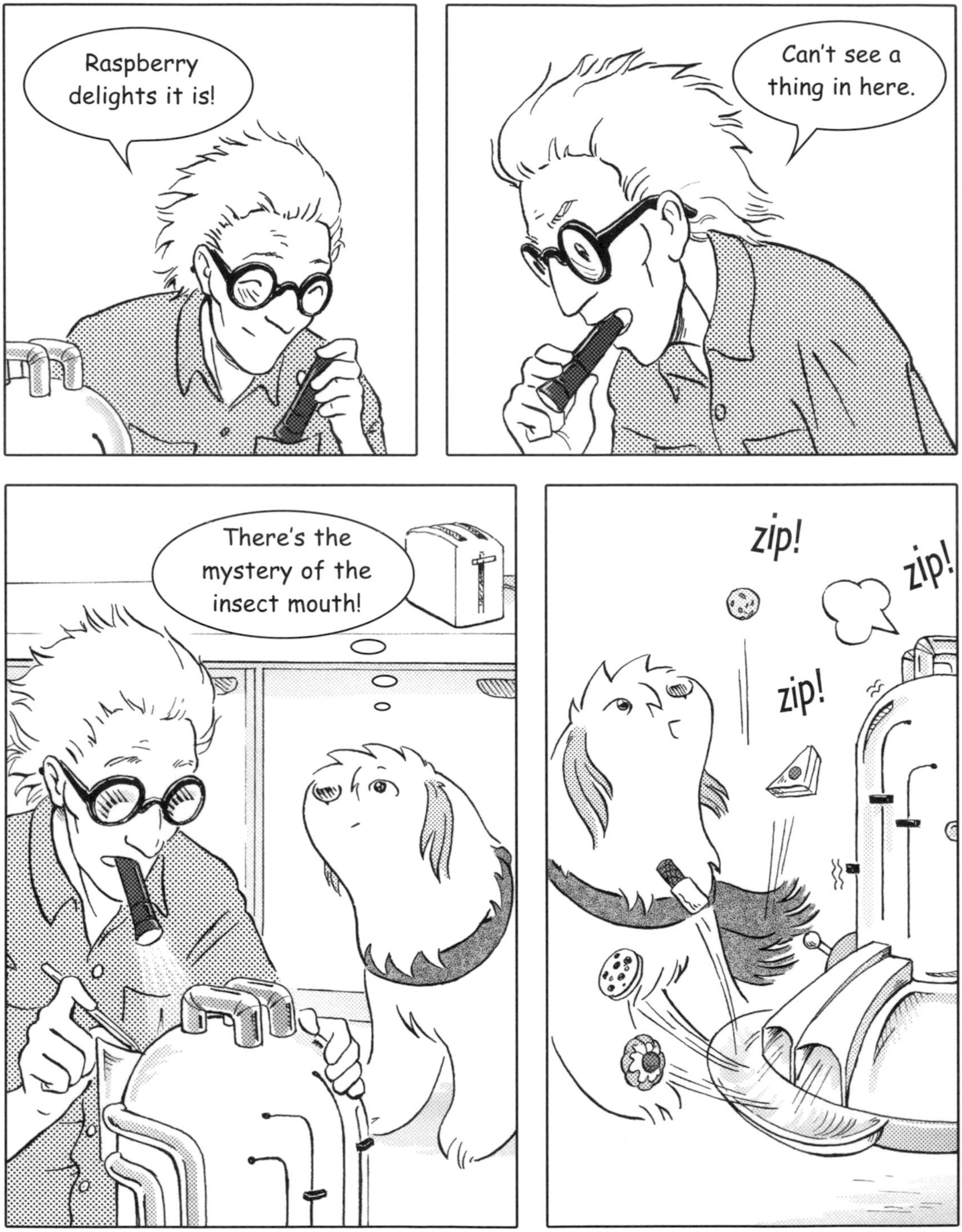
Raspberry delights it is!
Can't see a thing in here.
There's the mystery of the insect mouth!
zip!
zip!
zip!

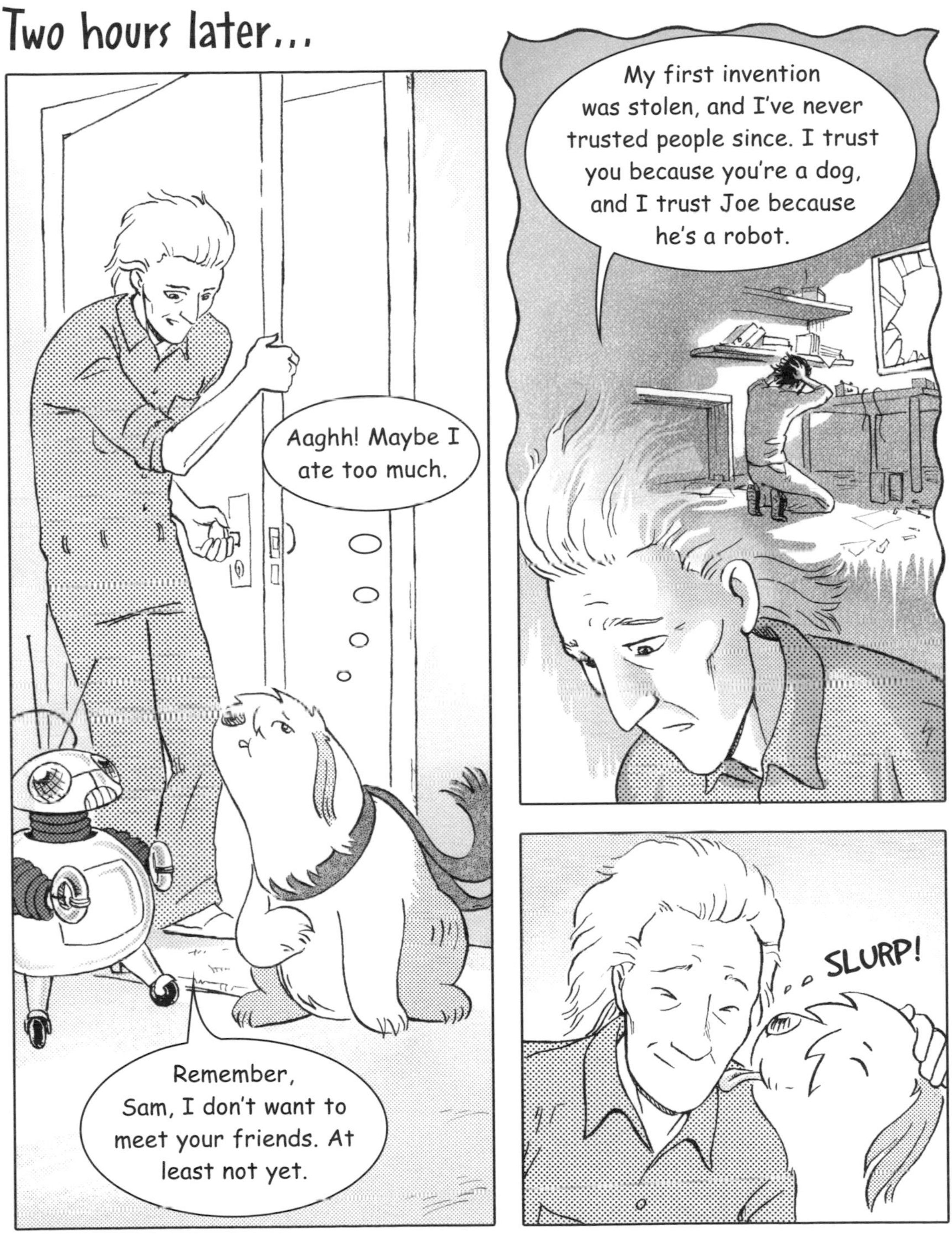
Two hours later...
Aaghh! Maybe I ate too much.
Remember, Sam, I don't want to meet your friends. At least not yet.
My first invention was stolen, and I've never trusted people since. I trust you because you're a dog, and I trust Joe because he's a robot.
SLURP!

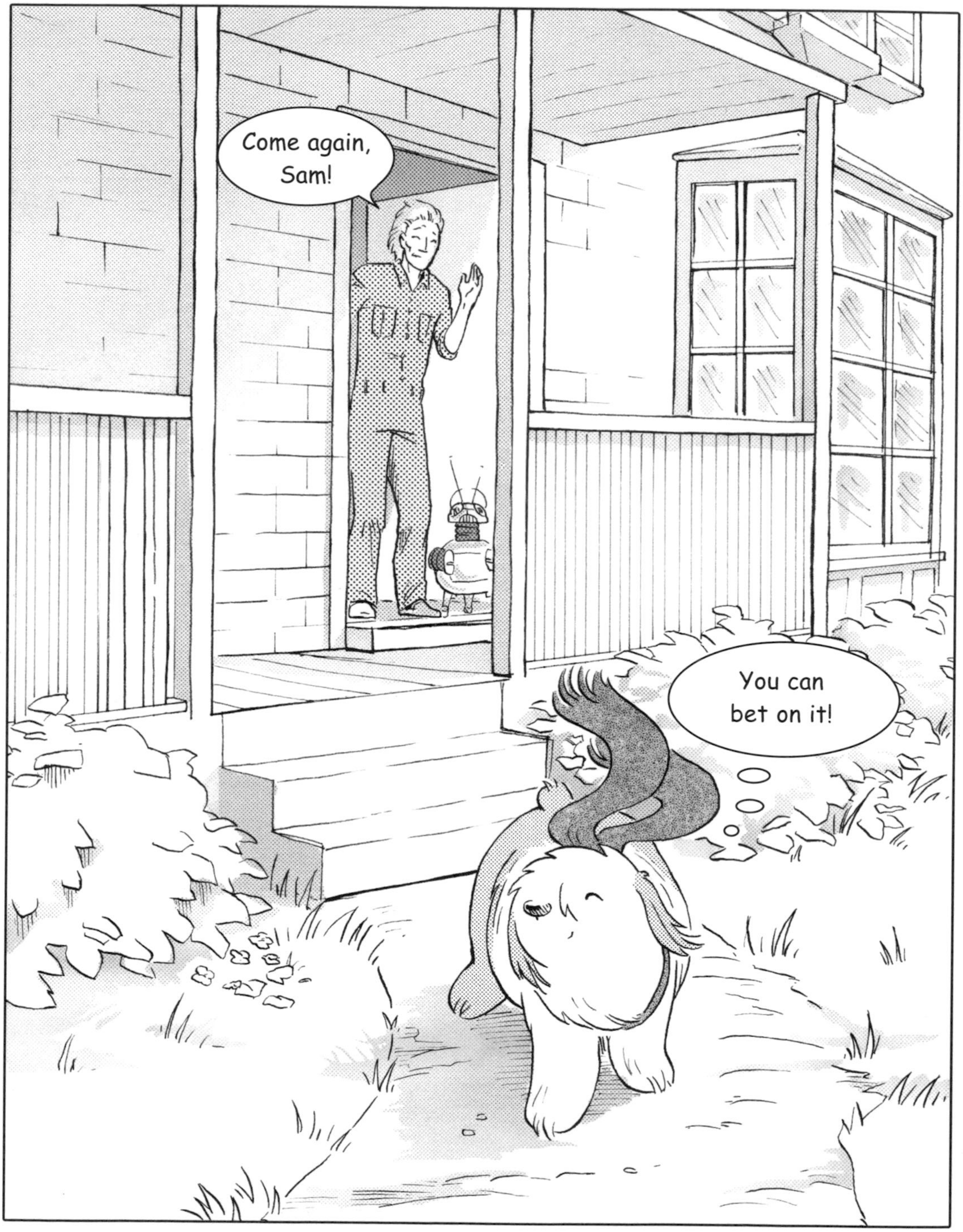
Come again, Sam!
You can bet on it!

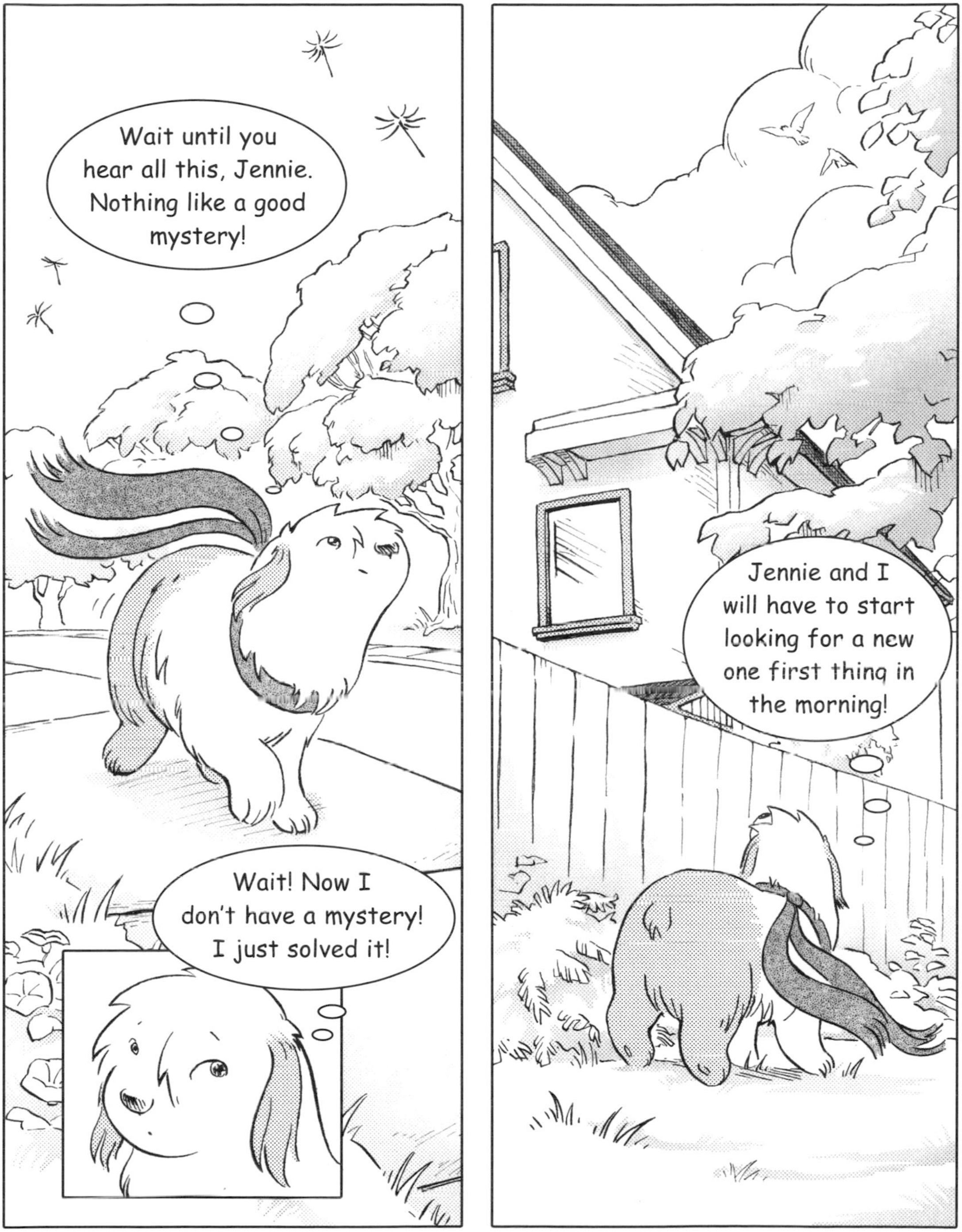
Wait until you hear all this, Jennie. Nothing like a good mystery!
Wait! Now I don't have a mystery! I just solved it!
Jennie and I will have to start looking for a new one first thing in the morning!

A Recipe for Adventure!

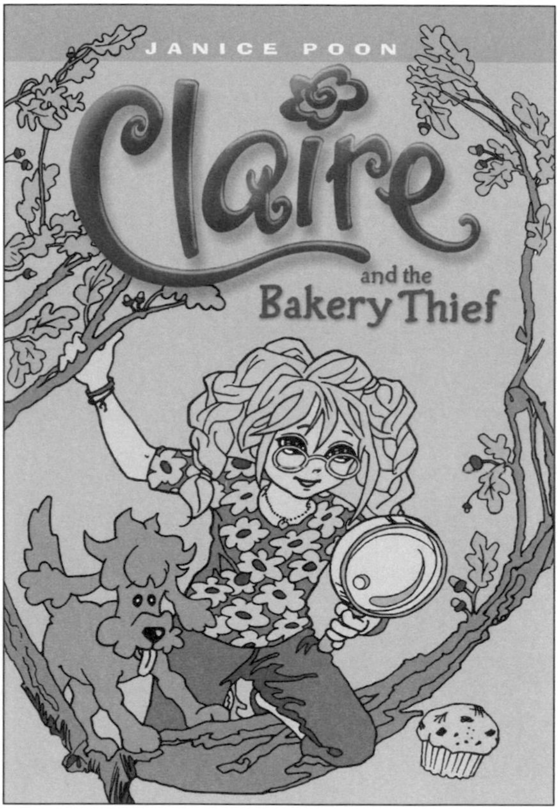

JANICE POON
Claire
and the
Bakery Thief

Claire and the Bakery Thief is a graphic novel that mixes friendship with a dash of fun.

Written and illustrated by
Janice Poon

Hardcover 978-1-55453-286-5
Paperback 978-1-55453-245-2

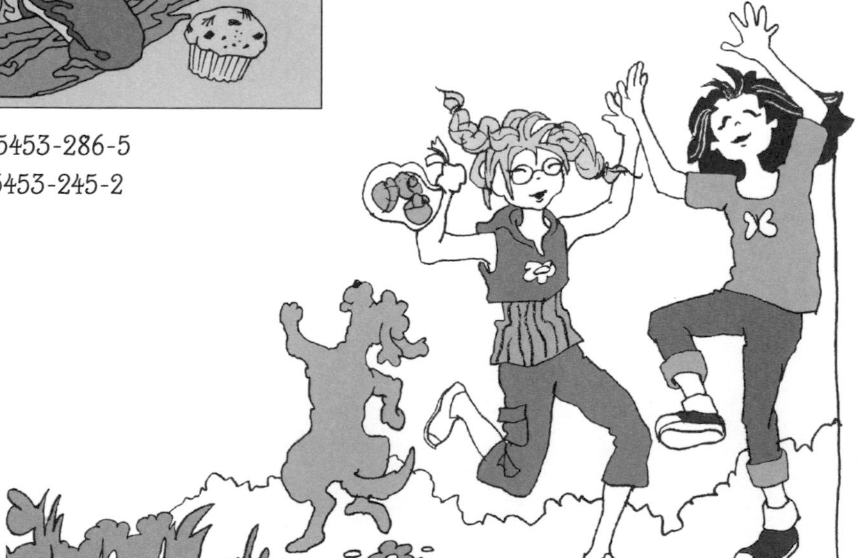